THE FINAL

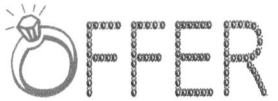FFER

Brenda A. White

CHOICES
WITHIN, LLC
HOUSTON

ISBN 13: 978-0-9819344-4-0
ISBN 10: 0981934447
Library of Congress Control Number: 2015903475

Cover Design: Chris Markland and Larry Newton, Determined Books
Interior Layout: Nakia R. Laushaul, A Reader's Perspective
Editing by: Michelle Chester, EBM Professional Services

Choices Within, LLC

www.choiceswithin.com

Printed in the United States of America

For my mom, dad, and Aunt Verba

Acknowledgements

THANK YOU! Another moment in history and I thank my God for it! Thank you, Jesus, again, for creating in me the talent, passion, and perseverance to complete my second novel! You are truly an awesome and incredible God, and you deserve incredible praise! I PRAISE YOU!

MY JOY! Thank you to my sisters and my brothers, my cheerleaders, for always supporting me. My sister, Juanita Robinson, set up her own table to sell my books. You rock! My sisters, Shirley Hicks, Tina Burton, and Cynthia Holmes, kept the books on hand and sold wherever you were. My niece Cassandra Quinney and my sister, Juanita, thank you for reading my manuscript and providing feedback. You helped me to tighten that thing up before sending it back to my editor.

MY LITERARY PEEPS! Michelle Chester, my editor, thank you for the feedback and pulling this story together and introducing me to others to get this project completed. Nakia Laushaul, A Reader's Perspective, thank you for an amazing job on the book layout. Chris and Larry at Determined Books, you guys are awesome. Thank you for the cover design. Victoria Christopher Murray, your "Ask the Author" calls, love them! I learned so much. ReShonda Tate-Billingsly and Pat Tucker thank you for sharing your knowledge on this literary journey.

MY HOMIES! Thank you to my hometown people, Yvette (Washington) Holley and Yvonne (Washington) McDonald, my very first book signing was at your party, Javaris Steward for taking some of my books and pushing from the trunk of your car, and Kendrick "Pops" Williams, Sr., owner of Pops Barber Shop in Pine Bluff, thank you for allowing me to sit, listen, and sell! I appreciate all of you!

MY GAL PALS! Sharon "Smooth" Bankett, my unofficial, works for food, assistant, who made sure my table was set up beautifully at multiple events and kept me in line. Angela Osborne, thank you for your assistance also making sure I don't have a mess in my suitcase. LaCheidra "LA" Hudson, owner of Studio 41 Salon in North Little Rock, AR and Demesha Haynes, owner of Shear Elegance Salon in Sugarland, TX, thank you for asking me if you could take my books and sell them to your clients. I am grateful for your support. Tarisa Busby, will whip out a book at any event, any house party, anywhere if someone asked, "Do you have any books with you?" Thank you Ramona Dalton, the woman who can sell two left shoes, will push a bookmark and a sales pitch about my book and t-shirts to anyone, anywhere. Shelia and Stephen Benson, my besties and Patrice and Charles Wilson, thank you for hosting events at your homes for me to sell to your friends. Thank you to all of my friends who purchased multiple copies to gift to friends.

Thank you to my First Chapter Book Club members for supporting me and choosing my first novel as the book of the month, twice! I have the best book club in the world. Who said a group of women can't come together and have great conversation topped off with great food, drinks, and no drama? Yes we can! Yes we do! I want to specifically thank the ladies who participated in the sleepover to read and critique several chapters of this novel—Angela Osborne, Karen Wooten-Miller, Sharon Bankett, Ramona Dalton, Lisa Roberts, Sheryl Robertson, and Tarisa Busby. Thank you for the sacrifice.

MY FELLAS! Thank you Ronald Punch, my pal from RP2 Entertainment, for sharing ideas and keeping me excited in this creative art thing. Thank you for writing my song for this love story, *You Have No Idea*. It's going to the top of the charts! We're going places! Dr. Michael McFraizer, thank you always for your support, thoughtful perspective, and for facilitating an in depth discussion on *The Best I Have to Offer*. I'm looking forward to the next one. James McKnight, thank you for your observation then powerful delivery of astute and profound comments. Tyrone Bennett, Kevin Williams, Robert Dunn, Charles Lucas, thank you for helping me to understand and validate ideas and actions from a male's perspective. Thank you, Dewan Smothers, for the best writing weekend trip ever! I appreciate you so much.

MY READERS! Thank you to all of the book clubs who chose my book as your book of the month and to all of my readers, my God, you're the reason I do what I do. Thank you for reading my work. I sincerely appreciate your support! Thank you Kay Williams-Dunkley and the Spirit of Sisterhood book club in San Antonio, TX! You all were the first to order paper-back copies and topped if off with a picnic in your living room to discuss the book. Brilliant! Thank you, again. Letha Walls, my buddy, thank you for your encouragement and prayers, they help more than you know. The book is here!

MY FRIENDS & FAMILY! My friends and family including nieces, nephews, sisters-in-law, brothers-in-law, cousins, AHS and PBHS Class of '87, Sister Sheretta West, and my church family at TCWW, my sisters of Delta Sigma Theta Sorority, Inc., Gloria Broumand, my Facebook, Twitter, and Instagram friends ☺ thank you for your support, prayers, and words of encouragement. I appreciate you! More to come...

THE FINAL

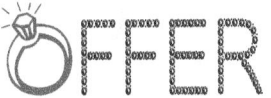

OFFER

Mia

T HE sound of a roaring car engine and falling glass interrupted our once serene and tranquil afternoon. I remember
that sound because it was the beginning of another change
in the relationship with the man that I loved dearly.

We had been engaged for almost a year and I had not made
a single step toward planning our wedding. I was paralyzed by
fear that had commandeered my entire being and had me completely idling. My best friend, Dena Thomas, on the other hand
was eager, willing, and ready to start the planning. She practically begged me to start. It was not about event planning as
her lucrative and main source of income nor was it about the
money she'd make because she had offered to do the wedding
for free. Dena just wanted us married and soon. She was still
riding the cloud of our introduction that she concocted over
two years ago, and I was running scared at the very thought of
marrying the wrong man whose past could potentially land me
six-feet under in a tragic way.

"I'm afraid, Gary! I'm afraid of what would happen to me
if I marry you and I'm stuck for the rest of my life in fear and
misery!" I had yelled those words to my fiancé, Gary Matthews,

as I packed my bags to run away to Arkansas two months after we were engaged.

He was definitely all I ever wanted in a man but drama followed him like a shadow. Gary is a partner at Matthews and Jefferson Consulting, LLC. His former assistant, Lynn, was in jail awaiting trial for trying to kill me by running through a red light and ramming a truck into my car, a Corvette. A tiny car compared to the dump truck like vehicle she was driving. Since the accident, Lynn's conniving children had vanished. They were not our current concern, but one of Gary's ex-girlfriends, Nina Briggs, resurfaced frequently.

Nina wanted Gary back and I was tired of dealing with her nonsense. I was tired of seeing her almost everywhere I went and I really wanted to pummel her. I wanted to physically harm her badly but I had been taught and got frequent reminders from others that a lady should not resort to fighting. Real women used their words not their fists. I thought that was a bunch of bull and I wanted to behave like Dena. I wanted to use my fists, my feet, and any other object to harm Nina. She would not leave us alone. Because of her, Gary and I stepped away from each other for a couple of months; well, I stepped away from him. During our hiatus, he went out with a lady named Roni, who was a bit of a psycho also. He says he never slept with her and did not understand why she was so obsessed with him. He pretended like he was clueless regarding advances and feelings from other women toward him. I don't believe him, but what can I say, I had left him at that time.

I was certainly not without fault. I had allowed Dena to pull me into so much mess over the years that both of us should have at least one misdemeanor, if not a felony. I carelessly recreated my own scene of drama while I was in Arkansas during my first hiatus. I just pray it doesn't reemerge at the most inopportune moment. I should've let that giant remain asleep.

It was a beautiful day, I had finished my yoga session and I was in the kitchen preparing breakfast. Dena called me every morning at seven-thirty. She was an early riser, regardless of the time she drifted off to sleep the night before. I saw her name and our picture flash on the screen. She was on time with her call.

I removed the ear bud from the Bluetooth device around my neck and pressed it into my ear. "Good morning, lil' devil," I joked as I twisted the wand to open the blinds over the kitchen sink.

She gasped. "I know you didn't call me a devil. I'm the furthest thing from it."

"Okay. I apologize." My voice dripped with sarcasm. I meandered around the kitchen opening all of the blinds to let the natural light in then back to the stove to check the omelets.

"You know you always try to act like Miss Innocent and Miss Corporate America and your butt did a one eighty when you left there. Just as ratchet as the next person now," she exclaimed.

I chuckled. "You're a lie. I have my quirks but I ain't ratchet, far from it."

"See there, I ain't ratchet," she mocked me.

"Whatever, Dena. I have an image to uphold. In this case, it is what people think of me. My reputation is how they choose me to present, to speak at their events, facilitate, consult, and yada, yada, yada. There's nothing in running around behaving rachettely. I know I just made up a word."

She giggled. "I heard you, but I know Jesus' disciple is not putting her fate in the hands of another human being. Your steps and your success are ordered by God! Anyway, Miss Angel Wings, why are we wasting time discussing 'ratchet' anyway? What are you doing?"

I was slightly taken aback by the comment, especially coming from her, but she was right. I sometimes forget that people are neither my source nor my provider, but the image and behaviors I was speaking of at that moment were also those of a mature Christian and I was tempted to pop back at her with such a comment but I changed my mind.

"I'm preparing a to-go breakfast for my sweetie before he rushes through here grabbing unhealthy stuff on the way out the door. He's running late today."

"Well, aren't you a sweetheart." Her tone had changed.

"I'm doing the best I can."

"Okay. I need to go to the park today. I just heard the weather. It's supposed to be a beautiful day, seventy-five degrees for the high, low humidity, no rain, a perfect day for swinging. What do you have on your agenda?"

"I just have a conference call for my life coaching class later today. Are you okay?"

"Yeah. I just need to get on the swings. Swing away some stress, some evil thoughts. I just need to swing."

Dena and I have been swinging away stress since we were kids. We'd meet at the park by the swings, spread out a blanket with food, swing for a little while, and then sit on the blanket and talk. It was always at her request though, at least once per quarter like clockwork.

"Oh, okay. What time?" I sprinkled shredded cheese inside the omelet, flipped it onto the croissant, added a couple of slices of avocado and quickly wrapped it in wax paper and foil, then slid it into a sandwich bag.

"Around eleven o'clock would work, not too early, not too late."

"Okay, I think I can work that in. My call is late afternoon."

"We shouldn't be long."

"Hold on for a second, Dena." I reached for the phone to put it on mute.

"Good morning, babe." Gary leaned in to kiss me as he rushed through the kitchen adjusting his tie with his jacket draped over his arm. He pulled the refrigerator door open and grabbed an orange juice. He took a swig and set the bottle on the countertop. His tailored navy blue pants swathed his firm glutes and rested neatly on top of his Dover Split toe shoes from Edward Green that I had picked up for him the day before.

"Hey, honey. You look nice. I like. And you smell good too." I stepped back in admiration and gave him a seductive once over.

"Thank you." He blushed as he adjusted his cufflinks.

"Here you go. I made two smaller ones today." I handed him a bag with turkey sausage, croissant with egg, shredded cheddar, Pico, and avocado and another one with a tiny omelet on a croissant with similar ingredients. He loved my little creations in the kitchen. He used to cook all the time but now I had turned into the perfect housewife without the title.

"Thank you. I appreciate you." He leaned in again for more kisses with tongue. "Ummm, I gotta go." He moaned and looked at me seductively. He winked at me and turned to walk out the door.

I followed him toward the garage. "Okay, see you later. Love you."

"I love you more." He hung his jacket on the hanger in the back seat of his truck and hopped in.

I yelled, "Knock 'em dead today. I know you will."

He gave me thumbs up.

I leaned on the door then blew him a kiss and waited until he backed the truck out of the garage before I pressed the button to let the garage door down.

I pressed the mute button and focused my attention back to Dena. "Oh, how I love that dude. Okay, ma'am."

"It took you long enough," she spat.

"It did not. Anyway, do you need to swing or do you need to chill? Because I was thinking, you should come here and I can expand this breakfast menu to add some grits and waffles or French toast or something."

"Can you add some wings too?"

"Ummm, now you're running out," I murmured as I looked in the freezer for wings.

"Yes, I can add wings."

"Swing, chill, it's all the same to me. I'm on my way. I'll be there in forty-five or less. Bye."

"Good-bye," I said for not, because she had already disconnected the call. She always hung up before I could say good-bye. My phone vibrated. I touched the text message icon and smiled as I shifted my weight to one leg.

Hey, love, I wanted to tell you how much I really appreciate what you're doing and all you do for me. This croissant is good as hell! I know you don't care much for the kitchen and other domestic stuff but you're awesome and I appreciate it and I don't take any of it for granted. I got you.

I could hear his voice saying those words and it made my heart smile. He loved me and appreciated me and I knew it. Before I sold my house and moved in with him, I had a maid, Millie, who came once per week to clean, do laundry, and sometimes cook for me. I abhor domestic duties. I kept things tidy because I didn't like a mess but I certainly didn't enjoy it. My parents made me do so many house chores growing up, I vowed to never do them when I got my own house. During my first budget sessions with Gary, that was the first area he reviewed to save money until we determine our expenses to income ratio while I worked to get my business running smoothly again. He promised it wouldn't last forever but we needed to make some observations before going overboard on "nice to haves."

I replied to the text after reading it a few times with a smile plastered on my face. *Thanks, babe! You really know how to make my day. :-)*

I could tell he was typing so I sent another quick note.

Does this mean I'll never see Millie again?

Ha, no, that's not what that means. You'll be able to see Millie for a couple of things soon.

Thanks, babe. Love you. Getting ready to fix wings and waffles for me and Dena.

Okay, love you too, have fun.

Dena arrived on time as she always does. We sat by the pool and lounged for over two hours talking, eating, and drinking mimosas as the light wind kissed our skin and the sun gave us our daily dose of vitamin D. She didn't complain about her deadbeat boyfriend, Monty, but actually said a few good things about him. He had been with the same company for more than a year. They were in love again. We talked about life and leaving a legacy for our children, grandchildren, our sorority, our alma mater, and the world in general. She shared some of the documents she'd started on like her will and her living will. I know this needed to be done but I was a little concerned about why she was all of a sudden focused on it now. I didn't push it; I reviewed the documents and handed them back to her and made a mental note to get mine done also.

"I'm really happy that you and Monty are doing better these days. It seems he's much better to you and everyone else when he's working."

"Yeah, he's one of those men who have a problem if his woman makes more money than him."

"I figured as much. When are you all getting married?"

She twisted her face. "I don't know. He's mentioned it a few times lately but he doesn't want a big to do wedding. He thinks that I want something extremely elaborate because those are the types of weddings I plan but that is so far from what I want. Simple is so much better for me. My nerves can't take it."

"But, you're pushing the wedding of the century on me?"

"Yes, because that's what you need." She smiled. "I plan extravagantly for other people and especially for my BFF."

"Oh, really?" I stared blankly at her.

"Mia, my treat today." She stood up. "Mani-pedis on me, before your class." She was good at changing the subject.

"Let's go."

"Wow. That was easy."

"You said the magic words—your treat. What's difficult about that?"

"You're silly. Let's go. I'll even drive."

"Well, you kind of have to since I haven't purchased a car yet."

"Gary has a fleet in the garage. Pick one. You're not driving yet because you don't want to. He's running and carting you around like Miss Daisy."

I shot her a look and she held up both hands. "But hey, I'm like Kermit, that's none of my business."

"Ha! You're stupid, Dena." I laughed as her reference to the social media memes with Kermit the frog where the tag would say something extremely messy, mean, or condescending and ended with '…but that's none of my business.'

"Help me clean the kitchen and we can roll."

I contemplated telling her about my encounter with Nina, Gary's ex-girlfriend, the other day, but I decided against it. I ran into her at the grocery store. She had intentionally bumped my shopping cart twice while I was shopping. I quickly completed my shopping and left the store and I mentally beat myself up for the remainder of the day because I felt I should have responded in some type of way. Later that night, Gary was so focused on his work, he didn't notice my irritation with myself. So, it was easy for me to bury myself in a novel and fall asleep but I remember when he turned off the light and pulled me close and planted a kiss on my shoulder before I heard his muffled snoring. If I told Dena the story she would've been ready to go find Nina.

By noon we were in our chairs getting manicures and pedicures. The place was crowded for midday on a Wednesday.

Something was certainly on my friend's mind but she wouldn't spit it out and I decided not to pressure her about it. We tried to maintain a mutual understanding. Unless it was life threatening, we would not automatically intervene unless it was requested. We'd had our issues in the past by one of us jumping into the business of the other one unrequested and it didn't turn out well.

Dena and I laughed and chatted for a few minutes, but then Dena leaned her head back on the chair as the massager shook her body to the different settings. I didn't like that thing so I decided to listen to "The Empress Has No Clothes" on my Audible app. The narrator speaking in my ear was low enough that I could hear and understand the book and hear anything going on around me, which is why I still heard the commotion at the register.

"I can't believe the type of service you provide and the people you let enter this establishment," the lady yelled as she looked in our direction.

Kayla, the shop owner, was trying to calm her down but the lady was too irate to hear anything.

I turned to look at Dena and nothing was lost on her; her eyes were wide open. "Who the hell is this trick?" She leaned forward. "She looks familiar." She narrowed her eyes as if that would help her to see clearer.

"She needs to calm down, looks like she's performing. I'm not giving her the satisfaction by looking her way."

"Girl, that's that chick Gary went out with."

"What? When?" I sat up straight.

"Mia, that's Roni."

She was about six feet tall with her stilettos on, sturdy, dark brown hair, nothing special, just a normal lady with an apparent attitude at the moment. Gary had never mentioned her physical attributes; he never said much about her at all. We both had agreed to 'wipe the slate clean' and start over, never asking about what happened while we were apart. Neither one of us knew at the time, that would be a huge mistake on both sides.

"What the hell are y'all looking at?" she snapped.

"Free my feet, Hannah." The nail tech appeared puzzled by Dena's request. Dena removed her feet from the bowl and leaned forward to wipe them off with the towel.

"No, no, no, Ms. Dena. You stay in your seat," Hannah begged. Hannah stood up to see what was going on.

"Now, Sarah, you know you're gonna have to pass me that towel. This woman just might be crazy enough to try us in this place today. You know good and well, you and Hannah can't protect us," I said.

"I know y'all just came in here to mess with me." She snapped in our direction but she wasn't coming any closer.

Dena and I looked at each other, confused.

"Is this heffa schizophrenic? We've been coming here for years and have never seen your crazy ass. What are you talking about?" Dena yelled as she pulled the arm of the chair up so she could stand.

"Dena, be quiet. Please don't entertain this fool unless she comes over here."

"Well, if she makes that bad decision, I'll be ready for her ass."

Kayla's husband, Mike, stopped working on his customer and walked to the front. "Ma'am, I'm sorry you're gonna have to leave, you're upsetting our customers."

"Upsetting your customers? They're upsetting me! I just stopped in here to get my nail fixed and y'all trippin'," she yelled.

"Ma'am, please leave or we'll have to call the police," he pleaded.

"Ma'am? My name is Roni, not ma'am, damn!" She snatched her purse off the counter and tried to storm out but her stilettos caused her to walk a bit more carefully.

Dena and I returned to our chairs and Mike watched as Roni got into her car.

"Well, so much for a relaxing afternoon. We can't go anywhere without freakin' drama. We're too old for this ish, Mia."

"I know, Dena. We're not starting it but somehow, we always end up in it."

As Mike and his wife were standing in front of our stations explaining to everyone what had happened, the sound of crashing glass and a roaring motor invaded the sound of soothing music and conversation—a sound that sent all of us scrambling to safety. Roni had driven her car through the building and my relationship with Gary had changed again.

PART ONE

HERE

WE GO AGAIN

Eighteen months later…

CHAPTER 1: MIA

VALENTINE'S Day had come and gone and it was 4:30 a.m. "Gary! Oh my God…that feels so, oh, good, baby." I managed a whisper after he touched that spot. My back arched into shallow breaths, shivers swarmed around my feet, marched slowly up my calves to my thighs, to my spine, and then back down. My eyes did a fancy swirl, my head flipped back, and my toes curled. "Ahh." My entire body shuddered and I collapsed onto the bed. Why is makeup sex the best?

We had just completed round four. I knew the playful tug would arrive just as it did every morning. I'm glad I'd always made sure cleanliness was at the top of my list of priorities. Using the flushable feminine cleansing clothes in the middle of the night if I got up to use the bathroom and the dab of toothpaste on the back of my tongue before going to bed made me comfortable enough to let him do what he did every morning which was wake me up with kisses, licks, and sucks anywhere on my body.

He lingered for a few minutes staring at the ceiling. The sun had made its way through the window and reflected off the mirror and onto our bodies sprawled on the bed. "You okay?" He smacked my thigh and got up to walk into the bathroom. I stretched out across the bed. Gary walked back into the room a few minutes later with a hot towel. We both turned toward the TV when the anchor announced the concert coming up at the end of the month.

"You still want to go to that?" he inquired as he moved the towel across my body.

"Of course, I do." I never turned my attention away from the TV. "Why would you ask that? You know I'm the biggest fan ever since…since before I was a teenager."

"Wow, okay, I just asked, making sure." He walked back to the bathroom, draped the towel on the rack, and returned to the bed. He kissed me on the cheek and gazed at me. "I love you, lil' girl and I'm sorry about last night."

"I love you, too." I snuggled into his arms.

I was in a car accident caused by his obsessive ex-Adminis-trative Assistant that resulted in a miscarriage and me being in a coma for several days. She's in jail now. I was getting my nails done when one of the obsessive women from his past, Roni, whom he had taken on a date, ran her car through the building and claimed failed brakes. I'm not sure what he did to her, but we have not heard from her since she changed her story after the first one didn't stick. She claimed she was in emotional duress and made a mistake and put the car in drive instead of reverse.

He wanted to "protect" me so I allowed him to talk me into moving in with him after we were engaged. Our wedding plans had been off and on at my emotional call. He still does not want me to work because he wants to "provide" for me which was the reason for our disagreement last night, and now we're here—emotions running high, then low, and then back to high again, all stemming from the pieces of me. I needed help badly. My current therapy sessions were beginning to make progress and he was scheduled to join me after a couple more sessions.

I snuggled in tighter, rubbed my leg over his, played with his nipples, and cooed. "Gary Matthews, baby you make me feel so good, and thank you for everything you're doing for me but you are very good at distracting me. We still need to talk about Nina. You want me to stay home so I won't encounter some of this foolishness on the outside. Me not working will not solve that. I'm done walking away from her."

I knew it was not the best time to talk about it but he had avoided this conversation ever since I told him she bumped my cart at the grocery store and he brushed it off, saying it was probably someone else and was more irritated because I had gone to the store without him.

"Mia Nixon, I'm not trying to distract you. I was just making love to my fiancée. The woman who I'm dying to marry but also keeps blowing me off. I'm not trying to distract you; I'm trying to love you and show you that it's time for us to move on with our lives, happy, raising a family, enjoying our families, and contributing to society, just living a simple, normal, and joyful life." He rubbed his fingers through my hair and then reached for my hands and pulled it toward his lips to kiss it.

I looked up at him and sighed as I contemplated my next comment.

He continued, "Babe, Nina is no longer a problem. I promise. Can we talk about that some other time? I'm not trying to spoil my day nor yours by talking about her. She should be the least of your worries."

"But, how do you know that? As long as I'm breathing and moving around this city, she will be a problem. She's in love with you and obviously wants you back, and she pops back up every few months in some kind of way. And I'm not sure if she thinks that harassing me would help her to get you back or what, but one thing it will guarantee her is an ass whooping. For sure."

He pushed up to press his back against the headboard with a frown plastered on his face. "No, she is not in love with me. She just likes drama. Don't worry about her, anymore."

I was slightly irritated that he moved from our cuddling position on the bed but I guess cuddling is not the perfect position for an imminent argument. I moved to mirror his position. "Gary, honey, look." I paused for dramatic effect. "I love you more than anything or anybody in this world." I paused again then continued in a matter-of-fact tone. "But I bullshit you not, if you don't get Nina's ass under control, I'm gonna kick her ass—hard. And I'm not playing. This is high school shit and I don't have time for it." I was looking directly into his eyes, my voice slightly elevated. I had allowed profanity to invade my vocabulary a lot more than usual.

He started shaking his head. "You need to calm down. Babe, outside of a lady, whose face you did not see, bumping your cart at the store, what has she done lately? And fighting over a dude is high school shit."

I rose up on my elbows. "Trust me, I will not be fighting over you, I'll fight because she crossed the line."

He rolled his eyes. "Now Mia, you know that's not who you are. That's not how you handle things. Is there something you're not telling me? Do we need to get a restraining order?" he bellowed.

His tone surprised me a little as I'm sure my tone and words had surprised him without notice.

"I, uh, yes, I do." I shook my head. "No, no I don't. I'll handle it myself." I threw the covers off me, stepped onto the cold, hardwood floor, and walked into the bathroom for a shower.

"When I finish with her silly ass, she'll want a restraining order against me," I mumbled.

"Mia, come on now." He followed me into the bathroom. "Don't start shutting me out again. Tell me what's going on. What happened?" He rubbed my shoulder with his massive hand and pulled me into a side hug. "I'm sorry, let's talk. Let's talk. Please."

"I don't have a desire to talk now. I need to take a shower. I'm meeting Dena at the gym in less than an hour." My tone was flat. I pulled away from him and looked toward the floor. Tears were threatening to gush out of my eyes. I was getting madder by the second. So, I put a shower cap on and hurriedly stepped into the shower to let the water hit my face.

Nina had shown up in a few places where Dena and I had been in the last month. Since the news spread that Gary and I were engaged again, she started popping up in the same location talking loud enough for us to hear her make claims about Gary. And as much as Dena tried to control her anger and tell me not to worry about her, I had allowed the drama queen to invade my thoughts enough for me to actually believe her. On about the fourth pop-up we were at Happy Hour in Uptown Park. She showed up as we were leaving and Dena leaned in as we walked by her and hissed with a fake smile, "You know I'll kick your ass and kill you, right? I owe you one anyway. You just keep showing up everywhere we go." Nina looked stunned but tried to maintain composure. Dena patted her shoulder and kept walking. I just glared at Nina as I walked by to cosign what Dena had said, not knowing her exact words until we were in the car.

My emotions were consistently in high gear at the mere thought of her.

He sighed. "Okay, we'll talk later." He walked back to the bed. Several minutes later, he leaned into the bathroom. "Hey, Dena is out front waiting for you."

I was brushing my teeth. "Huh, I was supposed to meet her." I quickly hopped into my workout clothes, brushed my hair back, and scooped it up into a ponytail.

Still looking at me with sadness in his eyes, he hunched his shoulders and returned to the bed.

Why was she here instead of meeting me at the gym? Gary probably asked her to come get me so I wouldn't be alone again in public. Though I sometimes appreciate the kind gestures and coddling at times, he's controlling and has trained Dena to behave in the same manner.

I finished lacing my shoes, grabbed my bag, and headed toward the door.

"Hey, hey, hey, hold on now. I know you're not walking out of here without saying good-bye, later, kiss my ass, or something." His voice was elevated slightly and eyes widened.

I stopped and turned to walk back to meet him as he stepped out of bed to walk toward me. I burst into a rambling spat, "I'm sorry. I'm just frustrated, that's all. I'm tired of all this drama. I gave up my life, my home, my everything to move in here and—"

"Huh? Sweetheart, we've been down this road before. We're getting married. There was a purpose for you moving in here. We're going to be married. You're going to be my wife."

His last statement gave me pause. I was certainly in a mood and I didn't want to sound like someone's property. *My wife.* Since the accident, I had progressed and healed but I was still struggling with my life. I had not gotten back into my work routine. I felt like I had given up all control of everything where I had a morsel of control—my career, my home, my independence. I felt like I was losing myself. Things were certainly moving faster than what I desired and in a direction that left me feeling vulnerable, out-of-control, and afraid most of the time.

I was in the midst of several ambitious entrepreneurs, which inspired me to step out on faith and start my own learning and development consulting firm, working out of my home and traveling a lot. So it was no surprise to me when Gary and Dena totally took my life into their hands and began to tell me what to do, how to do it, when to do it, and on and on. But in their defense, they wanted me to heal and get back into my daily routine without any worries or concerns about everyday life. I had no idea I'd experience all of the emotions that came along with it when I agreed. After my surgery, I had cancelled all of my events for three months so Gary and I hadn't bothered setting up my workspace in his house. I was supposed to let him know when I was ready, I just hadn't given him the green light yet. He had an office at home but rarely worked from home since he was leasing space with his business partner, Thomas Jamal Jefferson, or TJ as we all called him.

"I know that, Gary. I know. I just. I just still get frustrated that's all."

"There's no need to be frustrated. I got your back. I'm not going to let anything happen to you. Trust me. I'll handle whatever is ailing you. Today. And in the future. I got you." He rubbed down my shoulders and held my hands.

I sighed heavily. "Okay." I started to walk toward the door again.

He held my hand until I walked out of reach.

I texted my sister, Desilyn, on my way out of the door. *I was enjoying myself until the drama started again and I really got to know this man of my dreams. I'm not complaining, he still is the man I want to spend the rest of my life with, I'm just scared sometimes. I need to come home for a minute.*

I pressed Send and immediately regretted it.

CHAPTER 2: KAREN

"OH yeah, our beloved love child, Gary, is engaged to his cousin. I can assure you of that." I nodded my head.

"You've been running around here for two years, whispering that nonsense." Vaughn grabbed my shoulders and pushed me into the chair. He swiftly moved his hand as if he was going to hit me. "Do I make you nervous? Why are you flinching now? You were so tough when you walked in thirty minutes ago."

"No, I'm not nervous. Why should I be? Your yelling and flailing your arms do not scare me one bit. You're not a woman beater, Vaughn. I can recognize one of them a mile away. Now that, sir, I have experienced and that is not you." I tried to remain calm and not show my fear. I knew all too well what a beating felt like and I didn't like it.

The strength and confidence that I demonstrate outside my home was nothing like the demonstration inside the home where the doors were closed and the shades were drawn. I had learned how to make myself numb to the emotional and physical pain until it was over. My interpretation of that lesson I learned in my younger years from my mother landed me with two black eyes, three cracked ribs, and a broken wrist. It had also left a man clinging to life and me running for mine. I was tired and that was excessive treatment and unreasonable expectations for any human being to endure. I learned later that the nonsense my mother taught me was just that—utter nonsense. There was no way I should've tolerated that type of treatment just because a man was taking care of me. I should not have to shift who I am, so I didn't, I eventually fought back. The shift in corporate America as a black female was enough; I shouldn't have had to shift in my home.

"Oh but, you should be scared." Vaughn moved away from me slowly, never losing eye contact. He walked over and sat down behind his desk as he had a contemplative expression.

"Vaughn, you are not going to hurt me. You don't have it in you." I smirked and silently hoped he didn't have an abusive side. I didn't remember one. I only remembered how in love I had been with him at the time our son was conceived. I found out he was married and that crushed me. I think I allowed Judy Matthews to talk me into giving my son to her because I was hurt and didn't want to deal with anything connected to Vaughn M. James. I have regretted my decision for so many years as I struggled and fought to gain the trust and respect from my son, Gary.

"Try me." He smirked.

I don't know why we insist on getting into these arguments and make up later. I pulled my chair closer. I slapped my hand on the desk and responded slowly, "You listen to me, Vaughn, before you ever think about threatening to kill me, you remember this one thing, I don't take too kindly to someone wanting to beat my ass or who threatens to kill me. I got away with murdering my first husband." I sat back in my chair and stared at him. "Self-defense. Right after I tortured his ass. I'm not dealing with that again, though. I'll pay someone first."

I think Vaughn was just as evil as I. His tone matched mine. "There's a lot you don't know about me, Karen. One thing you should know for sure is that if you tell my son that cockamamie bullshit, I'll kill you myself. Strangulation. Don't push me." Vaughn spoke straight-faced bringing the conversation back to the reason I was there in the first place. "Why would you even think they're related? That's bull and you know it. You're trying everything you can to get him to like you, to need you. It's not going to work, Karen. You're going about this all wrong. Humiliation, stalking, sneaking around, it's all wrong. It won't work."

I dangled my crossed leg and tugged at my hair. "I have my reasons. That young lady's parents are my cousins. Second cousins."

"What? You're a lie. How is that? Run it down for me, Karen." He kept calling my name as if it would make me feel some kind of way by him doing so. "Run through your family tree and tell me where she fits in."

I brushed my skirt and sighed. I blinked a few times and folded my arms. "I have my reasons. Her parents are my cousins and that's all you need to know, Vaughn."

He stood up and leaned forward with his fingers spread and pressed against the desk. "Yeah, I bet you do have reasons. Just like I'll have mine when..." He paused.

His abrupt pause let me know that he had something up his sleeves and he didn't want to reveal it until he figured out what I was up to. He pointed his finger at me. "You've done enough damage in his life by leaving him at birth and not letting me know that he was mine."

I eased out of my chair, leaned forward, and pressed my fingers on the desk, directly in front of his. I was close enough to touch his nose against mine. He pulled away slightly. "I was young and afraid. Yes, I had given him away. I could have aborted his lil' ass and you would've never known."

I lingered there for a moment looking at him with lust instead of venom in my eyes. Standing so close made me remember the night our son was conceived. We both enjoyed that night and our most recent nights but this was all a game to me until I get what I want. I felt the warmness from his lips and heat of the breath from his nostrils so I backed away and sat back in the chair.

"But I didn't. I didn't want to give up my whole life for a kid. I was very young and I was not ready, so I gave him to parents I knew would care for him in a way I knew I wouldn't. And it was not at birth, he was several months old." I rubbed the back of my neck with both hands as I blinked back tears. My mood had changed on a dime. I needed one of my pills. I felt this coming. "Hell, I let him go after I had bonded with him. I breast-fed him, then Judy was helping me so much and she kept talking to me and I decided to give him to her and Clive." I dabbed a tear from my cheek.

Vaughn began to clap his hands and let out a hearty chuckle. All I wanted was a pass from him to understand what I was going through at such a young age.

"Bravo." He had composed himself from our intermingling breaths. I know he still loved me. He loved me years ago though I was much younger than him. He'd ended up divorced several years after his affair with me. I was too hurt at the time to continue a relationship with him. "That was a great performance; you know damn well Judy didn't coerce you into giving him up. You were not the first to have a kid at a young age and out of wedlock and damn sure wasn't the last. So don't you dare go there again." He rose out of his chair. "I'm his dad and you didn't tell me." He pounded his chest. "I could've raised him myself. I was stable."

I had managed to bring about a different reaction in Vaughn that most people had not seen. Most thought he was cool, calm, not much of a talker, a mentor, a father, and a hard worker. We had this *I shouldn't have given up my son* discussion so many times over the years, I stopped counting but I got the exact reaction and response every time.

"Oh, please, you were busy chasing women, as you still do. What were you gonna do, take him to the clubs with you? Let your old wife take care of him? Over my dead body." I fanned myself with my hand. "You don't realize how hurt I was to find out you were married. I was in love." I paused for a moment. I had never told him I was in love.

His eyes danced a jig of concern and he sat back in the chair.

I continued. "Clive and Judy were the best option for me at the time. They did well by him. I've provided support and protection for him all of his life. That's why he should be grateful and so should you. I was the one at his high school games, graduations, grand openings, everything. I have always kept up with him in my silent and incognito fashion. I have protected him all of his life even without him knowing it. I prayed for him daily." I paused as I rambled through my purse for nothing in particular.

He lowered his eyes but didn't speak so I continued. I was disclosing everything and prayed I didn't regret it later. "I had hired people to threaten anyone who brought harm to him in any way. Whether they lied on him or tried to harm him physically. Hell, I was the reason his aunt," I raised my hands to make air quotes, "and her daughter admitted they were lying about him having a kid, about him assaulting them, and all other lies they had told." I leaned forward and made hand gestures to every new piece of information I presented. "I got his record expunged when he and Sam got in trouble with drugs, when he got the DUI, and when they beat up the guy who stole money from them." I leaned back and crossed my legs. "Yes, I have indeed protected him most of his life."

Vaughn glared at me and let a long silence linger in the air. He decided not to respond to the "still chasing women" nor the "I was in love" comments. He rested his elbows on the arms of his white leather chair and pressed his fingertips together. "So you honestly think this protection you claim you've been providing from a distance was better than keeping him and raising him? That is the most asinine thing I've heard in my life. You know a lot of children still fall in love with their trifling parent and want so badly to be loved by them. Well as you can certainly see, this situation is different."

Sweat beaded around my hairline, my nose, and neck. Vaughn had probably purposely closed the vents. I looked up and noticed a piece of tape across the length of the vent. He had a small fan on the desk pointed directly at him. I started fanning with my hand then pulled my personal hand fan from my purse. I flicked it open in one motion and started fanning vigorously. The smirk on his face let me know that he suddenly realized he didn't need to cover the vents. My discomfort would have come automatically through conversation and hormonal issues at my age.

"Yes, I do. A mother's protection is always necessary. I couldn't provide him the direct love as a mother should, so I did what I could. I couldn't climb the corporate ladder with a kid. It's hot in here."

"No, it's not. And you're not the first woman to go to college, get an internship, go to Corporate America. Hell, you didn't even have a real job then. All of this sounds like an excuse to me. You're a coward, Karen. You were going on hope, alone."

"I was going on drive, dedication, desire." My voice rose slightly. "He would've slowed me down. Look at what I've accomplished. I couldn't have provided the support without a decent job. My internship provided me opportunities I would've never, ever, experienced had I kept him." I rolled my eyes and looked out the window when I recognized the stately lady who stepped onto the sidewalk. "I was simply not ready for a child." I had told myself that lie so many times over the years, I actually started believing it.

"So driving your 750 BMW, living in your...whatever Karen, stop beating around the bush with all this love and support nonsense and tell me why you think my son is engaged to his cousin." His nostrils flared showing his rising anger but he should have felt a nudge at that moment that told him, *Remember, you had a part in this too. If you hadn't stepped out on your wife, she wouldn't have gotten pregnant by you in the first place.*

He became extremely irritated for some reason, more than what I thought was necessary. I know he loved our son and fiancée as if she was his daughter but his response was different than in previous conversations about this. Maybe because now, he knows there's money involved.

"My son has been through so much in his life. The mental anguish of finding out he was adopted really took a toll on him. Nevertheless, he has worked hard and became a good and productive citizen in spite of it all."

"I understand that, Vaughn." I contemplated my next statement and how I could lighten the mood, especially when I knew we had a visitor strolling in soon. "Okay, if you must know. Can't you see they look alike? Just a little?" I teased. I'd only seen my son's fiancée once and it was in a dimly lit room.

I stood and walked around the desk to stand close to him. "Your children will be cursed because of your sins, Vaughn." I titled my head and rubbed my hand over his cheek. I had to admit, I enjoyed toying with him. He was extremely easy to rile.

Vaughn scowled. "Karen, get the hell out of my office before I strangle your ass. And if you go anywhere near my son with this nonsense I promise I'll kill you. Don't tempt me." He stood up.

"Her parents are my cousins." I sauntered toward the door.

There was a soft knock on the door, and it opened before Vaughn said, "Come in."

CHAPTER 3: GARY

WHEN I am determined, absolutely nothing can stop me. I'm determined to marry Mia and determined to stop Nina from getting in the way. I'm not the type to bring physical harm to a woman but I'm okay with a threat, if it'll get me the results I'm aiming for. Thoughts were racing through my head faster than the cars on the Autobahn. I wanted to leave a message on Nina's phone, I wanted to text it to her, but I decided I didn't want to leave any evidence, just in case. Even a simple-minded person knew that written communication could be saved and later used against you. I understood that words could get misconstrued over text or any other form of written communication, even in the tone of a voicemail if listened to repeatedly. I dealt with such cases daily. I needed to talk to her face to face.

I remember the first time I saw Mia several years ago. I was with Nina at a jazz café for her birthday. Nina's mood was extremely sour stemming from consistent bad days at work. I was miserable the entire night. My cousin, Dena, and Mia were having a girl's night out. When Dena saw me, she came over to chat and she introduced her friend, Mia, who was definitely a stunning first impression. She didn't say much so I couldn't get a particular vibe. Our eyes met but she made sure she didn't connect for too long. A dazzling smile and a nice physique, I had to break my stare. Of course, the introduction and my staring added fuel to the fire between Nina and me. She thought that Dena was purposely trying to break us up so that her friend could get her fangs into me. Her exact words. Little that she knew, Dena was so far from our problems. Dena and I grew up in the same neighborhood in Brooklyn and had known each other's families for years. She has always supported me with whoever I chose to date. Our cousins were married so we claimed each other as cousins. Nina was the reason that I let her go, not anybody else. I had tried several avenues to stay in the relationship—talking it out, being patient, trying to understand, but I was done. Exhausted. So, on her birthday, over two years ago, I had to let her go. I wasn't trying to be harsh, that just happened to be the day the scale tipped on my tolerance.

I remembered the email she'd sent six months after we'd broken up and after she saw me at dinner with one of my clients. The email was a one-liner from an email account that I know she created for bullshit emails. *Dear Gary, you hurt me and you'll never be happy with anyone else.* I saved it into my Nina folder and waited. I knew she'd be back with more.

Six months later, several emails later, and after I started dating Mia, a letter arrived in my mailbox like one of those stalker letters from TV with clippings from magazines and newspapers to spell out her thoughts. It was strange. She typed the last sentence in very tiny fonts. *I guess you and Dena got what you wanted. Your cousin's best friend as your girl. You dumped me for her? Are you serious? You will never be happy with her, not if I have anything to do with it. You will always be in misery with that joke of a woman.*

From the moment I met Mia, I knew without a shadow of doubt that she was the woman I wanted to spend the rest of my life with. I would give my life for her, but in my efforts to show her this, I felt like I was pushing her away, again. She thought I was trying to control her life. It's been a couple of years since her car accident but there seems to be one crazy incident after another which certainly slows our progress. When she left me and went to Arkansas, I went on one date with another pretty but crazy woman, Roni, who would not let go. She drove her car into the nail shop when Mia and Dena were getting their nails done. Since then, Mia had physically resumed her routine but her mood was on again, off again, from irritation and frustration to happy and blissful.

All I wanted was to be where I was supposed to be and doing as I was supposed to do. I've messed up enough in my life especially with women and I wanted to get this one right. She deserved it. I needed to talk to Dena though because I knew Mia very well and she didn't behave this way unless she was going through something that she had not fully revealed to me.

My phone rang and broke me out of the conflict that was going on in my mind.

"Hey, Gary," Mia's sister, Desilyn, chimed in an upbeat tone.

"Hey, how's it going?" I tried to match her tone and energy as I stretched and tried to sit up.

"What's going on with my little sister? She texted me but now she's not answering her phone."

Desilyn started this habit a long time ago. If she could not get Mia on the phone, she called me and expected some reasonable answers or else.

"She went to the gym with Dena." I pushed up and leaned against the headboard.

"Did I wake you? I'm sorry. I just bombarded—"

"No, no, not at all. I'm awake. I'm just chillin' and watching TV."

"Oh, okay. How are you doing?"

"I'm cool," I lied. Truth is, I was worried about where my relationship with Mia was going. I'm giving her all I got to give, my absolute best but I'm beginning to think my best is not good enough if I can't protect her from accidents, incidents, and drama from ex-crazies.

"That's good. How is she progressing?" Her chipper tone changed to worry and concern.

"Physically she appears fine but emotionally, I'm honestly not so sure. Since she moved in here she doesn't seem happy. I understand it's a big change for her and I try to be sensitive to how she feels but I don't think I'm doing a good job." I fidgeted with the sheet and felt slightly defeated after speaking those words out loud. Life and death surely does lie in the power of the tongue.

"Don't worry, honey, it'll get better. Have y'all started counseling yet?"

"Our first appointment together is in a couple of weeks. She went to her first two appointments solo."

"I know. She has probably wasted two sessions by not talking at all with her little stubborn self. It'll get better though. It has to."

"I believe so, too," I agreed and silently prayed. I know how I am and I know I can go full throttle in control of everything.

"Okay, well let me know if I can assist in any way. I know my sister very well."

"Okay, thanks, Des."

After ending the call, I tossed my phone on the nightstand and got up. I needed to find Nina before I got too busy and forgot about her as I've done so many times in the past. I had her numbers in an old phone but that phone was dead with no charger. I had no choice; I had to meet her at work or home. She shouldn't be too hard to find as she keeps finding Dena and Mia everywhere they go.

I thought Dena and Mia had left for the gym over ten minutes ago but I heard a car so I walked to the front door and they were still sitting there. I waved at Dena as she yelled a silly comment out the window and pulled away slowly.

I laughed at Dena as I walked back to the bedroom. I made a call to my barber, Breezy, because Nina lived in the same neighborhood as him. "Hey, Breezy. Man, what's up? I need a favor. Do you have Nina's phone number?"

"Hey, what's up, Brooklyn?" Breezy gave everybody a nickname usually named after the city or state where they grew up. "Hell nawl. That broad is crazy. I don't want her number. You can miss me with that one."

I chuckled at his voice, his tone, and his choice of words. He sounded like Tone Loc on steroids. "Clown, I'm not asking if you want her number. I'm trying to find her. I need to talk to her."

"Whatchu want with her? She wasn't enough drama for you while y'all were dating?"

I immediately regretted calling him. But I hadn't gotten to the real reason I called. I needed to park at his house instead of in front of Nina's house.

"Well, if I recall, you introduced me to this drama queen." I joked with him. Ever since Nina and I broke it off, I've teased him about not checking women out thoroughly before introducing them to someone. But I most definitely would never let him take the blame for that one. It was all me, a grown ass man making his own stupid decisions.

"Hell, man, I thought she was cool peeps until she started

acting a damn fool. I bet you I haven't introduced nobody else since then. She's a freakin' stalker, man. You better be careful. She was messing with this other dude who had to get a restraining order against her. "

"Oh, really?" I said as I thought about the same thing for Mia and me but I didn't need one just yet. I needed to talk to her. I wanted to be up close and personal in her space. "It's amazing how she leaves me the hell alone when she's dating someone but shows up acting an ass when she's not. Anyway, are you at home? I need to park at your house."

"Yeah, man. I'm here; come on through."

"Okay, cool, I have a stealth mission. I'll be in and out in a flash."

"You not gon' hurt the girl, are you?"

"No, I'm not." The regret I felt earlier returned. Truthfully, I didn't know what I was going to do. "I'll be there in a few."

I hung up.

I showered and dressed within thirty minutes and was prepared to walk out the door until the phone rang and slowed my stride toward the garage.

I pulled the phone out of my pocket and my face tightened as I swiped to answer, "What's up?"

"Hey, son. How are you doing today?" She was extra cheerful which irritated me even more.

"Hey, Karen," I grumbled. My shoulders dropped as I slowed my pace and stopped in the kitchen to find something to distract me for the few seconds, until I could get her off the phone. I was planning to talk to her, just not today. I immediately started replaying the scene with Mia earlier then quickly switched it to grocery shopping when I looked in the refrigerator since the scene with Mia didn't end the way I wanted.

"My, oh my, Gary, I thought these flat and dry greetings

every time I called were in the past. I see I still have a lot of work to do," she said curtly.

"Yes, you do." I let out a loud breath.

"Your lil' girlfriend is nicer to me than you are."

I was getting angry so I decided not to reply to her last comment and was trying my best not to hang up the phone while she was talking. I made a note to myself to ask Mia about her conversations with Karen. She had not mentioned any of them.

Karen is my biological mother. She moved to Houston around the same time as me because she claimed her husband was moved by his company. I believe it was to follow me. She claimed she's been with me and watching every major event in my life since she gave me away at three months old. I was adopted by two of the greatest parents one could ever ask for, and really believed it until I found out as a teenager that I was living a total lie and the two people I cared about most in my life, Clive and Judy Matthews, were a major part of the lie. Vance, my older brother; Jessica, my younger sister; and one of my best friends and cousin, Sam, were none the wiser and just as devastated as I was to learn the truth. Who cares that Karen was at a football game or graduation with hundreds or thousands of other people watching in the background. She wasn't there when it mattered like when I had the flu, when I had broken bones, when I decided not to play football anymore, when I got saved and baptized. She only showed up when it was glamorous or newspaper worthy and something that would impress her colleagues. I never knew she was there. Hell, I didn't know she existed. I eventually got past the ill feelings I had toward my parents and forgave them for keeping the truth from me for so long but Karen, I just wasn't there yet. And I didn't know if I'd ever be.

"Okay, well, just know that I love you, son, and I will go to my grave trying to prove that to you. It's been too long. I've wasted too much time." She tried to sound remorseful but I wasn't buying it.

"Yeah, that seems to be a pattern for you, wasting time." I hung up the phone and pushed it back in my pocket. I honestly felt bad about my last statement and for hanging up the phone abruptly but I'd have to deal with it later.

I needed to make some swift and inconspicuous moves so I decided to ride my motorcycle. I started the bike and made one last check to secure my phone and my wallet. I felt the phone vibrate. I looked at the phone. Sam had sent a text. *Hey G be there by 7.*

Sam was in route to Houston. He had always liked Houston since his first visit several years ago. He enjoyed his extended stay a few months back and decided to move. I was happy, concerned, and worried all at the same time. Since we were kids, wherever Sam and I resided in the same area too long, mayhem happened. We've matured and I'd like to think we would never cross those bridges of erotic dancing, playing women, and illegal activity ever again. I don't blame him though, I blame myself. All of the activities might have been introduced by him but the choice to participate was solely mine.

He was determined to move to Houston. He did some research, made some deals, and figured his business could thrive anywhere. Valet parking and car services had become two of the most lucrative businesses in Houston. He was confident he would be successful, so he decided to try something new while he was still young. He found a couple to rent his brownstone, put his home goods in storage, referred his steady clients to one of his friends, and took off to Houston. Brooklyn to Houston is quite a change but plenty of us have done it and love it. He planned to live with me for a few months then get his own place. I was actually looking forward to a slight change in pace, looking forward to the mellower Sam. So he was headed my way with his mantra, "I'm used to adversity, I was born into it. I know how to handle anything that comes my way. Anything. Nothing at all will break me."

I replied to the text, *Auight*. His relocation could be a help or hindrance. I kicked into first gear and off I went to find Nina.

CHAPTER 4: MIA

SOMETIMES love can be hazardous to your health and physical well-being. I texted Desilyn and dropped my phone into the side of my gym bag as I sulked down the driveway toward Dena's car. I opened the door, dropped my bag on the floor, and stepped in.

"Hey, Sissy, how are you today?" A smile spread across her face as she slapped me on the knee.

"I'm good." I leaned my head back on the headrest and closed my eyes. I could tell she was looking at me. After several minutes I opened my eyes and looked at her. "Are we leaving or no?"

"Uh, you know I don't ride passengers without seatbelts."

I turned away from her to pull the seatbelt over me to snap it. Holding my head down to find the snap was definitely like gravity for my tears because they danced along my eyelids and rolled down my cheeks. I blinked rapidly trying to stop them. That didn't work. I glanced to the right and saw Gary standing in the door. Dena let the window down and I prayed that she didn't strike up a conversation that would cause him to walk to the car. I leaned forward to grab some tissues out of my bag because I knew things were getting ready to go downhill.

Dena yelled jokingly to Gary, "Hey you, Jive Turkey!" She pressed the gas pedal and pulled away.

I leaned back in the seat and Dena noticed the tears as she was pulling away.

"What's wrong with you?" she asked accusingly.

"Nothing, my allergies are crazy this morning." I sniffed.

"Allergies my ass, Mia. What's going on?"

I remained silent and pressed my head against the head rest. Looking downward, I adjusted my bag in my lap trying to find the right words without getting into an all-out argument with her about my life, which is partly the reason I'm in a weird place now—everyone else trying to run my life.

"Mia?" I could tell she was getting frustrated.

"Nothing, Dena. I just want to go work out." I ran my fingers through my hair.

"Mia, now you know me well and you know dang well I'm not gonna sit here while you're crying in my car, talking about some damn allergies, and not say anything. Now either you start talking or I'm pulling this bitch over until you do." She slammed the brakes. "And I'll call Gary." Her voice was getting louder.

"You see that's it, Dena, all of you act like I don't exist anymore. No one is allowing me to make my own decisions anymore. Everything has to be run by Gary like I'm his property or something." Tears were flowing rapidly now. "And you're always yelling and ready to pop off like a sawed-off shotgun in the country."

"Mia, what are you talking about? You know we have your best interest at heart. Especially Gary, girl that man loves you. You're not far off…" she paused to choose her words wisely. "We just support you in getting back to where you want to be," she stammered.

"I want to be left the hell alone and living in my own space, and moving around freely, and making my own decisions as I used to." I folded my arms.

"Mia Nixon, are you serious? Look, I'm not trying to minimize anything that you've been through but you're going to be married one day." She put the car in park and adjusted herself in her seat to face me. "Gary Lamont Matthews would totally die for you."

"That's the problem."

Her eyes widened. She folded her arms across her chest and stared at me. "Enlighten me, what's the problem with that?"

"I'm just overwhelmed, Dena, that's all. I know y'all think I should be thankful and progressing after all of the drama from Lynn, the accident, the miscarriage, Roni, Nina, for the past two years. I haven't had the opportunity to get over one thing before something else happens." I stop rambling for a moment then started again. "I just have so much bottled up inside and I can't voice it because you guys will think I'm ungrateful and I know Gary always says he'll protect me but he can't be with me everywhere all the time. He was driving behind me when the accident happened and he couldn't stop it. I lost a baby that I wanted so badly it hurts; he couldn't protect me from that. Roni ran her car through the building sending all of us scrambling to safety; he couldn't protect us from that. I was moved out of my home and into the house with him. I haven't been anywhere by myself, I haven't made many decisions by myself, I'm always being told what I should do versus what I want to do." I rambled for what seemed like fifteen minutes. "I'm just tired."

"Girl, come here." She reached over for a hug. She pushed back. "We were…I was only trying to help you and relieve some of the pressure that you would probably feel dealing with all this stuff. I promise you, as controlling as I am at times, I don't want to run your life. I have enough darn drama in my own life. I was just honestly trying to help you and I'm sure I speak for Gary when I say he feels the same way."

"I know, I just feel some kind of way. Gary is not..." The honking from the security guy interrupted my statement.

Dena let the window down.

"Are you okay? Do you need any help?" he yelled.

"No, we're good. Just getting ready to leave. I was looking for my gym card."

"Okay, have a good weekend."

She turned back to me. "Okay now what? Gary is not, what?"

"He doesn't understand me. He keeps brushing everything off as if I'm overreacting to everything."

"He said that to you."

"No, he just acts like it."

"Now Mia, come on now. How does he act like it? Gary adores you and only wants the best for you. Dude texts me often saying thank you for introducing me to you. He loves you. You're it for him. All of those other relationships were a waste of time in his eyes. He told me that."

"Yeah, all that love is not keeping me out of harm's way."

She sighed heavily. "Did you tell him about the grocery store incident with Nina?"

"Yes, and that's what I'm talking about. He thinks I overreacted and thinks it was someone else and not her. He was more upset that I went to the store without him."

"Have you told him about Nina at all, showing up everywhere?"

"No, and don't plan to."

"Me, either. But you know what? If she keeps popping up, I'm going to pop her. I'll handle Nina, Lynn, and now I need to add Roni to the list. I owe all of their as— tails a beat down. Lynn, for trying to harm you, Roni, for trying to harm a bunch of people, and Nina, just for being a stupid bi—, oooh Lord, I'm trying to stop swearing so much. It's not working."

"I see." I mustered a smile. "But Dena, I don't want you getting into a fight for me. I got it. I'll fight for myself if I'm pushed to it. And besides, I don't want to live a life of tit for tat, and always in battle looking over my shoulder for an enemy. Hell I'm from Arkansas, in the country, we didn't have to live like that."

"Well. I'm from Brooklyn and that's exactly how we roll. And that Arkansas sheltered shit went out the window when we were in college. Remember?" She moved her hands in boxing and karate movements.

"Dena, stop it. Like I said, I fight when I'm pushed to it. Let's just go," I mumbled and tried to hide my smile.

She put the car in drive and headed toward the gym and I pondered the real reason I was so emotional all of a sudden.

CHAPTER 5: KAREN

"I get paid to be a bitch." I flung my bag over the sofa, plopped down, removed my shoes, and reached for the Bloody Mary my personal assistant, Alex, handed me. "Matter of fact, I've been a bitch for a long time, in a myriad of positions and a myriad of situations. My family, my friends, colleagues, enemies, everybody knows what I can become if I'm pushed. I've been a director, executive vice president, CEO, all of that and trust me when I tell you, being a bitch is required or they'll walk all over you. But where has it gotten me? Right back to Houston, Texas where I was born." I set the glass on the table. "My mother was on her own little journey and just happened to land here for a few months where she met my father but I'm so happy they raised me in New York instead of this country-ass place."

Alex scratched his head and raised his eyebrows. "Ahemm, you know I was born and raised in Houston, right?"

I fanned him away and took a sip of my drink because this conversation was not about him and his feelings. It was about me and how I had to make adjustments in my career because of my husband and now he's not where he promised he'd be in three years. So now I'm retired and consulting and he's struggling to hold on to the promise.

Alex had actually heard the same narrative when I first hired him. He knew whenever I was upset, he had to hear it all over again. The rant about Houston and my career was always safe.

"We followed my husband to Houston close to three years ago. Me, Chandler, and Breleigh, my beautiful eight year old daughter. I started with a small company that was eventually acquired by another, and after a span of control review, flattening of the organization, too many chiefs, and all of that corporate buzzwords bull, I was on the list of reduction in workforce. I really wanted to be a full-time mom; I was exhausted with the Fortune 500 corporate game, so I negotiated a retirement package, that's what I tell myself anyway. They made it worth my while. I had given a lot of years to that company, I felt they owed me that much." I gazed out the window for a moment. "Always remember this Alex, companies will always be more loyal to their bottom line than to yours. So you get all you can from knowledge to experiences to an entire compensation package because you never know when they will just walk in one day and say, 'we have to let you go.'"

I took a long gulp of my drink and set the glass back on the table. I continued in a tone that sounded more like I was talking to myself than to Alex. "I've made a lot of money in my day and received a lot in alimony from my ex-husband that I saved and invested, so I'm not hurting for money. But I still want all I can get; my daughter's future is riding on it. If something happens to me, I want her to be taken care of for the rest of her life." I walked over to stand in front of the window. I loved the view. The begonias Alex and I planted last week were beautiful. "The only reason I followed his no good..." I paused and changed my thought. I wanted to say something negative about my husband to Alex but I thought better of it. Alex does not know of the turmoil between us at the moment and I needed to keep it that way. "I allowed him to talk me into moving to Houston because I want to get to know my baby boy and to get my share of our inheritance and I'm not stopping until my mission is accomplished or it kills me, literally. And he thinks I only came because he had a promising career opportunity. Hmph! I always look for the possibilities, no matter what hand I'm dealt. I play to win." I finished off the drink.

Alex hopped up to refill my glass and I continued. "I have several things I need to get out of my way or get in my corner though, and it starts with Vaughn."

He frowned. "What are you going to do to Vaughn?"

Alex was fascinated by gossip. He's been with me for two years and I sensed that trait early on. I didn't mind it at all. I was only going to let him in on limited information anyway. His inquisitive nature has helped me more times than not. One of my very good friends owns a staffing agency and she sent him over. They sent him over with a list of qualities that complemented his competencies—prompt, persistent, resourceful, reliable, intuitive, assertive, critical-thinker, meticulous, and loves to shop. All of the qualities I needed in a personal assistant. I trusted her so I had no doubt she'd send me the best, and she did.

"I'm not going to do anything to Vaughn. I just need him and that little fat lady friend of his who's always interrupting our conversations out of my way of trying to get to know my son. He asks too many questions and she is always there unannounced to cosign."

"Oh. So what do you need me to do?"

"I just need to keep working on Gary's business partner, TJ

so you can become their temp then full-time assistant. You've done a really good job for me so far. I assure you, you stand to make a lot of money just by simply working for them and doing a good job. No funny business. Just work, listen, and do as I ask."

"I can do that. That's what I'm here for."

"Good." I massaged my feet as I took another sip of my drink. "I've been planning this for a long time and I want to make sure you have all the facts before you start. I want you to understand my son's personality—what he likes, what he dislikes—and find any information about that girl he's supposed to marry."

He nodded and reached for his notepad.

"My son, Gary, is engaged to Mia. I really need you to listen to see what you can find out about her. Strike up a conversation if she comes into the office to visit." I moved my index finger in a circular motion. "Dena is her best friend who's dating Monty. Sam, who lives in Brooklyn and visits Houston occasionally, is his cousin and best friend. Sean is also a best friend who's engaged to Holly, I think. TJ is his business partner and Vaughn, or V as we call him, is Gary's biological father. TJ is married, V is dating but neither of them matter in this story." I sighed heavily. "My goodness, that's a lot of people."

Alex was feverishly writing on his notepad. "I know you've told me this before but I want to compare notes and make sure I got it all correct." He held his pen to his mouth as if to contemplate his next question. "Now tell me if I got this right; for the Brooklyn crew, Clive and Judy are Gary's adoptive parents with one older brother, Vance, and a younger sister, Jessica who both have children who are not relevant to this story nor is all of the aunts and uncles and the Brooklyn ex-girlfriends, etcetera."

I held up my hand. "Yes, but hold on, make sure you understand the Brooklyn ex-girlfriends have no part in this, but the Houston ex-girlfriends might play a vital part here, so we need to keep them in mind, at least for now. The old assistant, Lynn, is out of the picture too. I believe she's still in jail for vehicular assault, attempted murder, or something. She was the one who tried to hurt his fiancée and her niece, Nola or Nyla or something, used to work for Dena, the best friend." I paused for a moment. This was all quite a tangled web. Lynn had children too. I guess they're staying out of sight for now. Two daughters. December and June, I don't remember her sons' names.

"You're good. How did you find out all of this information?" Alex asked.

"I know people. I know his family. I know his business partner, TJ. That's how he and Gary became business partners, because of me. I own the majority of TJ's half of the company. Gary owns the other half."

"As I stated earlier, you're good."

"Yes, I am. I work hard at it. When I tell them I have watched out for my son all of his life, I really have. TJ needed investors to start his company; I helped him with the majority of it. He didn't have the money. Then I coached him into a business partner because I knew Gary had finished law school, passed the bar, and started working. I wanted him to be an entrepreneur as he desired and not work in corporate America. I pulled that information from his law school friend, Sharon. You remember this if you remember nothing I tell you. Money will buy you almost anything you want. Remember that. Some people will sail their own parent up the river for money if the circumstances are right."

He nodded as he appeared to contemplate what I meant by

my statements.

I massaged my feet again. He walked over to me. "Let me do that for you, Mrs. Chandler."

I knew it was inappropriate but I didn't care. I leaned back on the sofa and allowed my assistant to massage my feet. He was much better than my abusive husband.

CHAPTER 6: MIA

T HE past can rear its ugly head at the wrong time, resuscitating a mistake that had flat lined a year ago. At least I thought it had until I got a text message just before my kickboxing class started.

Hey, Mia. been a long time. ~Q

I didn't reply. Q was Quan, a guy from a neighboring town where I grew up. I had not heard from him in over a year. I hung out with him a lot while I was in Arkansas during my last break from Gary. Hanging out with him was the biggest mistake I could've made. As with all relationships or friendships from the past, they ended for a reason and you should try to remember the reason so as not to repeat the mistakes again.

I was so emotional when Dena picked me up to go to the gym almost two hours ago and replying to a text from Quan would certainly heighten my frustrations. I had to keep lying to myself to get on with my morning. *Everything would work out fine.* My period was four days late and I was beginning to worry. I didn't mind being pregnant but I would mind if I lost another baby, so I kept telling myself that my period was late because it was always late, always sporadic. I was too afraid to be pregnant again. I had healed from a myomectomy surgery several months ago and Gary and I have been making up for lost time in the bedroom so the pregnancy probability was high. I had been drinking wine and working out like I was on one of the weight loss TV shows—two additional things I'm sure did not go hand in hand with a pregnant woman who had miscarried once.

Fifteen minutes into kickboxing, I felt the stress leaving. I released some of my frustrations in that room especially after the instructor incorporated the punching bag and speed bag intervals.

I walked to the back of the room to grab a drink of water and through the mirror, I saw a girl who looked like Nina walking with one of the trainers. My heart started racing and I paused for a second but I couldn't be sure as she was walking away from me. I really hoped it was not her because I was already in a mood and she would get a good beating today if she tried me. The gym was not like the grocery store, I was dressed for the occasion.

I looked toward the cardio area and saw Dena pacing back and forth on the phone with her hands flailing. I thought, *Oh gosh, she is letting Monty have it.*

I tried to push the thought of Nina out of my mind so I wouldn't get worked up and ready to fight for no reason. We finished the class including a cool down within fifteen minutes and I walked out to find Dena so we could do weights.

"Hey, you ready?" I asked Dena. She snatched her Bluetooth off and shoved it into her drawstring bag. "What's wrong?"

"Nothing. I just need to handle some things when I leave here. Let's finish this, I'm ready."

I placed some plates on the bar as Dena took her position on the bench. She did one set of ten as I spotted her.

She asked, "Are you still thinking about going back to Corporate?"

I thought that comment was abrupt and out of nowhere. We had not broached the subject in a while. I figured she was trying to get her mind off her previous phone conversation.

"Sometimes. I just don't know. I only thought about it because I want something steady and secure without having to work so hard for myself. But I keep resorting back to my thoughts 'stop being lazy' in my Mr. Brown's voice." I chuckled. "I think I've lost my drive for the grand scale and rat race of it all."

She smiled. "I know, right. I wouldn't go back if I were you. Not that you asked me. But I think your own ish is better than someone else's any day. You're representing you, your own brand, not somebody else's."

"Yeah, if your own ish is profitable."

"Yeah and you can make it so and where you can't, my cousin will pick up the slack. He's there willing and able to take care of you. You know that. And how hard do you have to work at talking. You do that well, just like me." She smiled.

I was silent. I lay down on the bench to do my set.

"Do you have an attorney on retainer?" I asked.

"Kinda, usually they won't just let you give them a retainer just in case you need them. They can't keep that money on the books without something to attach to it. I don't have that much litigious activity jumping off. But I do have this guy I've known for a long time who I can call and ask general questions. He always gives me advice or hooks me up to someone he knows with the specialty I'm looking for. His name is Gary Matthews."

I peered up at her from the bench. "Umph. Well, of course."

"Utilize your resources, Mia. The man is everything and you need to own the knowledge of that. Women would kill to be in your shoes."

"I know. He is a sweetheart. It's me but I'm getting it together."

"Yeah, you need to," Dena mumbled absentmindedly.

"Are you ready to stretch?" I asked Dena, noticing her distraction.

We were almost done lifting weights when the trainer walked Nina into our area. They stood a few feet away as the trainer explained the usage of the weights and the body parts she'd work to get her the desired results she wanted. I pretended not to see her and walked over to place the weights back on the rack. She's lucky I didn't ram one into her skull. I was feeling that kind of way.

"I know this bitchy-heffa is not in here trying to get a membership when she know her ass lives way on the other side of town. She's tripping," Dena said with disdain dripping from her tone.

"Yeah, I thought I saw her through the mirror while I was in class. I'm not sure what she's up to but I know I'm not in the mood. That shopping cart incident was the last mistake she was allowed to make without paying for it," I said as I watched the trainer continue the tour with Nina. "I certainly hope she doesn't take my current state of meekness for weakness. I'll take her out and she won't even see it coming."

"I feel ya', girl, but I got something for her today. I owe her. It's long overdue."

"No worries, Dena. If she doesn't cross us, we won't cross her. Remember your business. Remember your brand." I reminded her of her comment only a few minutes earlier. "We don't wanna be in here acting like we're filming a reality TV reunion show."

"Ummm hmmm, it'll be self-defense made for TV with her on the way to Ben Taub General Hospital."

CHAPTER 7: KAREN

I rushed across the heated marbled floor to get to my phone when I heard the song I had attached to his number.

"Hi, Vaughn." I smiled widely. I was beginning to enjoy every moment I talked with him. When I moved to Houston, we pretended to start off as enemies and over the past few months, we've become close. We stopped fighting the love we know we never lost for each other. Communicating on good terms can get us to the bottom of my son's connections to his fiancée and me closer to getting my inheritance. My parents had left both of us large sums of money. I could not receive any portion of mine until after I develop a relationship with my son. I believe they set it up in such a way because they knew it would be tough for me to do. The money would afford me the escape and courage to leave my husband so I will do what I need to do.

"Hey. Good Morning. I was calling to see if you were still stopping by for breakfast this morning."

"I want to really badly. I need to."

"Well come on. What's the problem? I'll have your plate in place before you could get into your seat," Vaughn said.

"I have a sore throat," I said as I studied my neck. The thumb-print bruise that Chandler left on my neck resembled a teenager's hickey and I didn't want anyone to see it. Wearing a scarf today would look a bit odd since the temperature was forecasted to reach eighty degrees. If Vaughn saw the bruise, he'd lose his mind. He was not too fond of my husband anyway.

"Really? You don't sound like you have a sore throat."

"Hmph. Well I do." I did not feel like it but I continued to smile because I enjoyed talking to Vaughn. We had redeveloped a closer relationship instead of the negative back and forth that we once shared.

I had learned that when you praise a man—especially one who you've had an intimate connection to—and show him respect and loyalty, he would desire you. I believe that to be true for most men. I knew that to be true for Vaughn. In contrast, a man who you ignore for whatever reason will definitely start to resent you and go the other way as well, I knew that to be true as well.

"So, what time are you coming?"

He probably wasn't trying to sound as sexy as he did but I heard a slight plea in his tone.

I sighed. "I'll be there in less than an hour."

I would never admit it to him or anyone else but I needed his attention right now.

I hung up the phone and called Alex.

"Did you get my baby to school safely?"

"Yes, ma'am, I sure did and I'm already in the office. I'm only working until noon today so I will grab your dry cleaning and head to your house before evening."

"My dry cleaning?"

"Well, it's actually Mr. Chandler's. I grabbed the bag because it was beside the door. I'm so sorry."

"That is not a problem, Alex. Of course you have to assist all members of the family, not just me. I'm meeting with Gary's girlfriend today for lunch, I'm picking up Breleigh from school, and I have a few errands to run so no need for you to come back this evening."

He paused then muttered, "Okay." He was probably stunned by the calmness in my voice. He doesn't know that I have assistance with my mood in the form of a small pill.

I got dressed and hurried to Vaughn's restaurant, Talk Sweet, to spend the morning with him. He made me feel special, he desired me, and anytime I could spend with him, I was happy about it.

I remember the day things started to change between Vaughn and me. I went to his office to discuss the possibility of our son getting ready to marry his cousin. I had leaned across the desk directly in front of him during a heated conversation. Our breaths intertwined and it was like magic, like a light switch that flipped and all of sudden, this was meant to be. After that day he had been calling and talking sweetly in my ear. Since I was getting so little attention at home, it was so easy for me to fall back into the arms of someone who I never stopped loving years ago.

Vaughn had the chef prepare an egg-white omelet and fresh fruit just for me. I had the same dish every time I met with him in his restaurant. We sat in the same booth by the window. He said it was to take in the sights and I said it was because he wanted to see who was entering and exiting his establishment while he was with me. Whatever the reason, I enjoyed our time together.

Vaughn sat across the table from me, his eyes studying me.

"What's wrong with you, Vaughn? Why are you looking at me in that way?" I pressed my hand lightly above my breast.

"I like what I see. I always have."

"Oh, really?" I pulled my fan out of my purse, flicked it open, and started fanning.

His eyes glimmered. "If you take that scarf off, you wouldn't be hot." He reached for the scarf and I pushed his hand away. He frowned and pondered. "What are you hiding?"

"I'm not hiding anything. Why would I hide anything from you?"

"What are you hiding?" he snapped and reached for the scarf again. "You know I'll kill that son-of-bitch if he hurts you." His tone had changed from a light-hearted chuckled to fuming.

"Vaughn, now you know I will not let anyone hurt me. He'd be pushing up daisies just like the last one."

He didn't speak, he studied my expression as if to determine if I was lying or not.

"Karen, did he hurt you?"

"No, Vaughn, he didn't." I started fanning again.

"You know you and Breleigh can come live with me."

I changed the subject. "Let's talk about my son's trust fund and her family tree."

"We can talk about the trust fund but I don't want to hear anything about her family tree."

"What? Why not?"

"Because I know she's not your cousin and I keep telling you, if you tell him that I'm going to do something bad to you."

"Oh, please. Here we go with that nonsense again. I'm trying to figure it out just like you are."

"Anyway, what does he have to do to get his money?"

"Let's review it together. These papers were couriered over to me before I left this morning." I placed all of the papers on the table and gave him a stack and I had a stack. "Find the section regarding age and I'll look for the section on family."

"How did you get these papers, Karen? I thought you lost your documents in the divorce."

"Don't worry about it; just look through them."

He glared at me.

"I know people, Vaughn. People who owe me favors, people who work for the attorney who drafted these documents."

He sighed. "They drafted these for you? Or they drafted them and you received copies."

"Copies from my mother's vault. Gary was the only one who was supposed to get a key to the trust after he reached his milestone and he is supposed to give me my portion."

For the next two hours, we flipped through pages and pages of paper and discovered that Gary was entitled to an additional five hundred thousand dollars at every milestone—complete college, advanced degree, marriage, and children. If I reconciled my relationship with him I'd received seven hundred thousand dollars. My hands started to tremble when I read that statement. He had received a lump sum after college and after law school. So, he was upholding his part of the bargain and I was struggling to complete mine. I had some hard working parents who were very savvy in their finances, including the windfall from the patent my father had on an airplane part used by all of the airlines. That's how my mother controlled everything and everybody—money. I showed her she had no control over me and what I did so I allowed Clive and Judy to raise Gary. My mother was so livid she made stipulations in their wills which is why I received zero dollars until I reconciled with Gary. What she failed to understand is, I loved my son and wanted a relationship with him, what I did not understand after all I had done was why my son didn't want a relationship with me.

CHAPTER 8: GARY

I was in Nina's neighborhood within thirty minutes. It was amazing the maneuvering one could do on a crotch rocket even when there was an accident on Highway 59. I pulled into Breezy's driveway, squeezed past his truck, and parked in front of it to hide my bike from the street view. I removed my jacket and helmet and walked down the street toward Nina's house. I didn't see her car in the driveway. She always parked outside because she had a lot of garage sale junk inside. I was not sure what I was going to do or say but I kept walking with irritation building in every step. She was causing unnecessary drama in my relationship and my honest intent was to get her to stop it. I rang the doorbell repeatedly but there was no answer. I knocked several times, still no answer. I put my ear to the door and heard nothing. I was tempted to peek through the window but thought better of it and started my walk back to Breezy's driveway. I rang his doorbell and he didn't answer but I could clearly hear the TV. I walked back over to my bike, put my jacket on, started my bike, and revved the engine to see if Breezy would hear me. I was getting ready to roll out to the street and leave a burnout circle so he'd see I'd been there but he walked out the door immediately followed by his son, Chance.

"Man, you wild, dawg. I was like Brooklyn out there acting a damn fool. Let me go out here and check his ass out." He grabbed my hand grinning widely and slapped my shoulder. Everybody at the barbershop calls me Brooklyn since I'm from there.

"I just wanted to holla at you before I took off. I was getting ready to leave you a ring of a present in the street but since you came out here, I don't have to."

He laughed. "Man, don't get me put out the neighborhood. You a wild dude." He stretched as he was looking down the street. "Auight man, I ain't doing nothing but chillin' with this lil' knucklehead for a minute." He grabbed Chance in a playful headlock and rubbed his head with his knuckles. Chance giggled and squirmed. "My first appointment is at eleven-thirty."

"That's cool. I'm just getting ready to turn some more corners."

"So Nina wasn't home?"

"Nah, doesn't seem like it. I didn't see her car but I thought maybe there was a chance she parks in the garage now."

"Man nawl. Sanford and Son still live down there, still park outside."

I laughed. "Man, you're a fool."

We both looked in the direction of Nina's house for a moment.

"Auight, son. I'll see you in a few days for a tighten-up." I rubbed my beard and then straddled my bike and extended my fist to bump his. I did the same to his son. "See ya later, Big Chance."

I pulled into the street and felt the phone vibrate in my pocket. I ignored it and kept going. A few seconds later it vibrated again and then again a few more seconds later. I pulled into the Walgreens parking lot to see who was so adamant about getting my attention. Dena had called three times. Before I could key in the password, she called again. I tried to remain calm before I answered but as soon as I swiped my phone, I heard her yelling.

"Gary, I kid you not, I'm going to kick the shit out of Nina if she don't leave us alone. Her ass keeps showing up everywhere we go trying to act like she don't see us or she'll make lil' snide remarks and shit. I promise you I'm—"

I cut her off. "Dena, hey hold on, wait. Where are you? What are you talking about?"

"This hussy has been showing up everywhere we go ever since you and Mia got engaged. And now her ass is at this gym taking a f-ing tour like her fat ass is really gonna work out. I swear to you, if you still messing around and still messing with this girl and making her think she has a chance and that's why she's causing all of this drama…oooooh I'm gonna hurt both of y'all."

I tried to remain calm and I was until she accused me of messing around with Nina. I started yelling in the same tone she had just given to me. "Dena, now you know damn well I'm not messing with Nina. I just left her house to snatch her ass up for harassing Mia at the store the other day. What do you mean, she's showing up everywhere y'all go? Why haven't y'all said anything about it? Hell I'm out here trying to fight a battle and I don't know all the facts."

"Cause Mia and I said we weren't going to say anything to you," she said calmly.

"Where is Mia?"

"She's in the kickboxing class and I just saw Nina's ass walk through here getting a tour. I'm telling you now, God as my witness, I'm getting her today." Her angry tone was back.

"Dena, don't do anything stupid. I'll be there in a minute."

"Bye," she said in a nonchalant tone.

The gym they were at was quite a ways from where I was. It would be a challenge to get there in forty-five minutes with no major traffic. I was up for the challenge so I tucked the phone back into my pocket and headed that way in a hurry.

I pulled to the stoplight and as soon as it turned green, I rolled the throttle, shifted up to second gear, then third all the way to fifth, rolling the throttle harder on each shift. I was on the Beltway and was riding hard until the traffic jam due to an accident slowed us to a complete stop.

"I hate this. Houston people can't drive worth shit," I yelled as my irritation was building. I calmed down enough to figure out a different route. I drove between several cars to get to the Sam Houston Raceway Park exit to take the feeder past the accident. I was almost there until one of those mean-ass-disrespectful-to-bikers-pricks blocked the shoulder so I couldn't get by. I waited patiently until I got enough space to fit my bike on the other side of the car with a little bit of space in front of the prick. He was so distracted trying to keep me from getting past he didn't notice the space had opened in front of him. I quickly maneuvered beside the driver's side door and slammed the side of my fist onto his window and yelled, "Bitch." I then pulled the throttle a little too hard because my front wheel was off the ground for about a hundred yards. I never lost control of the bike; I rode the wheelie out until I was able to set it down comfortably. "My God, I did not plan all of this today."

With each passing mile, I was getting closer to checking out the situation at the fitness center with Dena and Mia but each passing mile also gave way to the potential of more traffic issues before I arrived. As soon as the thought was completed, it happened.

CHAPTER 9: KAREN

ESLIE, my girlfriend, no-nonsense owner of the staffing agency had raked me over the coals for the last thirty minutes about my marriage. I mostly listened because I can barely get a word in when Leslie gets on a roll about failing marriages.

She thought I should just leave Chandler, Lawrence Chandler, my second husband of ten years, or kill him. But she doesn't understand that when you're in the position I'm in, you don't just leave, you have to plan to leave. It was not just about me, it was also about my daughter. My position was not unbearable. He gets aggressive occasionally but his actions hurt my feelings more than anything physical and it's only when he's been drinking which is too much lately. I had made the mistake of telling Leslie too many details about my marriage and now she wants to take him out.

"I'm okay, Leslie. It only happened twice," I lied.

She sighed then barked, "Even once should not be tolerated, Karen."

"I'm fine. I'll be fine."

She continued. "He should not put his hands on you nor

verbally abuse you. Listen, I hire people. That's my business. The people I hire do really good work. It's your move. What are you going to do? Let me know." We allowed a long pause to linger.

"I'll let you know." I finally said as I hoped I had misinterpreted the tone of her words.

"Good-bye, Karen." She hung up.

I drummed my fingers on the desk. I did not want to think about the decision I needed to make, but one thing I knew for sure is one of us had to go. However it happened, one of us had to go. I never thought I'd want him dead, though. I needed a plan.

Sweat started to bead around my forehead. I pulled the hand-fan out of the desk drawer, flicked it open, and started fanning.

I closed the fan, placed the phone on the desk, and continued to go through the mail placing each piece in its designated pile—trash, file, and read later.

"Mom, I think I want to eat at Cheesecake tonight." My daughter strolled into my office and plopped down in my executive office chair.

"Okay, is that Cheesecake Factory or are you just wanting Cheesecake for dinner? Honey, what did I teach you about being specific in your requests?" I looked over my glasses at her.

She smiled as she swirled around in the chair. I had rushed to pick her up from school earlier. Wednesdays used to be our eat-out day, wherever she wanted to go. As she had gotten older, I allowed her to choose the day and the place based on our weekly commitments. I made sure that I asked her daily how her day went. I needed to know; I'm her protector, her guidance, and her mother. She's such a sweet and beautiful girl with her caramel colored skin and light brown, kinky, curly hair. I made sure I told her daily how beautiful and smart she was.

My words were not merely words of encouragement but the truth. My husband loved our daughter but hated her hair. He's always barking about doing something different to it because his mother and sisters can't do anything with it when she visits them in Galveston. I fixed that, I just stopped allowing her to go there anymore without me. My baby was pretty, petite, and athletic with beautiful character. She was mature for her age. She keeps me grounded and I was not about to let any of them make her think differently with their negative connotations. I know there was a happy medium that I could have taken, like teach them how to care for her hair. But why? Cutting them off hurts them more. I would do anything to protect my children.

"Okay, Mom." She exaggerated her words. "I want to go to Cheesecake Factory that is near The Woodlands Mall at five-thirty p.m. today. I want to ride in your black BMW 745. I want you to wear—"

"Okay, little girl, I got it." I smiled at her and shook my head. I was so happy that she was well behaved and I never had to go to the school to discipline or scold her. Other parents can't say the same. All of her teachers loved her. They said she was a leader and very helpful. Her excellent grades proved she was a smart girl.

"Yippee!" She thrust her palms in the air as she twirled in her chair again. "God is good all the time."

I laughed. "You are something else, young lady. Finish your homework so we can get out of here."

After our twenty-minute drive, we ate dinner and then browsed in a few of the stores near the restaurant before returning home at Breleigh's bedtime.

We walked into the house and Chandler started in on me. "So, what took you so long?"

"What do you mean, what took me so long? We ate dinner and came home."

"You know Breleigh's bedtime has passed."

I let out a nervous chuckle because he appeared to be inebriated and that's usually when he behaved badly. I'm not sure why I appeared nervous or afraid in front of my daughter, and I think I demonstrate the same in front of Chandler. He knows I will protect her at whatever cost and if I could keep her out of harm's way by taking the brunt of the abuse, I'd do it.

"It's thirty minutes before Breleigh's bedtime. She still has time to take a bath, brush her teeth, and get in bed before her bedtime. She already completed—"

He interrupted me. "So, you did this on purpose? You kept her out so I wouldn't have any time to spend with her."

I turned to my daughter and kissed her cheek. "Breleigh, sweetheart, go upstairs and prepare for bed. Good night, sweetheart."

She walked over to him and wrapped both arms around his waist. "Good night, Daddy."

He rubbed her head, did not say a word, and never took his eyes off me.

Breleigh slumped her shoulders and walked up the spiral staircase by the pantry.

I listened intently and waited until I heard her feet cross the corridor and her door closed before I continued the conversation. "Do you realize what you do to her when you ignore her whenever she tries to show you any love and affection?"

"Do you realize how you make me so angry when you keep her out every Wednesday night?"

"Oh, I make you angry, huh?"

"Yeah, you little bi---, yes, you make me angry."

I glared at him and placed emphasis on every word that left my mouth, "Do you realize she looks forward to our time out together. You used to do it but now you're too busy with whatever you have going on in your little world. Nothing will make me take that away from her."

"Yes, I have a lot going on trying to take care of my family. You're the one running around Houston all day spending money on God knows what."

"I have a job just like you. Don't hate me because companies pay me for my expertise," I stated calmly as I thumbed through mail I had already sorted.

"Yeah, you have a job," he retorted sarcastically.

"Contrary to your unpopular belief, consulting is a job, Chandler."

"Unpopular? Unpopular?" he shouted. He slammed the refrigerator door shut and rushed across the room toward me. He grabbed me by the neck and squeezed his fingers into my flesh. "So, I'm unpopular now?"

I looked into his eyes as a tear rolled down my cheek. His grip was tight and painful. I did not panic. I tried to hold my breath until he loosened his grip or let me go. I did not fight back because I knew there would be too much commotion for Breleigh. I knew he'd stop soon because he would never want Breleigh to see him behave in that manner.

He was never this way when I was a full-time executive. He was more respectful, caring, and even submissive to a point. When he thought I needed him, he started behaving badly. I was so ready to get out of the marriage but I needed to make it just a little while longer with him or make it until he died. I knew what his exact response would be before he did it. He saw the tears in my eyes and immediately started to apologize. He buried his face into my shoulder and sobbed. I was done with this routine. It had become more frequent lately. His tantrums used to be once every few years, to once per year, to once every six months. I expected it to become even more frequent because that's usually how it went. But I wasn't running. I had a plan for him.

I did not see the unstable side of him until eight years into our marriage when he lost his "high profile" position at one of the large financial institutions. He's lucky he didn't land in jail for misappropriation of funds. Due to the small amount of money, he was able to maintain his dignity by repaying the money and submitting his resignation. He had allowed his title to define him and after his termination, he felt that all of his buddies in the club had started to treat him differently. He went from drinking scotch and cognac, to drinking beer and wine then from smoking cigars to smoking cigarettes and smoking a pack per day. He had definitely changed.

I needed to make sure I planned our escape properly and fighting with him would certainly rush things along faster than I wanted them to go at the moment. Fighting with him could potentially render me unconscious. Permanently. And I certainly did not want to leave my baby, Breleigh, nor my son, Gary.

I needed to remain calm. I allowed him to sob into my shoulder. I robotically touched his back. I stepped away from him and headed stiffly to my bedroom. This was another episode for the diary.

I heard a faint voice as I walked away from him and I heard the patio door close. "I'm so sorry, Karen. I'm so sorry."

CHAPTER 10: MIA

DENA and I finished our weights and walked over to the stretching area. I dropped onto the mat, stretched my legs wide, and leaned forward. Dena mounted on the machine to guide her stretching.

"Okay, I'm changing the subject before I run over and ram a weight into that girl's head."

"Dena." I snapped in a loud whisper. "Stop it. You're gonna get me all hyped up if we keep giving her the attention she doesn't deserve, and people would swear I'm fighting over Gary if the two of us locked horns."

"I know, right. But we both know that if you and her locked horns, it would be because she kept making the wrong moves and you tagged that ass." She tossed her hands in the air. "All is fair in hate and war."

A lady who had walked into the area overheard her and started to laughed and said, "I'm going to use that one."

Dena said, "Feel free."

I was very surprised Dena didn't snap at the lady for joining our conversation uninvited because that was definitely one of her pet peeves. We stretched in silence for a moment until the lady walked away.

Dena said, "You know who I think about a lot?"

"No, who?"

"Sylvester slash Brock. The man with multiple names and multiple women."

"Why on earth are you thinking about him? He vanished again. He's history." I frowned.

"Yeah for now. I got a sneaky suspicion he'll be back though," she replied distractedly as she held on to the bars and leaned backward.

"Why? He doesn't want you to tell authorities about his illegal activity."

"Mia, he's just that kind of dude."

"Oh. Well, I didn't get to know him that well. I was friends with him for only a few months."

"Thank God. It's bad enough we dated the same guy with multiple names. Geesh, it'll be awful to think he slept with my best friend before I met him. Ewww." She stood and placed her knee on the pad of the machine and moved her knee to stretched her quads.

"He seemed like a pretty okay dude but kind of distant, even weird at times."

"That's because he was juggling several of us at the same time. If he remained quiet, the fewer slip ups he'd make and the fewer questions he'd have to answer. He was dangerous though. Breaking into my house, writing on the mirror. Had his crazy daughter leaving notes on our houses. Just too much."

"I know, right."

"Did you sleep with him?"

"No, just dinner and movies a few times. Kissed him but that's it." I looked at her. "Ewww. We kissed the same guy."

"I know, ewww." Mia laughed.

Dena shook her head and frowned.

"From now on, we're telling each other everything about guys we go out with. Well, not everything, but you know what I mean. We can't have that happen to us ever again," I said.

She was looking at me blankly. "Uh, heffa, you're not ever dating anybody else. Don't make me kill you."

"Whatever, Dena." I placed the palms of my hands on the floor and raised my legs over my head to touch my toes on the floor. I asked, "Will you hold my legs back please?"

Dena remained silent and walked over to the mat and pushed my legs toward the floor. "If you fart on me, I'm going to kill you."

"Dena, my God, why would I do that? That's insane." My eyebrows were furrowed.

"I was only kidding. Geesh."

We finished stretching and headed toward the locker room.

"So, Dena, whatever happened between you and Dwight? He seemed like a cool dude."

"Girl, please. He was going through a divorce, remember? And he was irritating."

"More than Monty? Ooops, sorry. I know you loooove Monty."

"You're right, I do. He does irritate me but I know him. I know his drama, his faults, and his good qualities as well. But with Dwight, ugghhh." She fanned her hand. "No sense in going in knowing the drama is splattered everywhere. All of this back and forth with the wife, ugggghhhh just too much, too much. And he was too old to not be living his dream. He's still wishing and hoping and side hustling…nope no potential. Can't do it."

"So, then, when are you and Monty tying the knot? You keep throwing me and Gary in there."

"Ummm, I don't know. I'm having a blast planning your wedding but dang sure don't want to plan my own. I'm eloping."

Monty had proposed to her two months earlier. They were crazy in love which meant arguing all the time but couldn't do without each other. Lately, most of the arguments were started by Dena. She seemed irritated by him a lot more which is why I was surprised when he bought the ring. He had talked to Gary about it. I tried to accept him more since they were engaged. He wasn't abusive, but he was a cheater in his past, and I'm going to believe in reformation.

She headed for the scale and I headed to my locker. I was pulling my bag from the locker when I heard the tour-guide say "...and this is our locker room." I turned to see Nina smiling and twirling her keys around her finger. I thought, *This girl has a death wish.*

She had managed to get the trainer to give her a tour of the locker room while we were in there. Although I wasn't watching her directly I maintained my peripheral view of her. She browsed around the pool, steam room, and sauna while we were stretching and as soon as we walked into the locker room, she came in also. I really hoped I wouldn't have to fight her. My reputation was at stake. Public disturbance was clearly not my style but I was not against it, either.

Dena stepped off the scale and walked toward them.

"Hey, Dena," the trainer, Theresa, said. "Dena and...hey, Mia. Dena and Mia have worked out here for several years now."

"I know them," Nina chimed in.

"Hold on, wait a minute, Nina. You know I know your butt extremely well," Dena said.

I walked over to the area where they stood.

"Oh, that's great. You two know each other?" Theresa asked, her eyes lit up in surprise.

"Very well. We used to be cool until she flipped the fu—until she started acting a fool over a guy who doesn't want her." Dena was answering the question but never took her eyes away from Nina. I was actually surprised at her calm demeanor.

Nina sucked her teeth and rolled her eyes.

Dena stepped closer into Nina's space. "But now you keep popping up everywhere me and Mia go pretending not to see us, making little snide remarks just loud enough for us to hear you. You don't live anywhere near this damn gym and now you're over here wasting Theresa's time getting a tour, knowing damn well you're not going to join, nor work out." Dena paused and stared angrily at her from her hair all the way down to her inappropriate gym shoes and back up again.

"Who works out in sneakers with a heel on? She's looking for trouble today, and she found it," I added as I stepped closer to her.

"Better yet, who wears that shit?" Dena hissed.

Nina was not fazed by either of us. "Theresa, let's finish the tour."

"Theresa she doesn't live anywhere near this gym. You're wasting your time," Dena said.

Theresa's demeanor changed from chipper to deflated.

Nina shifted her weight from her right to left foot and said, "You don't know where I live. I—"

"Canyon Cove subdivision, North side, two forty-nine and Beltway Eight," Dena interrupted her and stepped even closer.

Her eyes widened and she scratched her head and glanced at Theresa.

Theresa gasped. "Yes, that is quite a ways." She looked back and forth between Dena and I then Nina.

"Now what, bitch?" Dena scoffed.

"She knows exactly what she's doing. This high school crap." I was trying my best not to use profanity as Dena was using enough for both of us. I'd like to think I have a bigger vocabulary to read her than resorting to those words. But when I became angry, I didn't care what I said or did until it was over.

"Listen, uh, girl. I don't know what your problem is popping up all over the city everywhere we are. Gary is with me now. I'm not sure what you're trying to accomplish by showing your face everywhere I go, but you'd better stop it and stop it quickly."

Nina folded her arms across her chest.

"We're happy. You got that?" I was furious but trying to maintain a calm demeanor as I thought back to Gary and my conversation earlier.

"May the best woman win." She snarled and glanced at Dena then turned to face me.

"The best woman will." I stepped closer to her. I was fed up with her nonsense. I was not about to back down and was struggling to keep my composure but stepped close enough that our arms touched. I was hoping she would push me so I could put her flat on her back and claim self-defense. She took a small step backward.

"You got that right and nobody got time for this stepping game." Dena grabbed Nina into a chokehold.

Theresa yelled and tried to step between them. "Dena, no, don't."

Nina elbowed Dena which caused Dena to loosen her grip. As Nina struggled to get away, she spun around and pushed Dena.

Dena ran around Theresa and threw a punch that scathed Nina's jaw because I was pulling her away and Theresa pushed Nina toward the lockers. "Dena, stop it! Now," I said firmly while trying to keep my voice low. "Are you even remotely aware that this girl can file assault charges against us?"

"Ask me if I care." Dena straightened her clothes and tried to walk around me.

"Stop it right now. This is too much. This is too much." I gritted my teeth. "Provoke her to attack you, not the other way around."

Theresa quickly grabbed Nina by the arm and said, "This is not good. I think you should leave, like right now."

Nina snatched away from Theresa's reach and stormed out.

CHAPTER 11: KAREN

had to take my mind off killing my husband in self-defense, so I shifted it to my son. He doesn't understand that I will get to know him one way or another. I will do whatever it takes. I tried to talk to him, but he hung up on me. He thinks I'm wasting his time. I've tried so many occasions and I'll keep trying. I cannot afford to lose him completely. He's part of my escape for me and Breleigh. I plan for the three of us to live happily ever after on our journey. His company, our company has to work. He's going to be livid when he finds my hands in his business. I get my monthly dividends from them and I don't think he knows. Well, he couldn't know. TJ pays me from his percentage. It's not much but it certainly gives me additional savings.

I do quite a bit of business sitting in my bed every morning. I had already taken care of my hygiene and Breleigh was on her way to a play date. I can handle conference calls, webcasts, consulting sessions all with my back pressed against the headboard, and that's just the way I liked it. My life had transitioned from executive to a working house-wife.

I noticed my husband had not left the house yet so I reached over to the nightstand and pulled out one of my pills I had hidden inside of a jewelry bag. I swallowed it and then took a swig of water from the water bottle that I made sure was within reach every night before I went to bed. I needed to ensure my nerves were settled and calmed before I encountered him. I asked my doctor to prescribe something for my anxiety about a year ago. Now I'm dependent on them; if I don't take them timely, I would probably have killed him by now.

Last night Chandler burst into the room yelling with his arms flailing shortly after he'd grabbed me by the throat. "You think you have control over everybody, don't you?" He huffed and stood directly over me as I was resting and watching one of my Real Housewives TV shows. He had slithered out the patio door professing his sorrow for what he had done to me and less than two hours later, he was in my face again.

I sat up in the bed. "Chandler, what are you talking about? My God, you're always so uptight."

"I am not uptight! I'm not uptight, Karen!" He huffed. "Did you tell my brother that he needed to get a job and take care of his own family because we couldn't take care of him anymore?"

He had to have spoken to his brother and listened to his sob story. I had spoken to him and his wife earlier and said "no" to their request. His brother was using him and he couldn't see it or he didn't want to see it. I wouldn't doubt if it was guilt or blackmail coming from his brother.

"Yes, I did. He needs to stop milking you for everything you've got because he's lazy and you know it." I yelled back at him.

"I can't believe you're being so cruel. We have the money. I know you own half of Matthews and Jefferson. What else are you hiding from me? We have the money."

"Chandler, what are you talking about?" I feigned confusion. I knew exactly what he was talking about but I had to perform as if I had no clue. That's money he and his family would never get their hands on. "I don't own anything. If I did, I wouldn't be here with you," I yelled back at him.

His phone buzzed in his pocket and distracted him briefly. He had been drinking and his attention deficit took over. "His wife is pregnant, Karen and she's on bed rest. He has to stay home sometimes to take care of her. They need help. You're just a stingy bitch. You don't control my money."

I flipped the covers off and stood face to face with him. My medicine had worn off because I was definitely on edge. "You got that right, I'm a stingy bitch and it's our money." I pointed my finger between us. "I'm not going to let that bitch brother of yours and his bitch wife take everything you've worked hard for or even better, money that you stole for our future. You have to manage what we have and we must invest."

"You stingy…" he raised his hand to hit me and I caught him by the wrist. He looked as if my actions surprised him. I was one hundred eighty degree different from the last time he saw me which was two hours earlier.

"Hit me and I'll kill you." The venom had swirled around my body and was squeezing me like an anaconda. I was ready for battle in that moment.

Chandler was taller and larger than me but I stood my ground when I needed to. He knew that I'd been a battered woman before, a victim, now I'm the opponent because I can get with the best of them. The smart thing I do is not do it in public. As far as the public was concerned, I was the victim.

"Don't think I don't know what you've done. Don't tempt me, Chandler. I have proof and I have backup in multiple places. Even my death won't bury what I have on you."

He looked stunned. I was so sick of his crap. I revealed more than I should have. He was a wimp, a yes-man who easily got his feelings hurt, and then he'd drink and drown his sorrows, start yelling, trying to harm me, afterward he'd sob and cry about it.

I threw a pillow and the duvet at him for dramatic effect. "You need to get out of here and sleep in the guest room or the sofa or anywhere you'd like. Try your mistress' house, I don't care, just get out of here. I don't need your drunk ass in my bed." I certainly did not want him to come down from his high and try to have sex with me either; that would result in accidental death.

I knew the effects of the pill would calm me in the event he walked back into our room with another performance. I prayed he did not and he didn't.

He walked in quietly, shoulders slumped, not giving me eye contact. "Good morning." He walked into his closet.

"Good morning." I watched his every move.

Fifteen minutes later, he walked out. "Have a good day, Karen."

I knew how to handle my business and I was doing it. His brother would never touch another dime of the money that I could be stashing for my future.

CHAPTER 12: GARY

I was on edge in a major way trying to maneuver Saturday morning traffic. I finally made it to the gym but not before the fight. Dena had already allowed her emotions to get the best of her. According to a couple of my buddies who were in the parking lot, it all ended soon after it started. Nina was on her way out of the gym yelling obscenities while Dena and Mia were still in the gym talking to Theresa and the manager. Dena, as usual, was always ready for any altercation, never thinking about her reputation or causing herself or anyone around her harm. She's ready for the attack. She has anger issues that seem to have gotten worse over the last year. She had a difficult childhood and some issues into adulthood but I'd think some of that stuff should've been resolved by now. Contrary to popular belief, everybody could use some type of therapy.

Dena and Mia were like sisters which meant they were always there for each other, but the expression on Mia's face and her body language showed major signs of irritation. As I walked through the door, she saw me but immediately rushed toward the other door to exit. I didn't go after her because I didn't want to cause a scene. So, I walked toward Dena.

"Dena, what happened?"

"Hey, Gary. I choked Nina. I told you I was gonna do it," she said dryly. "Now, Mia is pissed at me saying I didn't have to take it that far. All of us were standing there talking shit and nobody was doing anything, so I choked her."

"So, you couldn't stay calm long enough to walk away?" I glared at her with furrowed brows.

"Whatever, Gary," she said as she stormed past me.

"Dena, hold on, wait." I reached for her arm.

"What?" she shouted and she spun around to face me.

My eyes widened. "Oh, really?" I tried to keep my voice low. "Is that how you're going to act in front of all these people? You'd better calm your ass down. What did Nina do?"

She folded her arms across her chest and shifted her weight to one leg. "She showed up—one too many times."

I had so much that I could've said at that moment but I decided to keep it simple. "Let's get out of here." I guided her toward the door.

"Hey, Gary." Theresa came around the desk.

"Hey, how are you doing, Theresa?" I kept my grip on Dena's arm.

"They don't have to worry about her coming here anymore. You know Dena and Mia are my girls. We can't have anybody coming in here harassing my people. But you might want to consider a restraining order," she said.

"Yeah, I need to do something. Thanks, Theresa."

"Thanks, girl." She reached for a hug from Dena. They embraced then we turned to walk out the door.

"Gary, contrary to you and Mia's beliefs, I don't act a fool all the time. Only when pushed. She pushed me and I was fed up."

"So, she pushed you?" I asked with skepticism in my voice.

"Well, not physically." She twisted her face.

I shook my head. "Dena, you have got to calm down."

"We all need to calm down," she said.

Mia was leaning on the car talking to someone on the phone. I walked toward her as Dena pressed the key fob to unlock the doors. She tried to get in the car before I got to her.

I made it to her and pressed my hand against the door. "Baby, wait. Look…"

She tried to pull the door open and I pulled her closer to me as she struggled to get away so I loosened my hug and place my hands on her shoulders. "Hey, hey, hold on, Mia." I leaned down to look directly into her eyes. "I'm trying. I went to find Nina this morning and I had no idea she would be over here. I'm sorry, baby. All I can say is let's get a restraining order before somebody gets seriously hurt."

"I've already been seriously hurt by your assistant, remember?" She snatched the door open and got in.

CHAPTER 13: KAREN

I watched her get out of her car, a silver sedan with a dent in the side. I was a bit perplexed. I never pictured her driving such an ugly little car. My son is in love with her? She approached the patio, wearing blue scrubs. She had gained some weight. I thought it was because she had been in recovery mode for some time and hadn't taken the opportunity to go to the gym. Her hair was different as well. Short, honey blonde twists. Though cute, I just didn't see her with my son. She didn't look like his type, well she didn't look like the type I'd want him with but I understand I can't pick for him. She appeared shorter than I remembered but maybe she had on those high heels the women are wearing nowadays. Her appearance makes me want to absolutely make her my cousin, even if I had to fake it, so they'd break up. I studied every step she took in my direction.

"Hello there, lovely lady. How are you doing?" I stood up to hug her.

"Hello, Mrs. Matthews."

Her hug was weak.

"Mrs. Chandler, sweetheart. I've never been a Matthews. But I asked you to call me Karen, remember? No formalities necessary. Especially if you're going to be my daughter-in-law."

This is really strange. Gary's fiancée is acting like she's never met me before. Women usually try to impress the mother of their fiancé. Mrs. Matthews? I had spoken to her several times over the phone. I told her to call me Karen, anyway. She looked different. I was trying my best to like the girl.

"Oh, I'm so sorry." She wiped her forehead.

The waitress came to our table and asked for our drink orders. We both asked for water.

"Are you okay?" I reached across and placed my hand over hers.

"Yes, ma'am. Yes, ma'am, I'm okay. I just had a uh—a uhh altercation at the gym earlier this morning and it's still rolling through my mind, that's all." She brushed her hand over her hair then put the menu up to cover her face.

"An altercation? With who?" I was curious.

She adjusted herself in her seat and tugged at the corner of her hair. "One of Gary's—never mind. I should not have said anything."

"Okay, I won't have you relive that moment by rehashing it now. So, how are you and my son doing?" I smirked.

"Oh, we're fine." She let out a deep sigh as she smiled a fake and wide smile.

I smiled back at her and slowly clasped my fingers in front of me trying to determine my next question. "So, didn't you tell me you grew up in Arkansas? Tell me about your family."

The waitress came back and interrupted us again. We ordered and before I could launch back into the conversation, she excused herself to the restroom.

I grabbed my phone and texted Alex. *I'm not getting far with this one. Nina is fidgety and slow with the answers to anything I ask.*

My phone rang within five seconds of pressing send. "Uhhh,

Karen. Gary is with Mia not Nina. You have the names mixed up. Do you even know which one you're having lunch with?" Alex's voice dripped with concern.

My jaw dropped. I could not believe what had just happened. I'm having lunch with the woman who has caused my son a lot of grief. I pulled the folder from my Tumi tote and there it was—Nina Nixon. I had mixed the names of my son's friends. Shoot, Chandler has me so mixed up that I messed up. The picture I had from a newspaper clipping looked nothing like the woman who was once sitting in front of me.

I looked up from the folder when I heard tires screeching. It was Nina in her raggedy car leaving the parking lot. She didn't realize she'd just made a new enemy.

CHAPTER 14: KAREN

made a mistake." I slammed the folder on the table in front of Alex and planted my palms on the desk. He flinched as he always does when I throw things. "I messed up, damn," I spat as I dramatically demonstrated my frustration with myself.

I walked into the laundry room to change clothes. I stepped into the room, switched my shoes, pulled my hair up into a ponytail, slid out of my skirt, and pulled on some sweat pants. I removed my jacket and hung it on the drying rack and slipped a t-shirt over my head. I had a certain look I wanted to convey to Gary's girlfriend and I was impressing upon the wrong woman. I stood in the laundry room talking to myself. "I cannot believe she tried to trick me." All this time, she's been faking me out. I stepped out of the laundry room and walked toward the kitchen to join Alex again.

"Gary is planning to marry Mia not Nina. I took that troll Nina to brunch and I figured it out, well not until I heard the screeching tires and when you called. I knew something was very strange though. She lied to me. I should do something to her. But as I think about it, it was a blessing. I'm glad I found out sooner than later. I didn't like her anyway. I'm glad she's not the one but I'm not glad she tried to play me. I've been talking to this girl for months," I rambled. "But she's about to meet my mother's other child and nobody likes that bitch." I pulled the refrigerator door open, took a bottle of water, twisted the cap, and took a long swig.

Alex stared at me blankly. "Yes, you mixed that one up. And technically, she didn't lie; you assumed a lot and went for it. What happened?" He shook his head and started thumbing through the papers in the folder I had labeled Nina Nixon. "Let me fix this."

I ignored his probing and frustration. "I needed my son. It just occurred to me. I didn't have an escape route because God had already planned it for me." I smiled widely and looked at Alex. "My son." I smiled some more. "My son, Gary, is my escape route. That dimwit I was meeting with is not the one, she just wants to be and after I tell him he's about to marry his cousin, that'll be over and we can live with him happily ever after."

Alex's eyes widened. "He's about to what?" He appeared horrified. "I thought you were just trying to find out some information on her."

"I am trying to find out some information on her. Alex, my dear, if you're going to continue to work for me you can't continue to react to the things I tell you." I fanned at the horrified expression and continued talking. "I'm trying to find out if she's my cousin. I don't know for sure that's why I need you to do this research for me. I mixed things up so badly. I've been saying Nina was his cousin now I don't know if it's Mia." I needed a pill.

Alex sat there looking confused so before I got irritated with him, I reached for a piece of paper and scribbled everything I needed him to research and pushed the paper toward him. "Put that in the folder."

He took the piece of paper and looked at it. He slid out of his seat and pouted toward the door. "I'll talk to you later, Mrs. Chandler. I have to digest this."

Alex left and I picked up the phone to call Nina. She didn't answer right away so I called Leslie. I needed her to find Nina and put a stop to her madness.

CHAPTER 15: GARY

MY ride from the gym was less than fifteen minutes but when you're regretting an impending argument it trudges on like an hour. My mother, Judy, called as soon as I turned the bike off. I took a deep breath and answered. "Hey, Ma."

"Hey, son. How you doing? Why you sound so down?"

"I'm doing good, Ma. I'm not sounding down." I unsnapped the chinstrap on my helmet.

"Yes, you are. What happened?"

"Nothing. I just pulled into the garage."

"I know you're not telling me the truth. But anyway, is Sam there yet?"

"No, ma'am. He said he'd be here by seven o'clock."

"What are you doing, all of that noise? Where's my Mia?"

"Which question do you want me to answer?"

"Boy, don't get smart with me with all that darn noise in the background. I can hardly hear you."

"I'm sorry, Ma. I just pulled into the garage. I was taking off my jacket and putting my helmet on the hook. I don't know where—"

"You've been on that ol' motorcycle driving all fast."

"No, ma'am. I told you, I always ride my bike as if you were on it with me." I chuckled at my own lie.

"Now I know you're lying. You'd have my whole entire forehead peeled back going so fast."

I laughed. My mother was so cute with some of her comments. "You won't let me try, so you don't know what your forehead would do."

Never forgetting her question, she asked again, "Where did you say Mia was?"

I paused for a moment before answering. I didn't want her to ask to speak to Mia. The truth was I didn't know if Mia was in the house or somewhere with Dena.

"She's at the gym with Dena."

"Okay, well, I know you're not telling me the truth, I can sense it but tell her I said hello. I'm praying for you two. Something told me to call and check on y'all this morning. I know it's always something with those crazy ass Houston women down there. I wonder if it's something in the water." She paused briefly. "Or the food or something. But you and my Mia will be all right. I just know it. I'm praying."

Her intuition was amazing. I don't know how she can read the tone of my voice and my chosen words to discern when I'm not telling the truth. She never misses a beat with me. It's almost like she gave birth to me. I guess it comes from the bond we developed from three months old to adulthood.

"Okay, Ma."

"Have you talked to your mother?"

I paused again, and then added, "I'm talking to my mother now."

"Sweetheart, you know who I'm talking about."

"She called this morning." I sighed.

"But did you talk to her."

"For a minute."

"Gary, I think you really need to hear her out."

"I will, one day, just not today."

"Hmph. Okay, well, call me when Sam gets there. He didn't answer his phone when I called a few minutes ago. Okay bye, love you."

"I love you, too. Bye, Ma."

I hung my jacket on the hook, walked in the house, and went straight to the bedroom to see if Mia was there. She was standing beside the bed wrapped in a towel. Two suitcases were on the floor. Her hair was wet and pulled up in a ponytail and water was still on her back. She was beautiful.

"I hate leaving a situation feeling like I should've done something different but didn't," she said as soon as I planted my foot onto the hardwood floor.

"What do feel you should've done?"

"Killed her," she said gravely.

"Mia, stop it. You know you don't mean that."

She stopped packing for a moment and glared at me.

I casually walked over to sit on the chaise and said, "I'm serious. You don't mean that, so stop talking like that. Where are you going?"

"Arkansas." She picked up her suitcase and threw it on the bed. She stacked underwear, socks, and bras into it.

I couldn't stop a determined woman so I watched.

"You do realize that all of us are one decision, one mistake away from a felony?"

My words became staggered. "Mia, why are you talking like that?"

"'Cause I'm tired, Gary. I'm so tired of trying to live my life for other people. I'm tired of trying to be the bigger person and walk away. I'm pissed. I wanted to kick her feet from under her and land her straight on her back. I wanted to grab her by her hair and slam her head on the concrete floor until all of the blood comes running out. I need to do what's in my gut, and right now, its murder." At that point, she was slamming so much junk into the suitcase. I walked over to her and pulled her into my arms.

"Mia, you don't mean that. Don't talk like that." I rubbed my hands down her arms and lifted her hands to kiss them. "Please, don't talk like that."

She didn't move. I pulled her close and held her and didn't say a word for several minutes. She raised her arms as if she wanted to push me away but she didn't. She allowed me to hold her. I thought I was hugging some of the pain away. She leaned her head into my chest but she didn't cry. I had held her many nights as she awakened after a nightmare and cried but this time, after a real life nightmare, she did not cry.

I kissed her hair then her forehead. "I'm so sorry I hurt you. I promise it was not my intent. I went out this morning to look for her. I'm so sorry." I held her face in my hands. I kissed her forehead, her nose, and then her lips. I pressed my forehead against hers and looked into her eyes.

"You know what she said?" she said stiffly.

I stepped back to look at her. "What?"

"She said may the best woman win."

"This is not a competition or a game, babe. I'm with you. I want you. You don't have to worry about losing."

"You got that right."

"I'm trying to figure out why Nina's behavior has changed. I have not had any conversations with her. I haven't seen her. I don't understand either."

"How do you feel about that?" She moved around me to start throwing more stuff into the suitcases.

"How long are you staying? Why are you packing all of this stuff?"

"I don't know how long I'm staying. Now you answer my question."

"Mia, what do you mean? How do I feel about what? I don't like this stuff any more than you do."

"I think there's a little hint of pride riding in your heart that there are two women or maybe more, who want you so badly that they'll fight over you."

I shook my head. "No, that is not exciting to me at all. I just want one wom—"

She interrupted me. "With all due respect, Gary, you're not all that. You're not as good as you think you are."

Her words caught me off guard. I thought we were connecting a moment ago.

She continued. "You're controlling, you're evasive under the guise of getting it all out in the open…with ev-ry sin-gle passing day it seems a new issue pops up and you're saying, 'oh that's my past, I don't understand what's going on.'" She threw up her hands and stormed into the closet.

"Mia, what? What the hell are you talking about? Where is all of this coming from?" I shouted with flailing hands then immediately calmed down because I believed she wanted an argument. She wanted us to argue more than what our current situation called for which would give her more ammunition to leave. *Every single passing day?* I was confused but I needed to defuse the situation. "Hey listen, I love you."

She replied, "I don't care about love right now. Love is just another word…most people don't even know what it means anymore. And from the looks of it, you certainly don't."

"Mia, baby, please just calm down. You're talking about murder and you don't care about love. Mia, this is not you. Look at me. What's going on?"

"Gary, I can't be looking over my shoulder all the time for the next tragedy. Women walking up to me every time I turn around. I can't even go to the freakin' gas station and pay at the pump without a crazy bitch coming up to me."

I had the most dumbfounded look on my face. She was talking like a mad woman and I was certain that actions were soon to follow.

"Okay look, I'll do whatever it takes. Whatever you want." I gently positioned my hand to the back of her head then rubbed down to her shoulder. "God, I'll pump your gas from now on, just baby, please."

She glared at me and shook her head. "You just don't get it, do you? It's not about you serving me; it's not about pumping gas. I am so sick and tired of running scared, on the defense, ready to fight all of the time. That's not who I am. When I drive, my heart is palpitating so rapidly, I'm surprised I haven't had a heart attack. And I'm just tired of it all."

I didn't respond. Me, Mr. Fix It, didn't have a clue what to do next.

"And I'm afraid." She stuffed another pair of jeans in the suitcase.

"Why are you afraid of me?"

"I'm afraid you won't do what you say you'll do. Afraid you won't be there when that fatal blow drops. Afraid that we will break up after all of this wasted time has passed. And all of the energy I've put into this relationship will be wasted. I'm just plain, old afraid." She was in full blown sobs.

I reached out to touch her shoulder and turned her toward me. "Sit down. Sit down, right here." I guided her toward the bench at the end of the bed. "Mia, there's no wasted time and you don't have to be afraid. We have both put a lot of energy into this relationship and we can fix this if you stay with me. Just please don't leave. I promise, you don't have to be afraid of me. Please, Mia." My eyes pleaded.

Crisis brings about attitude changes and we had definitely changed. Mia had never spoken to me in that manner before.

"Gary, I need to do this for me." One tear rolled down my cheek. "I must do this for me."

"Mia, I got—"

"Gary, I love you but the only thing I need you to do for me right now is to let me go."

"So, are you breaking up with me? What's going on, Mia? Why such drastic measures?" I tried to keep my composure but I felt like I was entering the fight of my life.

"No, Gary, I'm not breaking up with you. I still love you and this is not drastic. I just need to get away. Have you noticed that I went from accident, to healing, to another accident, to healing, to surgery, to your house, to no control over anything I do anymore?"

"Baby, that's not true."

"See, that's just it. No one sees or feels what I'm feeling. It's been over a year and—"

"Okay baby, I'm sorry. I just want to be here for you. I don't want to harm you in any way. I just want to love you. I want to protect you and provide for you." I leaned in to kiss her, softly. "I'm sorry. I do understand." I kissed her again. "I understand, I promise I do. I promise. I do. I understand."

"No, you don't," she whined.

I held her and she allowed it without pushing me away. I tried to wipe the tears that made a consistent flow down her cheek. This experience was almost as heartbreaking as seeing her in the hospital in a coma. She looked up at me, swallowed hard, but didn't push me away.

I planted soft kisses all over her face and then to her neck as I began to remove the towel. "I love you so much, Mia." I was turned on from the moment I walked into the room but the argument derailed it for a moment. I lifted her up and pushed her back on the bed and made love to her like it was the last time I'd see her.

After she finally succumbed to my begging and allowed me to take her to the airport, I had moved out of the way to allow her to finish packing.

I sent Dena a text.

Thank you for saying no to taking Mia to the airport. This is the last time I'm allowing her to leave; this must stop.

She replied with a text.

I gotchu bruh. She asked and I politely said if ur goin' let Gary take you.

Thanks

I totally agree with you. Running is NOT the answer to everything. She knows I'm mad at her ass for leavin' again.

After we arrived at the airport, I reached into my pocket for the note that I had written while she was packing. I pushed it into the side of her bag. "Read that when you settle in."

"Okay." She pushed the note deeper into her bag.

I pulled her close and rubbed the back of her head. "Listen, I love you, girl. I don't want you to go, so whatever it is you're searching for in Arkansas. I want you to find it this time because this is the last time I'm going to allow you to go home mad and upset with me over some nonsense, because this we're going through right now," I pointed my finger between us, "does not require separation."

She raised an eyebrow.

I continued. "Yes, I said allow. The next time we're fighting this thing, whatever it is, together, head on. Okay?"

She nodded. "Okay, but I'm not separating from you." We chatted for a moment then she delivered a few departing words that stung worse that all she'd said earlier. She had a way of letting me know that I had my own issues that I needed to handle.

CHAPTER 16: MIA

GARY didn't know the magnitude of all my frustrations I had unleashed on him. I was so wrong for that and he didn't deserve it. He was not the root of every issue we had. I had created some of the turmoil and I needed to get to Arkansas to make an attempt to silence mine.

Gary had made love to me and then gave me space to pack what I needed to go home. I loved the way he made me feel when our bodies were intertwined, so it was on rare occasion that I turned him down when he made an advance. Nevertheless, physical feelings mattered not, I was an emotional wreck. I was in love with him, I knew that, but I had to determine if he was who he said he was, if he was indeed the one God was telling me to spend the rest of my life with—I just didn't know. I needed time to figure that out, for the third time.

We rode to the airport in silence. He stepped out of the car, opened my door, and hoisted my bag from the back seat. He rolled the bag with his right hand and reached for my hand with the other. We walked through the parking garage, across the walkway, and over to curbside check in. After I finished, he walked with me inside then pulled me into his arms and delivered an ultimatum in which I responded, "Okay," then I had said a few words of my own.

"So, how long are you going to stay?" he asked again as his eyes diverted as far away from me as he could.

"I don't know, maybe a month." My eyes searched for a glimmer of hurt in his eyes. I had to admit, I wanted him to hurt at least a little. I wanted him to feel the way I felt and I believe he did.

His eyes widened and his head snapped back slightly. I knew this was hurting him just as much as it was killing me but I knew I needed to leave, if only for a little while. I could feel the suppressed anger that I had withheld for so long rising up and threatening to burst to the surface. I needed to continue therapy but I decided I needed to go home more to make a visit to the cemetery, again.

"Did you hear anything I just said? Okay, okay, I'm not going to fight it. I won't try to get you to change your mind, although I want to. You do whatever you need to do. Just remember this for me." He placed his hand gently on my chin and I tilted my head upward toward him. "I love you. I'm here to provide for you, pray for you, protect you, or whatever. I'll get better at all three. I promise."

"I know, Gary." I held the tears at bay. I wrapped my arms around his neck and kissed him softly on his lips. We stood there as if we were the only two people in the world. "I do love you, Gary, so much, but can you do me one favor while I'm away?"

"Yeah, what's that?" Concern filled his eyes.

"Can you contact your biological mother and get to know her? I think that's one of the roots feeding some of our issues. I'm going to take care of my side of the issues in Arkansas."

He sighed and looked away. His eyes met mine again. He sighed heavily, "Okay Mia, I'll see what I can do."

"Think about it like this. You have two women who love you as their child and would probably do anything for you. I have to go to the cemetery to talk to mine."

He lowered his head. "I understand."

We hugged so tightly and more tears rolled down my cheeks. I shivered at the touch of his hand in the small of my back that ignited an explosion inside of my entire body. No man has ever done that to me. I love him, but sometimes love is confusing and maybe not enough.

"I have to go, baby."

"Okay, but read that." He tapped the side of my purse and kissed me.

He walked with me to the security gates.

We said in unison, "I love you."

I stopped to wave goodbye. A tear rolled down my cheek. I almost changed my mind right on the spot. I loved him but I needed to get away if only for a moment.

I made it through security, grabbed something to eat, and arrived at my gate. The flight to Little Rock was delayed. The desire to read the note Gary gave me was burning inside me but I decided to wait until I got to Arkansas. I didn't know what was on the paper but I felt I was too weak emotionally to read it in public. I feared I'd call him and say I'm sorry, please come back and get me.

I sat down and scrolled through my phone. Another text message popped up from Quan. His previous thirteen messages had not left my thoughts all morning, they just kept twirling through my mind like an Olympic ice-skater. He was relentless. *So I c u been ignorin' me. U know what, I need my $$, now!!!!*

I still didn't respond. I absolutely hated the way he texted. I had to stare at the screen to decipher what the hell he was trying to say. I don't know why I got involved with his ignorant ass anyway. And even more, I don't know why I entertained him when I was home during the first time Gary and I broke up. I should've known better. Vulnerability will get you into a lot of trouble if you're not careful, and I clearly wasn't careful.

Quan had sent nine text messages today and I had ignored every one of them. I was sick of the cloud he had over my head about the money I "owed" him for paying for my last year of undergrad. I was going home to settle it with him once and for all. I couldn't have owed him any more than six-thousand dollars. He was part of the frustration I had with myself. I had made some of the dumbest mistakes when it came to men and they always seemed to come back. The mistakes usually involved money or some material things purchased as gifts for me. I had never had intercourse with Quan although we did other things, well he did. He always thought he'd go further but I never allowed it.

My mother used to say, "Don't give in to the legal prostitution. Buy your own shit. Don't let a man get it for you because you'll always owe him. He'll feel like you do anyway." I didn't listen to her advice because I wanted to finish school and I didn't want them to have to pay for it. I was working but I wasn't making enough for my tuition and I didn't want to go part-time, I was ready to graduate. Quan offered to pay and I accepted. I should've gotten it in writing as the gift it was and I wouldn't be in the situation I'm in now…owing him and not trusting the man I really love at one hundred percent because I fear he'll turn into a clown like Quan or others.

I texted Dena, *I'm headed home.* Then I sent a second text, *Wedding plans on hold for now.*

My Bluetooth started to vibrate less than one minute later.

I pressed the ear bud into my ear. "Hello."

"So you decided to make a run for it, huh?"

"Yep, you talked to Gary?

"Yes, I did. He's distraught but trying not to show it. I know Gary."

"I need to go. For me. He can't control everything, Dena." I folded my arms.

"Don't think I didn't catch that sarcasm in your first text. I wanted him to drop you off. I think you're making a mistake, but who am I to judge? I can't believe you're ceasing all wedding plans." Her voice dripped with disappointment and disgust.

"Dena, are you serious right now? I can't even think about getting married at this moment." I pounded my fist into my hand while awkwardly trying to keep my voice low. I got up to walk toward the gates where there were few passengers. "I'm so pissed off I don't know what to do."

"I'm just trying to cheer your ass up," she barked.

"How is what you just said supposed to cheer me up? Gary has a woman who wants him so badly that she's following me around town everywhere I go. I don't know if this fool will try to hurt me, or kill me, or what. Especially after you just tried to kill her in the gym."

"Girl, please. That bitch ain't doing nothing but taking her tail back home and cry. She needs to make a hair appointment."

I almost laughed at her last comment. "Dena, you're going to have to settle down or I'll be forced to leave you standing. You have anger issues that you need to work on and you have me all worked up with you," I grumbled.

"I don't have anger issues. I just react to what other people bring to me. If people leave me the hell alone, then they won't have any problems. Don't start none, won't be done. That's my motto and you know it."

"You've gotten worse."

"No, I haven't. People have gotten worse, especially, Nina. And Monty. I'm sick of people trying to act as if I don't have feelings and acting like they can say or do anything to me or my friends and expect me to stand back and say nothing. Not going to happen. They say stupid shit. I respond to stupid shit."

"Well, you need to stop it."

"What about your hateful-ass attitude now. You're no better than anybody else."

We both sighed after a brief pause. Both of us knew where this would go if we kept doing the tit for tat. I know what she's capable of and I know me. I usually try to suppress my temper and remain silent but at the moment, I was letting it flow. Dena and I are like sisters, we argue, we fight, but we still love each other and want the best for each other.

"I need to get out of here for a few weeks. I can't take it anymore. I need to get away."

"Girl, let's just do a spa—"

I cut her off. "No, I need to get away. I need to go to the country. My country. Where I can go and chill and work on myself, search and find myself again. I'm not letting anybody hurt me again. People only have power over you if you give it to them. And I have given my power away to...to other people."

She didn't speak. I assumed she contemplated my comments.

"Gary is wonderful but—"

"There's no but, Mia, when it comes to Gary. I know that man loves you with everything in his being."

"Yeah, that's why I'm putting the wedding planning on hold until I get my heart and mind on the same page as him. So I can love him with everything in me, uninterrupted by all of this nonsense."

"So, you're saying you don't love Gary? This better not be about that bitch-ass, Quan."

"No, that's not what I'm saying. Girl, you know I love Gary. I said I want to get my heart and mind on the same page as him so I can love him with everything in me, and Quan has nothing to do with this."

"Whatever, Mia. Trust me, he hasn't started calling and texting you for nothing. He always wants something. He's a snake and I don't trust him."

"I don't either, Dena."

"Well, stop entertaining him then."

"I'm not."

"You're not what?"

"I'm not entertaining him," I lied.

She knew Quan was part of the reason for my abrupt decision to go to Arkansas. He was usually quiet if I entertained his mindless conversations and deciphered his text messages enough to respond. If I ignored him at any point when he reached out, he started yelling, *I want my money*. He was missing in action for many years and all of sudden he reappeared with the same old tactics.

Quan used to be kind and helped a lot of people in college. What all of us didn't know at the time was that those he helped would be indebted to him for the rest of their lives.

He had started texting every day since I made the huge mistake of telling him I had moved in with Gary and was getting married. That bit of information was none of his business and I was stupid for sharing it. He was married but always claimed he was headed for divorce even after she married him during his first year in prison over twelve years ago. Truth be told, I enjoyed hanging out and talking to Quan when he was level-headed.

Dena lowered her voice and let out an exasperated sigh. "Okay, Mia. You better not be entertaining that fool. Call me when you get there. Love you, bye." She hung up before I could respond.

I have certainly gotten myself into a bad situation.

CHAPTER 17: GARY

I parked my cars parallel in the driveway so I could see anyone approaching. I thought Sam would be pulling up soon so I took a few minutes to finish a project that I had been putting off for several weeks.

I got set up—cognac on ice, cigar, leather conditioner, and cloth. I walked over to the shelf and turned on my old school music. The first song on the mixed CD that I'd left in the player was "A Woman's Gotta Have It" by Bobby Womack.

"Of course," I mumbled.

I hoisted the chair out of the corner and into the center of the garage. I always completed a task that requires a certain amount of focus when my mind was racing. I couldn't help but think about Mia. She was indeed filling a space in my heart that I didn't know was there. We had met and made a pretty good run despite all of the outside forces not wanting us to be together. It was nothing against her, it was all of the people wanting to get to me, but I am nothing special. I'm a hard working young thug at heart from Brooklyn who left and made some different choices to be successful.

Mia had hurled some harsh words my way while she was packing. I couldn't seem to get them out of my mind. She headed to Arkansas to rest, work on herself, and to think. Again.

You're controlling, you're evasive under the guise of getting it all out in the open…with ev-ry sin-gle passing day it seems a new issue pops up and you're saying, 'oh that's my past.' I don't care about love right now. Love is just another word…most people don't even know what it means anymore.

Gary, I can't be looking over my shoulder all the time for the next tragedy. Women walking up to me every time I turn around. I can't even go to the freakin' gas station and pay at the pump without a crazy bitch coming up to me…

You just don't get it, do you? It's not about you servicing me; it's not about pumping gas. I am so sick and tired of running scared, on the defense, ready to fight all of the time. That's not who I am. When I drive, my heart is palpitating so rapidly, I'm surprised I haven't had a heart attack. And Gary, I'm just tired…

Her words played over and over in my mind and while some of them may be true, I knew there was something else bothering her and I needed to figure out what it was.

I needed to do some soul searching myself. My way of dealing with issues was to block them out and not think about them. Any woman from my past would tell you that they would've experienced some harsh comments back at her and I would have sent her packing. Mia's final words stung the most because of the truth in those words. "You need to get to know your biological mother; I think that's the root to some of our issues." I hadn't thought that was the root of my issues, but what if it was?

An hour later, Sam whirled his car into the driveway going too fast. I raised my head and prepared to move just in case his brakes failed.

He got out the car and stretched, loudly.

I chuckled. "What's up, yo?"

"Not much, son. I'm stiff as shit. I know that. What's going on?" He shoved me playfully. "Where's Mia?"

"She's not here." I stopped long enough to greet him but I had to keep working, I had to stay preoccupied. After I dropped Mia off, I spent two hours at the gym trying to burn off some built up tension. Other times like this I would bury myself in my work or I would've called Sean but he took a teaching assignment and moved to Dubai for a year. I think that's part of the reason I didn't hesitate when Sam called and asked if he could stay with me for a couple of months until he got settled. Sometimes I need another perspective and Sam and Sean have played my conscious and devil's advocates plenty of times when I went off the path. Sam can be wild at times but for some reason, he can always keep me going in the right direction when I get off course, especially when it was matters regarding my relationship with Mia. I had never showed so much love and admiration toward a woman.

"Well, where is she, yo'? What's going on, man? You auight?" His face had conflicting expressions. His lips curled into a smile while his brows furrowed as he paused before continuing.

"What is this, fifty questions?"

"Nah, I just know you don't partake in labor like this unless you're pissed off or worried about something. Yo' ass usually pulls out the checkbook or credit card to pay somebody else to do stuff like this." He looked around the garage. "So which is it?" He paused. "And you're listening to the blues and drinking brown liquor with yo' southern ass. Yah mean."

I smirked at his southern comment. "Both." I put more conditioner on the cloth.

He looked around the garage again, then walked over to grab

a folding chair and placed it directly in front of the leather chair I was conditioning.

"Auight yo, Sean ain't here. Start talkin'."

I paused and looked at him. "I don't feel like talking about that right now. How was your trip?"

"Son, you know damn well you don't care about my trip. Are you serious?" His tone was accusatory. "It went. I texted you throughout the trip. I made it with no accident or incident. I'm here, yah mean." He stretched his legs out, crossed his ankles, and shoved his hands into the pockets of his hoodie. "And, I'm hungry as hell."

"How hungry is that?" I managed a chuckle. I stood up and dropped the cloth on the table next to the conditioner. "Let's go inside."

He stood to follow me. I pressed the button to close the garage door, then walked over to the sink to wash my hands.

"Man, you can ignore my question all you want but I'll ask until I get tired."

"Look, man, everything is cool." I pulled a bottle of water from the bar and took a long swig.

"No it's not, son. I just gotta say it; this is what, the third time Mia has left to go 'find herself.'" He raised his hands to make the air quotation marks. "And you let her go. What happened to the G I know, who would've said, 'hell no, enough is enough, you staying yo' ass here'?"

I guffawed and shook my head at his comments. "That G is still here. I got my point across in a slightly different way this time." I paused. "Trust me, I let her know. We're good though."

"You've changed, man. I'm not saying it's bad but you have definitely changed. The wild boy is gone." He laughed and threw a fake punch at me.

"Yeah, I have. Things I used to fret over don't matter to me no more. I really do believe God sent Mia to slow me down, to focus on Him more to help me solve these daily issues I have. She's a beautiful person and I just can't seem to keep things going in the right direction for the long run, you know."

"I understand, but it might not be you, son." He looked at me then folded his arms across his chest.

"Yeah, you're right." I had to agree with him.

The truth was I knew Mia had something else up her sleeve. The emotions she was emitting couldn't have possibly all come from the incident with Nina, then again, maybe it did but I saw a name from a text message pop up on her phone while she was packing. The display showed *Quan(8)Text Messages*. I know Quan was someone she knew from Arkansas. I remember her telling me about him.

"Okay, whatever you say, yo. But you know I'm ready when you make a move." He washed his hands, dried them, and walked over to the refrigerator. "Man, what you got in here? All this healthy shit, but beggars can't be choosy, yah mean. I gotta grab and make a few runs to prepare for Monday." He grabbed some grapes, turkey, and cheese and prepared to make him a sandwich. "I have some people to meet downtown in the morning for information on permits and licenses and all of that." He tossed a couple of grapes in his mouth.

"Auight, man. You need my help with anything."

He shook his head. "Nah, not right now. You've done enough setting me up and letting me stay here. The rest I have to go get it. I'm gonna chill for a minute then head to the library."

I frowned. "Library?"

"Yes. sir. I visit the library occasionally. You know, I found a new library the last time I visited here." He flicked his fingers and started speaking in an orator tone. "There comes a time when a young man must expand his horizons and explore opportunities beyond those in which he had previously become accustom." He moved around the kitchen with ease. He took a knife from the drawer then spread mayonnaise and mustard on the bread. "Reading expands the mind and allows one to explore the world without leaving the city in which he lives." He opened the refrigerator, then the vegetable drawer for lettuce, tomatoes, alfalfa sprouts, and cucumbers. "And one can do all of this world exploration," he paused, "in the library for free."

I laughed. "Boy you are wild indeed."

He looked around the kitchen as if he was missing something and stepped back to admire his sandwich. "Yeah, I fixed this joint up gourmet style. I'm gonna need a diet soda to wash this down."

I laughed. "You're a clown, man. Anyway, what are you working on in the library?"

His facial expression and tone became serious. "I need to sit and read over these documents for my business. I need a better understanding for my meeting in the morning, and I need to tightened up my business plan. As I think about it, I will need your help again."

"What's up?" I twisted the cap on the water and set it on the counter. "Let's go in here." I walked down the hall and down a few steps and into the media room. I plopped into one of the large black recliners and he fell into the other one.

"First thing, I need you to let me drive you around for a few weeks," Sam said.

"Drive me around?"

"Yeah, like your chauffer."

"Sam, have you lost your mind? I'm not doing that."

"Come on, son. It'll be easy. I'll drop you off at your office or wherever you go during the day and pick you up. People will see your driver and they'd want to hire me."

"Really, that's your business strategy?"

"Yes, yes it is part of it and I know it'll work because I did it in New York and I know it'll work here because people don't have time to sit in this traffic behind the wheel. They hate it, actually. If I'm driving them, they could be in the backseat working."

"Sam, I'm not a celebrity and I don't have the funds to pay you to take me from point A to point B and then sit around waiting all day while I work." My eyebrows furrowed.

He set the plate on the end table between our chairs. He held both palms up. "Check this…hear me out. You don't have to be a celebrity, I'm not asking you to pay me, and this doesn't have to be forever. I will take you to work on days where you'll be in the office all day. You do have days like those, don't you? I can have other clients during the day and come back to get you when you're ready to leave."

I sat there and looked at him like he was a nut case. I didn't speak. I picked up the remote and flipped channels. He took two bites of his sandwich, chewed what seemed like one hundred times, and started talking again.

"I bet if Mia was here she'd let me drive her around."

"Now there's a thought. I like that and you can be her bodyguard, too," I said sarcastically but was beginning to think he had a good idea.

"I'll definitely do that for her." He paused. "Remember when I told you I won the lottery?"

"Yeah. Don't drop any crumbs in that chair."

"I'm not." He looked around to make sure. "You never asked me how much?"

"Because it's none of my business." I pressed the power button on the remote to turn the TV off.

"Well, it is now."

I looked in his direction and waited for him to continue. I grabbed the remote to the surround sound to listen to music.

"I won a lot of money—a lot of money. And I need your advice on what to do with it."

CHAPTER 18: MIA

had been in Arkansas for almost three weeks. Although I had talked to Gary several times, I pulled the note he stuffed into my bag and read it again for the twentieth time, I almost had it memorized.

I love you, Mia. I know I keep saying it but it's true. I want you, Mia. I need you, Mia. I feel like I'm on a battlefield that I didn't choose to be on and quite frankly, not prepared for. Things are going from one crazy scenario to the next, in my opinion, neither of us are inviting. But our pasts have a clever way of catching up to us. I say this with conviction, I have never and will never get involved with another woman as long as I'm with you and I request the same from you. In all things my intent is not to be evasive, but it is certainly to keep those things, which are not necessary away from you. To me, that's protection. I give my best to whatever I touch which includes my relationship with you, Mia. Again, I say, I love you. I have learned that trials, struggles, strongholds, and disappointments will come but at the same time, blessings will also come. I will remain vigilant in what I know I'm supposed to do and that is to give you the best I have to offer in every area of our lives. I'm going to allow you this last time to go away but in the future, we will handle things together not separately. I've said this many times before, I love you with everything in me and I will fight to my dying breath to care for you, to provide for you, to love you, and to protect you from anyone or anything that threatens to harm you. No matter what.

   ~*Gary Lamont Matthews*

I missed him so much but I wasn't ready to go back to Houston for more impending altercations, but I knew I needed to go back. I really felt safe in his presence but the problems came when he was not around. Since he couldn't get Nina under control, I'd have to do it myself. But I also needed to finish what I came to Arkansas to do. I had cried and sulked long enough and needed to make some decisions. I had prayed, turned it over to God, and then took it back from God when I didn't hear an immediate answer. It had turned into my daily routine but I was determined to change that. So I started on my plan. I needed to pay Nina a visit.

   I was stretched out on the bed reading when Desilyn knocked on the door and walked into the room. I regretted sending her the text message when I was upset because she had pressed me a few times for more information but I simply said, *It was nothing, I was just being dramatic.* I could tell she didn't believe me but she didn't go any further.

   "Mia, darling?"

   "Yes." I rolled over and rested on my elbows and placed the book face down on the bed.

   "Hey, chica. How you doing today?" She sat on the bed and brushed her fingers through my hair. If she only knew how that gesture reminded me so much of my mother and lovingly brought me to the brink of tears rolling rapidly along my eyelids every time she did it. I was sixteen years her junior and she treated me like a daughter. They used to call me the mistake baby until I started falling into the name by making all kinds of stupid mistakes growing up. Still do.

"I'm good, just resting, trying to finish some of the books I brought with me."

"Are you sure you feel okay?"

"Yes, Des, I'm okay."

"Okay, honey, I'm just saying. Your skin looks a little blotchy."

"Thank you." I smiled with my voice oozing sarcasm.

"You talk to my brother-in-law?"

"No, not today." I swung my legs over the bed, stood up, and walked over to the mirror to examine my skin.

"You miss him?" She pushed herself back to lean against the headboard.

"Beyond measure."

"I know you do."

"I think I'm going back sooner than later this time. I just need to get clarity on some things. I keep praying and telling God, 'I'm going to turn it over to you.' But when I get up, I pick it up and walk away with it."

"Well, you know that's not going to get you going in the direction you want."

"I know."

"How's your arm?"

"It's good." I turned toward her and held out my arm to show her. "It healed nicely. It hurts occasionally if I overwork it but it's really healed. It's been over a year."

"That's good, you know I have to check. When you get old, that arm is going to hurt like hell from Arthur Riley." She laughed at her attempt to sound like my mother mispronouncing the word, arthritis.

"No, it's not."

She sat there looking at me awkwardly.

"What is it now? What did Chris say?" I folded my arms and leaned against the dresser.

Chris is my brother-in-law, Desilyn's husband. He was jovial, very popular, and well-liked by many people. He had a habit of telling Desilyn what he thought about me and my relationships so I knew her awkward expression had to follow a comment he had made.

She sighed. "He ran into Quan at the store a week or so ago and he said that you owed him some money."

I plopped down on the bed and shook my head.

She scooted to the edge of the bed and threw her legs over to sit beside me. "It's true? I argued Chris down that it wasn't true. Did you borrow from him?"

"Not exactly." I sighed. "Do you remember my last year of college and they wouldn't allow me to get more student loans or grants? He volunteered to pay for my last year. I thought he was just a nice guy to help me and now in the last two years, he's always throwing it up in my face."

"Damn." She rubbed her eyes. "How much do you owe him?"

"I shouldn't have to pay him—"

She cut me off. "Stop it! Yes you should pay him, you owe him. Anytime a man pays for something for you, especially a man like Quan, a freakin' ex-con, drug dealer, assault and battery felon, assist anyone, it's never the end of it."

"He's all of that now but he wasn't all of that then. And I don't owe him anything, he volunteered but I'm going to pay his stupid ass."

"How much?"

"Less than five thousand. I called the Financial Aid office and they confirmed what I paid."

She gasped and stood up. "I'm going to pay him."

"No, Des." I stood up. "I'm going to pay him. I need a few days to calm down from his silly text messages and threats and I'm going to call him."

"He threatened you?"

"Yeah, just that he's going to spread lies about me," I lied. He had actually threatened to harm Des and Chris.

"Why do you care about that?"

I hunched my shoulders. "Reputation."

"You ever slept with him?"

"No, I just let him kiss me then eat me out once, but I've never had intercourse."

Her eyes widened and she grabbed her chest. "You're so graphic."

"What? You asked."

"When did y'all do all of that?"

I frowned. "When I was in college."

"Okay, okay." She shook her head. "Well handle it, please and soon. If you don't, you know I will."

"I told you I will."

"You hungry?"

"Ummm, kinda." I walked to the mirror.

I continued to examine my face but didn't comment because I agreed with her. Throwing up all morning will cause that, I guessed. My stomach was queasy which I contributed to stress. My eyes were sunken, my mouth was dry, the back of my hair was pushed up, and I looked a complete mess. I still had no car of my own, my house had recently sold, most of my household contents were in storage, I didn't have another consulting gig set up, my fiancé was constantly telling me 'I love you—I got you,' and I'm still afraid and now I have a felon contender.

Des stood up, fixed the bed, and headed toward the door.

"Mia, you're just going to have to mature in this area. Strong marriages, long marriages last because they have staying power. Fighting power. You can't fight if you're not in the ring. You keep running and that's not going to work. You know you are welcome here any time but you must stop running. And you know Gary will beat the hell out of Quan's lil' ass if you told him Quan was trying to blackmail you."

I looked at my reflection in the mirror and then looked at her but I didn't speak because I knew every bit of what she'd said was true.

"Come on, let's go eat." She walked toward the door.

CHAPTER 19: GARY

SAM was focused. He was pounding the pavement to get his business up and running, hanging out at the library, setting up meetings, and staying up late to handle everything he laid out on his business plan. He had always been old school with everything so he forced himself to use current technology. We had golfed on the greens and in less than a month, we had given Top Golf so much money it was ridiculous. He was in love with the place. He didn't know it but he really helped me to keep my mind off Mia. I even surrendered to his persistent prodding and allowed him to drive me to work a few times. I really enjoyed sitting in the back seat reading my cases before I got into the office. I could really get used to the idea.

He had walked into the media room earlier in the morning as I was sitting there in my robe drinking my coffee and reading the paper. "What's up, Clive?"

I managed a laugh as he called me by dad's name because I had truly become him. He used to get up early, make his coffee, and read the newspaper. "Man, shut up."

He let out a hearty laugh as he pulled up a chair and sat down. "All you need are some reading glasses."

"Dude, you silly."

His tone turned serious. "G-man, I need to talk to you about something that's been weighing on me."

"Yeah, what's up?" I folded the paper to give him my full attention. I was genuinely concerned and never suspected the conversation was about to turn all the way around to me.

"Man, you my cuz, yo, and I want you straight. I want you happy, but what's up with you and Mia? No, wait. Let me start over. What's up with you, yo? You seem so different or depressed or something. I watch you as I'm driving and you're staring out the window for most of the trip. I'm concerned because I don't want you to go back to the other G-Man that I knew before Seattle. The one who didn't give a fuck. The one who would shut people out at the drop of a dime. You know how you are when you get pissed off, you hold it in and act out in a dangerous way. And where you go, you know I go with you and I came here to settle down not to start the old life again. So, you auight?"

I tilted my head trying to figure out what the hell Sam was rambling about. "What?" I frowned. "Are you serious? I'm much more mature than I used to be, I'm good."

"Auight. Okay. I'm just making sure."

"Auight, yo." We stood up, shook hands, and that was the end of that conversation.

I drove to my first appointment at ten o'clock and was there for two hours, then headed over to Vaughn's restaurant for lunch.

The hostess escorted me to Vaughn's office in the back of the restaurant. "What's up, Pops?" I joked. "Thanks, Minnie." I'd been to this restaurant hundreds of times and they always announced me, and then escorted me through the restaurant to his office. He was so smooth, he probably orchestrated it so he would have time to stop whatever he was doing, end a call, or hide the evidence from the crime he committed. I never could tell with him.

"Hey, son." He grabbed my hand, pulled me into an embrace, and patted my back. "How are you doing? You hungry?"

"Starving." I took my suit jacket off and hung it on the hanger then adjusted my tie. I'd had a rough day. It appeared every client who called today was pissed off and letting me have it. I was acting as the legal mediator trying to come to an agreement without going to court but the insurance company representative thought I was only trying to get the claimant more money. I had never met the lady before but he implied that my interest in her was due to our race. I had to threaten him with going to court and losing versus settling out of court. I wanted to threaten bodily harm but that may have gotten me a dial-tone and a court date as the defendant.

"Hey, Minnie." He called out to her.

She stepped back into the office. "Yes, sir?"

"Will you…" He paused. "You want your usual?"

"Yeah, that'll be fine."

"Can you get us two Porterhouses? You know how we like it."

"Yes, sir, I do." She turned on her heels and walked out.

"Thanks, Minnie. You're the best."

"I know." She teased as she smiled and pulled the door closed.

Vaughn wasted no time in getting into my business. "So, you talked to Mia?"

"Not today."

"How long has it been?" He rocked back and forth in his chair.

"Man, I don't know. I honestly try my best not to think about it."

"Well, we both know that won't make it go away."

"Yes, I know."

"So, did you get rid of the threat?"

"Huh?"

"Did you get rid of the threat? Nina, what did you do about Nina?"

"Dang, dude you sound like it should've been a murder scene or something." I shook my head. "I guess, I got a restraining order and I haven't seen her since Mia left."

He nodded slowly, never diverting his eyes away from me.

I continued talking. "I tried to call her just to try to get some things straight but never could catch her so I just got the restraining order."

He continued nodding. So, I allowed the silence to fill the room.

"You didn't do anything to her, did you?" I asked with a quizzical expression.

He gave a wry smile. "No."

I sighed. "I don't know what I'm going to do. Mia is gone again. She's afraid of me. Afraid of what might happen being with me. I just don't know."

"It'll work itself out. Just give it time. You talked to Karen?"

I was grateful he changed the subject but not so excited about what he changed it to. "Yes, she's called a few times. Not long, though. I do more listening than talking. She's too sarcastic and sometimes condescending. I can't stand…I don't like that." I frowned.

"I had a conversation with her about that. Several actually. She's allowed that corporate mombo-jumbo to go to her head."

"Hmph."

"But you should probably hear her out. Like I said, I had a

long conversation with her and I think she gets it—finally. She's been through a lot. She really does have a good heart though."

"Oh."

"I promise if you sit down and talk to her, you can ask anything you want to know. Look at it like this, son, you forgave me, you forgave Judy and Clive. Why not Karen?"

"She's the cockiest of them all and she started it all."

"I know, but she didn't start it by herself. I helped her. I think she finally got it. Start slow and build some trust with her. She has quite a story. I think you'll see her differently."

"You're not getting soft on me, are you? Are you messing around with her, again?"

"No." He smiled and shook his head.

He was so reserved, so smooth, poker-faced and rarely showed his emotions, regardless of the situation. I never knew if he was lying or telling the truth.

Minnie and a server delivered our steaks and we devoured them and the Cabernet Sauvignon. I was actually enjoying my evening until we heard a knock on the door and it opened before Vaughn could acknowledge. I could've spilled my entire contents onto the table when I recognized who it was. I wanted to talk to her but not today. Vaughn had set me up.

"Hey, Slick." She walked around the desk to hug Vaughn. He stood to hug her. The hug lingered longer than I thought it needed to.

She looked at me as if she was trying to determine if she should hug me or continue to launch into conversation as if I wasn't sitting there. I decided in that moment that I would acknowledge and respect my biological mother. I was alone; I did not have any distractions at all, with the exception of my career, so I decided it was time.

I did not speak from my seat. I stood up and took a few

steps toward her and reached to hug her and even kissed her on the cheek. "Hello, Karen."

She stammered in her response. "Hi, Gary." She looked back at Vaughn.

He waved his hand for her to sit down. I pulled the chair out for her to sit; she waited until she felt the back of the chair bump her leg and she sat down. My mother was stunning. She was tall; runner's build, with short, wavy salt and pepper hair, manicured nails, perfect white teeth, and was impeccably dressed.

Vaughn stood. "Well, let me get someone to get these plates out of here," he said as he began to gather our plates and napkins. "Are you hungry, Karen?"

"No, no, Vaughn, I'm fine." She had a smiled plastered on her face and never took her eyes off me.

"You sure? I'm putting it on Gary's tab." He chuckled.

"No, I don't want anything but to sit here and talk to my son."

I felt a softball sized knot form in the pit of my stomach.

CHAPTER 20: GARY

was surprised by the sudden discomfort I was experiencing while sitting in the room with my mother. I thought I had forgiven her until I was face to face with her. So, I did what most people do in this decade, use their smart phone as a distraction.

"So, where do we start?" She reached over and touched my knee, which diverted my attention from my phone up to her.

I stared at her for a moment and then said, "With you. You know so much about me but I have no clue about you."

"Okay." She crossed her legs and leaned forward slightly. "I guess I'll start from the beginning. I was eighteen years old when I got pregnant with you. By Vaughn, of course, who was significantly older than I was."

I smirked as she quickly tried to ensure I knew she was much younger than Vaughn.

"My parents were livid because they knew I was pregnant by him, who was older, married, obviously didn't want me to be with him in the first place." She paused, rambled through her purse, flicked out a fan, and started fanning. "They didn't want the embarrassment. My parents were strict and upstanding and had my life all planned how they wanted it and being with a married man was not part of the plan. And you know the whole rebellion thing; doing anything but what your parents wanted you to do. That really was me. Always was." She closed the fan and pushed it back into her purse. "Well, anyway, I carried you nine months and then…" she paused.

I shifted in my chair. I was beginning to feel uncomfortable, emotionally.

She continued, "I really felt like I was going to die during labor. Oh my God, it hurt so badly."

She stared at the floor as she spoke as if she could see the pain coming up through the hard wood. "I was still torn between whether I would keep you or give you to a family member. The adoption system was never a thought." She fanned her hand in the air.

I rested my elbow on the arm of the chair and remained quiet.

"Three months after you were born, I felt like…I felt like… umm, my uh, milk had dried up." She sighed heavily, rambled through her purse, and pulled out a hand fan and flicked it open and started fanning in one motion, again. "I was young and naïve. I had read so many articles about keeping a baby healthy, what was best for a baby and breast-feeding was the best. I'd told myself that I would wait until you no longer needed breast-feeding, then I'd approach Judy and Clive. I had spent a lot of time with them after you were born. I could tell they were falling in love with you." She smiled as she spoke of my parents. "They are two wonderful people. I knew them very well. They had one young son and wanted more but were having a hard time trying to conceive at that time. Judy used to snatch you out of my arms as soon as I walked through the door." She let out an uncomfortable chuckle. "I know they had Jessica later but…" A long pause then, "Gary, sweetheart, I really thought I was doing the right thing. My mother hated me for giving you up but she wasn't doing anything to help me to take care of you either. She tried to punish me. She wouldn't babysit; she wouldn't help out with anything. I didn't know what I was doing. Judy was right there all the way, showing me how to do everything; including how I should hold you and how I should hold my breast so you could eat. She was like a big sister."

I adjusted in my chair and crossed my leg. I had resigned to the fact that this entire conversation was going to be uncomfortable, now the breast-feeding talk was on the docket. I had to treat her like one of my clients during mediation. I felt like that would keep my emotions out of it. The difference was, this "mediation" was all about me and it was extremely difficult to separate myself. But I was willing to try it because I did not intend to let go of the reigns of my life and allow her to get her fangs into me. I had heard she was very powerful, well-known, and influential. She knew how to get what she wanted whenever she wanted.

"How do you know my mother?" I asked the question without even realizing the impact it would have on her.

She gave a somber expression and then said, "I met her when I was a teenager through this girl's mentoring program that I was in. She was a great mentor, a Christian lady." She smiled widely as she spoke of my mother. "She introduced me to the director in the Career Planning and Placement office, which was essentially how I got my internship. My mother wanted me to be in education like she was and I didn't want that because…to be frank with you, they didn't make the kind of money I desired to make. And honestly, I liked everything that my mother didn't and vice versa. My father was a partner in some type of invention for farmers and received an enormous amount of money for it and his success changed my mother, negatively, in my opinion." She frowned and shook her head.

"So, tell me about you. Outside of loving money and notoriety, what kind of person are you? What are you like?"

Her eyes widened slightly. "Well..."

Vaughn walked back into the office without knocking.

"How's it going in here?" His eyes danced from me to her and back to me.

"It's going." I glanced at him but tried to keep my eyes on Karen, waiting on her to answer.

"You didn't give us much time, Vaughn," she whined. "Well, Gary we'll have to pick this up later. Will you go to dinner with me soon?"

"I'll consider it. Let me think about it."

"Fair enough. I'll wait on you to call me." She paused. "You will call me, won't you?"

"Yes, I will." I stood and prepared to leave. I reach for my jacket and turned to Vaughn. "I know you set this up. You're just that tricky. I know you, man." I shook my head as I put my jacket on.

I was honestly not mad. I actually enjoyed listening to part of her story, but I wouldn't dare let her know it. I noticed how she was relieved that Vaughn interrupted just as I turned the question to the core of her existence.

I closed the door on my way out.

CHAPTER 21: MIA

I finally texted Quan to let him know I was in town. I dreaded talking to him but I knew I needed to pay him and just cut all conversations for good. I really was thankful that he helped me pay for college but this silliness he had going on was past its expiration date. I had spoken to him a couple of times and ignored several of his text but I finally called and he asked me to go to lunch. I wasn't hungry but I went anyway just to get the process over with and to keep him from showing up at my sister's house acting a fool. I asked Desilyn to go with me but she had an appointment so she allowed me to use one of their cars. I met him at this new restaurant in the mall. I wore sweats, a t-shirt, and sneakers. I didn't want to give him the impression I was trying to dress up for him. I just wanted everything to be above board.

I stopped at the bank to get a cashier's check for six thousand dollars.

"Hey, Mia, how you doing? You look good." He was already there sitting and never bothered to stand as I slid into the booth in front of him. He never liked the fact that I was slightly taller than him.

"I'm good and thanks."

"So when is the wedding?"

"Soon."

He sat there awkwardly smiling at me. He was a small framed guy but his time in prison had allowed him time to pump up his muscles. He had been out over two years and he seemed to have kept it up. I couldn't help but wonder if I could take him out if he tried me. I was ready to leave as soon as I arrived.

"Mia Nixon. The cheerleader and valedictorian."

"Why do you say the same thing every time you see me?"

"I don't know, I'm just reminiscing."

"Well cut it out. I'm long gone from cheerleader and valedictorian." I stretch a smile as I mocked the way he'd said it. "So how are your kids?"

"They're good, in school. My oldest is in high school this year."

"Wow. That's good. So, you're still married this time, right?"

"This time? Well yeah, no, sort of. My wife is at work but we're on the outs." He licked his lips and it irritated me.

My stomach gurgled. "Huh, sort of on the outs?" I frowned and picked up my phone.

He grabbed the phone from my hand. "Who are you texting?"

Thank God I hadn't keyed in the password. "Quan, give me my phone."

"I'm not giving you anything. What's this, incorrect pass code number five. Ten times a charm." He started pressing buttons. "I'll reset this bitch and you won't have a phone at all." He touched it again.

"And if I don't have a phone then you can't bug the hell out of me. That might not be a bad idea."

He tossed the phone onto the table. "You think you're better than everybody, don't you, since you're getting ready to marry this big shot lawyer? I thought me and you would eventually have something together."

I texted Gary. *Call me.* I felt I needed a distraction, and a call from Gary would do the trick. I also wanted to show Gary I was not hiding anything from him and I wanted Quan to witness how in love I was. I know it was childish but I did it anyway.

I sighed and looked away. "Quan, are you high? You have really bumped your damn head." He was annoying the hell out of me already. "How much do I owe you?"

"Why you think me and you can't have something? You too good for me?"

It really hurt my heart to see someone that I honestly thought was a semblance of a friend behave in such a nasty way one minute and try to show love the next.

"So, what's up?" He pulled a piece of paper from his pocket.

The waitress set two glasses of water on the table.

I frowned. "Quan are you drunk? Nothing is up and nothing will ever be up between us." I said it in dramatic fashion so the waitress would hear me. She asked if we'd like something else to drink. Before we could order, the look on his face changed from a smile to a look as if a team of masked gunman had entered the building. I turned around to look and came face to face with a short, stocky lady with black, brown, and red hair down to her waist. She looked like a test mannequin.

My phone started to vibrate, I swiped to answer.

She yelled out, "Who is this bitch, Quan?"

I politely stood and casually grabbed my purse, pointed to him, and said, "Lose my number." I turned toward her and pointed. "Call me a bitch one more time and I'll flatten your little fat ass. Think I'm playing?" I flicked the envelope across the table and sashayed out.

"Mia, hold on, wait a minute. Don't start that today, Constance."

"I hate conniving-assed people," I said to no one in particular as I moved with intention through the restaurant and out toward the parking lot to my car, ignoring him calling out for me to come back.

I heard Gary yelling, "Mia, what's going on?"

I placed the phone to my ear as I stomped toward my car. "Hey, babe. I was trying to be nice and go to lunch with one of my classmates, Quan. I knew things were about to get weird, so I texted you to call me."

"Oh, so you used me?"

"I'm sorry; I wasn't trying to. I didn't know that was going to go that way. I was expecting him to hear me talk to you. Did you hear all of that?"

"Yes, I did," he said dryly.

"I'm sorry. I thought I was getting ready to show him how in love I was by talking to you and you get to hear a lady call me a bitch."

"Yeah and I heard you invite her to try you again. Go on with your spicy self."

I snickered. "Stop it, Gary."

"Who is he? Who are you with?" He questioned as if he didn't hear me say the name the first time.

"I was trying to have lunch with a guy from college, Quan."

"Oh, the same dude who wants you to leave me alone?"

His response shocked me. "What?"

"So you forget what you tell me. I remember everything you told me about this Quan guy."

"No, I haven't forgotten." I hadn't forgotten but I felt stupid. "There's nothing going on between me and Quan. Why would I have you call me?"

"Look, Mia, I know you're not that naive. Dude wants something from you and you act like you want something from him. If that wasn't the case then why is he the very first one you call every time you go to Arkansas?"

My words were temporarily stuck in my throat. My mouth became dry like I was trying to swallow a spoonful of cinnamon. I managed a fuming response. "He was a friend, Gary. What are you talking about? You must've gotten your information from Dena."

"No. Should I talk to Dena? Never mind, Mia. I'm not trying to start an argument. I'm just trying to see where your heart is. You still love me?" he said, ending the argument before it started.

"Yes. I. Do," I said with emphasis after every word. I pressed the key fob to unlock the car.

"And I love you too, so, drama just seems to follow you too, huh?"

I stared blankly as I closed the door and caught on to where he was going with his comment. "Yeah, seems like." I had said some harsh words to him before I left Houston and in this short conversation he helped me to remember that very thing. He knew where he was going with the comment and I didn't catch it until it was too late. He was one hundred percent correct; I had drama, too and he wasn't running from mine as I did his.

"Are you ready to come home?"

"I think so."

"When?"

"I don't know."

"Well, make it soon. You know I'm always here for you, right? Always."

"Thank you, baby. I really do appreciate that." I paused for a moment trying to think of a way to change the subject.

"Okay. Well, I'm gonna get off. I need to talk to God for a minute."

"Okay."

"Love you," we said in unison.

I touched End, started the car, and began to pray.

"Heavenly Father, I can do some stupid things at times, please have mercy on me..."

Gary had just held up a mirror and scolded me without raising his voice. I felt like a total fool. All of the stuff that I accused him of had just landed on my side of the fence. He showed me that solicited and unsolicited drama can certainly go both ways.

CHAPTER 22: KAREN

SINCE the day I talked to Gary in Vaughn's office, I was all smiles. I picked up the phone to call Vaughn. The phone rang once and as soon as he said, "Hello." I started talking.

"Vaughn, he actually listened, talked, and was engaged. I am so happy right now." I threw my head back and clapped my hands.

I had talked Gary into hanging out with me. I knew he enjoyed golf so I brushed up my skills in my backyard and at the driving range then invited him out to the country club. I needed him to feel confident that I wasn't wasting his time, so I needed to practice. He accepted and we had an opportunity to talk more.

"Karen, don't get too chummy. When you tell him that bull you've been holding onto for years, it's going to ruin all that you're trying to build with him," Vaughn said.

"I have to tell him my concerns, Vaughn. That would ruin the relationship if I don't tell him."

"Okay, if you tell him, I need to be there when you do."

"Okay, that's fine."

"So when do you plan to do this?"

"I don't know," I lied. I had no intention of involving Vaughn in my conversation.

He sighed. "Okay, Karen. When you find out, please let me know," he said, his voice oozing concern.

"I'll talk to you later." I pressed End and placed the phone in the chair.

I stood in my two-story closet turning in circles. I had not planned my escape properly and I'm disappointed in myself for it. Procrastination is a killer, so now I have to stay a little while longer subjecting my daughter to this foolishness. My husband was so mean at times; I should not have stayed so long.

I stood in the closet moving from one rack to the next, thumbing through clothes, not looking for anything in particular but reminiscing about my past. From Houston to Brooklyn to Los Angeles to Miami back to Brooklyn to Seattle and back to Houston. I had moved a few times over the years through college, first marriage, now my second marriage. Chandler had followed me around for several years of marriage. When the offer came to move to Houston, his opportunity was bigger so I followed him and it was time for me to retire. I was exhausted in the rat race anyway. I guess that was better than divorce since his career opportunity to work with that firm blindsided me. So, I hadn't planned for it and lack of planning is not my modus operandi. I have always had a 'plan B', but I've never had to use it because I always made sure 'plan A' worked.

I thought about Mia for a moment. I wanted to talk to her. I had gotten her number from Leslie who got it from her best friend, Dena. I really wanted to understand if she knew her family's history. I couldn't just call her and come right out with it.

The phone rang, interrupting my thoughts. I flipped it over

to see my daughter's surrogate. I had invited her to visit. I sat down in the brown leather wing-back chair.

"Sharon, I was just about to call you. Please do not tell me you're calling with another delay."

"No, no, Ms. Chandler, I'm not. I'm actually here and the driver is not here."

I leaped from the chair, "What?" Danny is not there?"

"No, I've been waiting for over thirty minutes and he's usually here but I haven't seen him."

"Arrrgghhhh! Okay, sit tight and I will call you back."

"Okay." She sighed.

I pressed End and searched for Danny's number. "Hey, Hi, this is Karen Chandler, I ordered a car service to pick up at IAH at three fifteen and my client has been waiting since then and still no one has come to pick her up."

"I'm so sorry, Ms. Chandler. Our driver was in an accident on the way to the airport and we were so caught up in making sure he was okay, we forgot to call. It was pretty bad."

While I was certainly saddened by the situation, they were still running a business and I would've expected some type of alternative solution. After a long pause and not hearing one, I decided to find one for myself. "Oh, okay. I'm sorry to hear that. I will, uh, try to find another driver." I didn't wait for a response. I noticed another call coming in so I answered it.

"Hey, Gary." I was frustrated but tried never to show it when my son called.

"Hey, I was just returning your call."

"Oh, I wanted to see if we could change our dinner to Thursday night instead of tonight. I got my dates mixed up and I have a client coming in tonight and the driver didn't make it there to pick her up so I need to find another car service to get her."

"Okay." He didn't sound disappointed at all.

"I'm so disappointed but I promise I'll make it up to you." I was frustrated with myself. I can't believe I got my dates mixed up.

"Not a problem at all. I have some other things I need to do tonight anyway. And by the way, you can call Sam to get your client. He has a few drivers."

"Sam?"

"Yes, Sam."

"Sam who?"

He paused. I could tell he was baffled I was pretending not to know who Sam was and pretending I didn't know Sam had moved to Houston. I knew exactly who Sam was and I knew he had moved to Houston. I assisted Sam with some legal issues a few years ago and he still owed me.

"My cousin, Sam."

"Sam, from Brooklyn, Sam?"

"Yes." His tone let me know his eyebrows were furrowed.

"Okay," I said excitedly and continued my lie. "I was not aware that Sam actually lived in Houston and had a car service. Will you text me his number?"

"Sure."

"Okay, thank you so much, honey. I'll talk to you later." This was working out in my favor. Sharon knows Sam from Seattle in his brief time there.

"Yeah." He ended the call.

I really didn't like the way he spoke in such a casual and slanged manner when he talked to me, but I'll address that later or maybe I'll get Vaughn to do it.

I called Sam and talked him into picking up Sharon at the last minute. He hesitated at first but eventually I influenced him to agree to pick her up. Money always talked.

CHAPTER 23: GARY

I arrived at my office at eight o'clock. It took me an hour and a half to get there with the people in Houston who just can't seem to move around without playing bumper cars on a rainy day. Mia had been gone for too long, almost a month and a half, and I was getting more irritated with each passing day with the traffic compounding the issue.

I walked through the lobby, greeted Mr. Richard, and rounded the corner when I noticed a guy dressed in a suit with the slim fitting Capri-styled pants. He was shorter than me and much smaller and wore glasses. He looked no more than sixteen. He hopped up from the bench next to the door and extended his hand toward me. "Mr. Matthews?"

I automatically extended mine. He seemed harmless but I looked at him quizzically. "Yes, and who are you?"

"My name is Alexander Martin Ferre. But you can call me Alex." His voice was as deep as mine. I wasn't sure if it was natural or he was performing to appear larger than his slim five foot eight frame.

"Okay?" I raised my eyebrows.

"Oh, I was sent over from A True Careers Staffing Agency. Mr. Thomas Jefferson requested a temp."

"Oh, okay, yes, we discussed getting a temp. But how did you know I was not Mr. Jefferson?"

"Oh, I, uh, met Mr. Jefferson, yesterday."

Before I could respond, TJ appeared. "I see you two have met."

"Yes." I pushed the door opened and they followed me into the suite. There was something weird about this dynamic but I decided not to explore it yet.

"Gary, I need to talk to you about something after I show Alex around the office."

"I'll be in here." I walked in wondering what the heck was going on with this situation. I sat down and quickly searched through the stack of resumes on my desk. I found Alex's resume. I reviewed it and was impressed. He was in Thurgood Marshall's Law School at Texas Southern; he graduated from Prairie View with a degree in Criminal Justice. He had worked at an insurance agency, retail shoes, and fast food. A somewhat weird combination but I think we can work with it. He had several temporary placements in law firms around the city so I would guess he's well connected unless he left all of them on bad terms.

TJ leaned into my office. "Hey, G, man put me on your calendar for one-thirty."

"Okay."

I made a few phone calls that lasted too long, asked Alex to schedule a couple of appointments for me, read some files, and headed out the door to meet Dena for lunch at 11:30.

She called yesterday to ask if I could meet her for lunch, well actually she demanded I meet her since Mia was not here. She needed to clarify some things about the wedding. I didn't have a clue what she was talking about and quite frankly didn't care what her and Mia came up with for the wedding. I was just ready for Mia to come home. We could get married anywhere but Houston. I didn't feel comfortable our wedding would go off without a boatload of shenanigans. I hadn't discussed it with Mia but I wanted to have a destination wedding, with a select group of people or no people. At this point, it really didn't matter to me; I just wanted to marry Mia.

I parked my truck and was in a purposeful stride toward the door of the restaurant. "Hey, Gary! Mr. Matthews?" I heard a male's voice yell across the parking lot. I turned to try to figure out who it was. An older, silver haired gentleman approached me with his hand extended. He looked familiar. I'm sure I had seen him in several courtrooms or meetings over the years. "How are you doing, sir? Randy Chadwick, with Chadwick and Chandler."

I certainly recognized the name. I had never lost a case against them. "I'm good. How are you, sir?" I'm sure I had a *what the hell do you want?* expression plastered on my face because that was exactly how I was feeling.

"I'm doing great now that I'm finally getting a chance to talk to you." He fumbled in his pockets.

"Is that right?" I folded my arms to contain my irritation. I remembered seeing him in passing at meetings, mediations, golf tournaments, and restaurants all over town but never did more than greeted him and kept moving.

"Here's my business card. When you have a moment, I'd like for you to call me. I own a law firm here in town and our clientele is expanding and has started to reach into more corporate structure. I've kept my eye on you for some time now and I had the opportunity to watch you during mediation several months back and we liked the way you handled both of the clients who came to an amicable solution without a lot of nasty battles."

"Hmmm, Chadwick and Chandler, I recognize the name. Yes, I've been in battle with you guys a number of times."

He smiled as he pushed his hands into his pockets. "Yes, you sure have. Some of our boys don't stand a chance against you," he mumbled, rocking back and forth on his heels. "You really know your stuff. I'd love for you to come work for us to run our newly expanded corporate division."

Okay. He's vague and he ended that statement incorrectly—*work for us*. I don't want to *work* for anyone but myself, now work meaning partnership, I would consider.

I started to shake my head. "I'm going to have to decl—"

He interrupted me. "No, no don't make the decision right now. Please think about it. Please. Maybe we can meet up for a round of golf or something. I know you have a pretty nice game."

I raised my eyebrows. This guy has really been watching me.

He grabbed my hand to shake it. "Please think about it."

I saw Dena round the corner with that Lexus on two wheels. She had to be upset about something. I needed to hurry away from this guy before he sees her perform.

"Okay, Randy, I'll think about it," I lied as I shook his hand and turned to walk toward the restaurant to catch up to Dena. I didn't want to think about working for anyone else.

"Men get on my damn nerves with all their bullshit! I'm so tired of crying and being upset. I'm exhausted." Dena stomped across the parking lot toward the door to Pappadeaux's. She shoved her phone back into her purse. "Between traffic and Monty this morning, I was almost late for my mammogram. I do not need to get off my schedule today. I have too much to do."

"Dena we can skip lunch if you want. Go ahead and finish what you have to do. I can grab something quick. I'll be okay,"

I offered. I silently hoped she wasn't going to launch into how the mammogram went.

"No," she shouted. "Focusing on someone else today will help me to calm my nerves. We need to finalize some more of the wedding plans. I know Mia is off in Arkansas doing whatever the hell she's doing. I talked her into putting the plans back on, so now I need you to look at some stuff in her absence. She won't be gone long." She sighed heavily and tried to pull the door open. I grabbed it from her and waved my hand for her to walk in.

"So have you decided if you're getting married at the church or at the chapel y'all found in The Woodlands?" she continued.

"How many?" the hostess asked.

"Two." I smiled at the young lady and acknowledged her since Dena appeared irritated and didn't seem to notice her. Though I know she did. "We haven't decided yet but she, well 'we' were leaning more toward the church."

"Right this way." Another hostess led us to our seats.

"You know what? Planning this wedding is the most exciting thing in my life right now."

"You must have a pretty boring life." I smiled at her trying to help her release the scowl that had taken over on her face.

"Good afternoon, can I get you something to drink?" The waiter greeted us.

"Yes," Dena quickly replied. "I'll have a glass of Pinot Noir, a Greek salad. Gary do want to share one?"

"Sure."

"Okay, the Greek Salad for two and the crab cakes, and a glass of water." She handed the waiter the menu.

"For you, sir."

"Pasta Mardi Gras."

"Wine to drink for you, sir?" he confirmed.

"No, just water," I said as I handed the menu to him.

"So, getting back to your yelling when you got out of the car, what's going on with you and Monty?"

"Monty has to go for real this time. I just can't take him anymore."

"Why? What did he do?"

"He's always accusing me of everything. I'm just sick of him." She rubbed her forehead and then began to twirl her finger around her already naturally curly hair.

"Did he hurt you?"

She snapped her head back as if that was impossible. "No. I wish he'd try."

"No, you don't. What did he accuse you of?"

She fanned her hand in the air. "I'm leaving him anyway."

The waiter put our drinks on the table.

I didn't probe any more. I was trying to determine if I believed what she was telling me. The anger she demonstrated walking in didn't stem from a simple accusation. Something else was going on and I was just waiting on her to tell me what it was.

She was fidgeting quite a bit. She rubbed her hand underneath her left arm and around her breast a few times as she looked absentmindedly around the restaurant. I almost asked about the mammogram but I know if she wanted me to know, she'd blurt it out eventually. I just prayed for the best.

"So, oh, let me show you pictures of the chapel and the church and you can decide, and we need to finalize a date."

Our food arrived just as she pulled out the pictures. The waiter tossed the Greek Salad and served us.

"Shrimp for the lady?" he asked.

"Sure." I nodded.

I reached for the pictures as we maneuvered our hands around the waiter placing food on the table.

"Can I get you anything else?"

No, we're good. Thanks." I looked at the pictures for a moment. "Dena, what would you say if I told you that I wanted a destination wedding instead of getting married in Houston?"

She stared at me blankly for a moment.

I continued, "I'll still pay you the same amount to organize it for us. I just don't think getting married in Houston would be a good idea. I honestly feel like there is someone or something lurking to make a spectacle of it."

"I would say, make up your mind, choose a date, and give me my marching orders. Have you told Mia?"

"No, I actually thought she was on hold with the plans until you called me last night and I thought about it then."

"Did you two talk about the wedding plans?"

"Yeah, this morning. But it was brief. I just wanted to hear her voice, see how she was doing."

"Awww. Gary you're so sweet." She smiled genuinely. "I told Mia you loved her dearly."

I rubbed my hand over my face. "Hmph, please don't call me sweet. And trust me she knows." I managed a frowned

"Well, hell, you know what I mean. You're a good man."

"Thank you."

As soon as I took my last bite, I saw Nina walk past the window. I wasn't sure if she was coming here because she saw my truck or if it was a coincidence. Dena didn't see her. I immediately asked the waiter for the check as I kept my eye on Nina until she was out of view.

"You know what? I think I'm going to leave Houston. There are too many memories, too many bad memories."

Dena shot a perplexed look in my direction then turned around to look behind her as if she was trying to determine where that comment was coming from.

She shook her head. "Lord, I don't feel like fighting today."

The waiter put the bill on the table. I glanced at it and pulled out several bills. I waved my hand to get the waiter's attention, handed him the money, and told him to keep the change.

I focused my attention back to Dena and said, "You won't have to because we're getting ready to go."

Thank God Nina didn't see us. I walked Dena to her car. I opened her door after she unlocked it. Before she got in, I hugged her and said, "Look, I know there's something you want to tell me and you're just not ready, but know that I'm here at any time you need me. You got that?"

She nodded and I saw a rare tear struggle down her cheek.

She hugged me. "Okay, I love you, man."

"Yeah, love you, too." I walked back to my truck and waited until Dena drove away.

I hurried back into the restaurant. I looked around until I found Nina. She was seated alone in the corner, near the restroom. The place had gotten crowded. I strolled to her table and sat down. I had to hurry with what I had to say because I didn't know if she was meeting someone. "I've been looking for you. It's extremely disappointing to know I was right about you. I thought after our last conversation you would move on and start your life with whoever you wanted to, but you keep coming back, and for what? If you're dating, you're okay, if you're not, you're insane. I misjudged you, Nina, but I think you misjudged me more. Stay your ass away from Mia and anybody in my family. You got that? Think I'm playing and your ass will be faced down in dirt."

Her eyes widened then she folded her arms. "You ain't gon' do nothing to me."

I was taken aback by her dialect. "Oh, really?" I grunted. I stood up then leaned into her ear with a fake smile. "As I said before, I will tie your ass up and take you over to 23521 Garden Meadows Lane and let you watch while I slash a couple of throats and take out everybody with a pulse and never get my hands dirty." I paused.

She appeared surprised. She inhaled and panted each exhale.

"Yeah, your parents moved. I know." I stood up and adjusted my jacket as I glared down at her. "I don't want to see your face or hear about anybody I know seeing your face."

She started to sweat above her top lip and her brow. She used her napkin to dab the sweat but she maintained her composure. I knew my last comment put a certain level of fear in her. The address I rattled off was that of her beloved grandparents, her mother, and her nieces whom she loved dearly. If she wanted to harass people I loved, then I was ready to torture people she loved.

A short, bald, well-dressed, old dude came to the table. He removed his fedora and placed it on the table as he looked back and forth between me and her. "What's up, baby? Is everything okay? It took me a minute to find somewhere to park after I dropped you off." He pulled the chair out where I was previously seated.

She started to speak, "Uh, ye—"

I interrupted her. "Yes, everything is cool, sir. I have a restraining order against her so now she's all yours."

I walked away as she started to explain to the old dude.

CHAPTER 24: MIA

HANGING out with elderly people, you will more than likely hear the same stories over and over again. I hung out with Aunt Edna for the day, and we decided to go to the mall just to look around. I drove her Cadillac along East Harding toward the mall, as she talked nonstop. She had just repeated two stories and then started on a third.

"So, Mia, how is Gary's mother doing? I'm not talking about the one who raised him. I talk to her all the time. I'm talking about the other one. The one who had him, the snooty one."

"His biological mother, Karen? I guess she's fine."

"That's a shame that woman didn't raise her own son. And he still turned out to be a fine young man. But she ain't the first one to do that. Plenty women have done it, some by choice and some because their grandmother begged for them. You know Gertrude did the same thing for one of her cousin's children and raised her as her own. Shol' did."

"Aunt Edna, who is Gertrude?"

She fanned her hand at me. "You know Gertrude. She used to live right down the street from your mother. Used to go to the same church and everything. Big lady, tall, real tall, with big ol' pipe legs, long hair. You know her."

I laughed. "You and these descriptions." That could've been several women. "Pipe legs?"

"You know her, she raised about twenty-five kids in that lil' house."

"Oh okay, I remember her." I had no idea who Aunt Edna was speaking of but I had to pretend so she could go on with her story and stop throwing out random descriptors.

"Well, anyway, that girl she raised found out later and she didn't care. She was just glad to be in a loving home. The only problem I saw with that deal was the girl didn't know who her folks were and she almost married her brother."

"What? How?"

"Well, they hadn't told her she was adopted and then she got to high school and wanted to go to the prom and found out when he came to the house. Gertrude told them."

"Oh, my goodness. That's not almost getting married though."

"Yes, it is. First the prom then the wedding."

I slowed to a stoplight and looked over at her. "Oh." I didn't want to comment because I had heard the same story the last time I was visiting Arkansas. Aunt Edna believed what she believed and I didn't want to upset her by disagreeing as I did the last time. That did not go over well. My comments got me cussed out and given the silent treatment for about thirty minutes. It wasn't worth it so I remained quiet.

I couldn't help but wonder if there was any way possible I was related to Gary since he was adopted. His family is not from Arkansas, though. His roots were extremely difficult to trace. Aunt Edna had told me before that we were not related to anyone with the last name Matthews or James, which didn't matter in our case because Gary was not the biological son of the Matthews. I didn't know Karen's maiden name but Aunt Edna said she knew Karen's family because they were from Alabama, the same town as her husband, Uncle Herman. Aunt Edna didn't think we were related, but what if she was wrong? After I asked so many questions, she said she'd have to do some asking around for Karen's background. I remember her saying, "It's easy to find information on the mother of the child but only God knows who the father is…momma's baby, daddy's maybe."

We made it to the mall within fifteen minutes. We walked around for a couple of hours browsing for the most part. She tried on a few dresses until she found one she liked. I purchased it for her birthday. She was so happy when she found out I purchased it while she was in the fitting room.

"Are you ready to get something to eat, Aunt Edna?"

"Yes, chile, yes I am. And thank you so much for buying my dress. You are such a lil' sweetheart. Always have been." She hugged me then looped her arm around mine as we waddled out of the store.

We were sitting in KFC eating and chatting when we heard sirens and emergency response lights.

"Lord have mercy, I know that woman, right there." She rose from her seat slightly as she looked out the window. "Crazy broads get on my nerves," my aunt chimed in as we watched a woman destroy a car. "I know her momma and she's out here beating on that boy's car like she done lost her mind." She settled back into her seat. "Those police officers got her quickly though. Look at 'em."

I turned to look out the window when my phone vibrated. I glanced at my phone, a text message from Dena.

Hey headsup…Gary's mother is going to call you. I have a client Leslie who is very good friends with her and she asked for your number.

We heard the sirens stop then started again ten seconds later. Aunt Edna continued to strain to look out the window. "That's good for her lil' fasss tail."

I thought about Nina as I placed more potatoes in my mouth. "She has lost her mind. She reminds me of Gary's ex-girlfriend. She just hasn't gone that far but I wouldn't put it past her."

"Girl, if that ex-girl or whoever she is, ever come at you, you do your best to disable her ass. That is just crazy." She shook her head as she stabbed her green beans and took in a mouthful then shoved a piece of chicken in her mouth.

"Auntie, that's why I came here again because she just keeps messing with me and I don't want to fight. Well, yes I do. I want to hurt her, badly, but I'm too old for that and I don't want to end up in jail."

She sighed. "Lord have mercy. Mia, you won't go to jail for defending yourself." She shook her head.

"Yes, I will because of what I'd do to her when I touch her."

"You gon' have to stop running every time something happens. If you get married to him, what are you gon' do? You can't run every time, honey."

"I know. I'm going back soon."

My phone vibrated again, I glanced toward the phone on the table and saw Quan's name.

I put the phone in my purse because I knew he would keep texting until I answered.

"Yes, you stop running. Stay there and deal with it. Whatever it is. You stay there and deal with it. Stop running."

"Yes, ma'am." I picked up a napkin to dab my mouth.

"You're opening the door for such foolishness to occur. I love to see you here but you need to take your butt back to Houston. Remember what happened the last time you broke up with Gary because of that ex-girlfriend. He's a young man. He has needs, chile." She took a swig of her drink. "Remember he went out with that ol' new crazy girl that drove that car up in that place on y'all." She shook her head.

I stared into my drink as I stirred with the straw and remained silent. There was no need to speak because I knew she would only repeat herself and talk over me until she made her point.

"Yes, ma'am," I finally said.

I needed to prepare for an impending battle.

CHAPTER 25: GARY

DIFFERENT tragedies bring about a change in the lives of some people. I went back to my office for a 1:30 meeting with TJ.

"Hey, G." He walked in and closed the door.

"Hey, TJ. How much do you know about this guy? His credentials seems pretty good for what we need him to do, but is there anything striking you? We've been without and through a couple of assistants since Lynn."

"I know, man. Lynn, despite all of her issues, was the best assistant out there. But this young man is cool. He came highly recommended from a few people so I scooped him up. Hopefully we can work around his schedule."

I noticed he winced as he adjusted in his chair.

"Are you okay, TJ? I noticed you limping earlier and now you...you don't seem comfortable."

"Yeah, man. That's why I wanted to talk to you. I went to the doctor the other day and they said the cancer is back."

I stared blankly for a moment. I didn't expect him to say that. "Ahh, man. I'm sorry to hear that."

"Yeah, it's a bummer, man. I'm trying to stay positive. I haven't told my wife yet and I don't know how long I can go without telling her."

"Today would be a good day to do it. How long have you known?"

"Well, only a couple of weeks. I know my body, man, so I went to the doctor. I don't procrastinate like I used to do. But I know this; I'm not doing chemo again."

I scratched my head and listened as he continued.

"I just can't do that again. I'd rather spend my time traveling the world, marking some things off my bucket list."

We allowed a long silence to linger between us.

"So what do you need me to do for you?"

"Well." He leaned forward and placed a flash drive on my desk. "That's the plan I've worked on for the past week. It's nothing fancy but a lot of information nonetheless. I want you to take some time to consider it all and let me know what you think."

I reached for the flash drive.

He leaned back in the chair. "And if we can get this young man up to speed reading the files before you get them, briefing you on the new ones or any new developments on the old ones, typing letters, keeping up with facilities, and giving you a report of everything on a regular basis. I can work remotely making calls to keep the business flowing in here. But once you finish reading the plan, we need to discuss it. If we change the business model, you might have all you can handle."

He was rambling.

I contemplated all he'd said. I turned to place the flash drive into the USB connection. I couldn't help but think of what it would be like to have him gone forever.

He continued again. "The other side gig stuff, like the P.I.

and surveillance can go to the side for now unless you want to pick it up."

"No, I'll have enough." Although I thought about the possibility of Sam doing it.

"I know. So, it can go to the side. I'm going to be in the office for a few more days and then I'll be out until I beat this thing for the second time."

"TJ, you know I can handle this, if this lil' dude can keep up. If not, I'll get someone else. If I have to, I'll get Mia or Dena in here to help me. You need to get going on your road to recovery. Get out of here. Take care of yourself. I got it."

"Okay, I need to bring closure to some accounts and then I'll..." He stood.

I stood up to walk around my desk. I reached out to shake his hand and gave him a encouraging squeeze on the shoulder. I didn't know what else to do or say. TJ and I had become good friends. He was like family; I had learned a lot from him and really hated to see him go through the same illness again.

"Take care of yourself, man, I promise I got it."

"I know, I know. You did it before."

He walked out and I put my head in my hands.

CHAPTER 26: MIA

I walked Aunt Edna to the front door and got chastised for treating her like an old lady. I didn't respond when she said, "Mia, you could've walked your lil' tail on to your car, I don't need your help." She fumbled the keychain I handed her for the house key. I waited until she was safely inside then walked to the car. I pulled out of her driveway and waited until I got on the I530 to dial Dena's number.

She answered the phone singing, "I just ate lunch with your sweetheart. He's lost a few pounds."

"Who?"

"Mia, stop playing around. You know damn well I'm talking about Gary." She sounded annoyed.

"Dang, I see I can't joke with you today. What do you mean he's lost a few pounds?" I was sure not to match her tone.

"His face looks slimmer. His cheeks."

"Oh." I paused. "I miss him."

"Well bring your ass home." She huffed. "What is the problem?"

"You sent a text that you gave Gary's mom my number." I cut straight to the point because I was not interested in getting into another argument with her.

"Yes, I know Leslie and she told me Karen wanted to find me so she could get your number."

"Oh." I had no problem talking to Karen. I wanted to form my own opinion of her and not necessarily mirror Gary's feelings. I know it's easy to do so I hope she calls.

"So, what is Quan stressing you out about? Trust me; I know he's up to his tricks."

"Yep, he's back to threatening me about his money again. One moment I owe him another minute I don't."

"That's why I paid him that lil' five hundred dollars I borrowed to get my car fixed. He'll hold that mess over your head forever. He was cool and all but I couldn't deal."

"I know, but he's up to fifteen thousand dollars for me. I paid him exactly what I owed him. I hated to go in my savings but I had to."

"Man, I don't know what's gotten into him. Maybe he's broke." She suggested.

"I don't know. But if this six thousand makes him rich then so be it. He gave me a piece of paper with a bunch of handwritten numbers on it and then at the bottom he wrote fifteen thousand. I was like boy bye. He's threatening to harm my family and everything."

"Girl, no!" She hissed. "He's just too much. I'm sure he's just bluffing. Chris will flick Quan's lil' ass like a bug. But you need to pay that fool and bring your butt home."

Ten minutes into the conversation, my phone vibrated and I noticed a number that I did not recognize. The number showed on the screen with Seattle, WA underneath it.

"Somebody is calling me from a number I don't recognize from a 206 area code."

"That's Karen, answer it," she said anxiously.

"Okay, I'll call you back."

I cleared my throat as I pressed End and answered, "Hello."

"Hi, Mia. This is Karen Chandler. How are you?"

"Oh, Hi, Karen. I'm doing well. How are you?" I held the phone to my ear then decided to drive hands free. I pressed the speaker button and pushed the phone underneath my bra strap.

"I am doing fantastic. Hey, I wanted to call you to see if you and I can go grab a cup of coffee or tea or something. Since you're engaged to my son, I thought it'd be good if you and I got to know each other a little better. I'm trying but I'm taking it slow in pushing myself on him, I'm allowing him his space and getting whatever time he gives me."

I pressed the brakes as I slowed to a stop light passing The Pines Mall. She finally took a breath so I jumped right in with a reply.

"Oh that'll be great. I'm out of town right now, though."

"Oh really? Okay, well we can do it when you get back. When will you be back?"

I coughed. "Ummm, in a few days," I stammered.

"Oh, okay, good. Let's say we meet on Monday around noon. Is that good for you?"

"Sure."

"Uh, Mia, can we keep this between us for now?"

"Yes, uh okay."

"I just don't want Gary getting upset with me."

"Okay." I suddenly felt weird. I know that Gary would be upset with both of us if he knew we were meeting.

Now I have to keep another secret and figure out how I'm going to get to Houston and back to Arkansas in a day.

PART TWO

NEVER

GIVE UP

CHAPTER 27: GARY

EACH day had vanished like the wind and I still couldn't get past the fact that TJ's prostate cancer had returned. He seemed a bit at peace with it this time, as if he was ready to leave. I, on the other hand, was sad for him and anxious about my own life. I had spent many hours staring out the window and thinking, wondering what my next move should be. I talked to Mia via text followed by a brief conversation. I read through the document, it had a lot of details but not enough, leaving his options open to his 24 percent. Who owned the other 26 percent? If TJ decides to leave, should I get another business partner, or should I sell? Our office space lease was close to expiration, should I move and work out of my home? Should I keep the assistant that TJ hired or get a female in here, since I had reservations about him anyway? Should I go back into corporate environment, since I've been approached so many times? What should I do about my personal life? Should I really fight for Mia for a final go at it? I wanted her to be safe and feel safe. Should I make an attempt to get to know my biological mother? Too many questions and too many decisions to make. I needed to pray. On my knees.

I walked over to the doorway. "Alex, please hold all my calls for the next hour or so."

"Yes, sir." He pressed a few buttons on the phone then paused to look at me with concern in his eyes.

"Thanks." I closed and locked the door before he started asking a lot of questions, which he was good at. I absolutely hated the way he looked at me.

I removed my jacket and hung it on the hanger behind the door. I walked over to the leather sofa against the wall and stared at the abstract artwork that Mia and Dena had placed above the sofa after they begged me to redecorate my office last year. I stretched my hands toward the ceiling then paced back and forth for several minutes, folding and unfolding my arms across my chest, studying the squares in the carpet. My life at the moment felt abstract. I loosened my tie for more comfort.

I walked back to my computer; I leaned over to find one of the daily email devotionals that I sometimes read but most of the time deleted. I clicked sort by sender, scrolled down to the emails beginning with the letter "J." There were several I had not deleted from various dates. "Bingo. God, let this be what I need to get me focused, get me started," I said to myself as I eased into the chair to decide which one to read. My eyes settled on one from exactly one week ago. It was as if I'd heard an audible voice say, "That one." I doubled clicked the title, *Worry or Pray, You Can't do Both*. The scripture was spot on: *Do not be anxious about anything, but in every situation, by prayer and petition, with thanksgiving, present your requests to God. And the peace of God, which transcends all understanding, will guard your hearts and your minds in Christ Jesus.* (Philippians 4:6, 7 NIV).

The devotional ended with a prayer but I felt I needed to get on my knees and talk to God with my own words. "Lord,

I don't even know where to start. I just feel like I need to say something. I need peace, they need peace. Lord, give them peace," I mumbled as I walked back to the sofa and knelt down.

"Heavenly Father, the all knowing, all powerful healer and provider of all my needs. I ask for forgiveness of my sins. I thank you for everything you've done and everything you're going to do in my life. I'm here now asking for healing for my friend Thomas Jefferson. For some reason the cancer is attacking his body once again. This time worse than the last. You healed him the last time and he had quite a testimony afterward about his experience. Heavenly Father, can you grant him that same healing again? I ask that Your will be done in his life. Your grace and mercy be with him. Heavenly Father my mind has been racing none stop and I'm tired, I need Your help. I know I'm a fixer and try to run ahead fixing things sometimes without even asking for Your help. I need help that only You can give right now. I'm sorry I didn't ask You sooner. Sometimes I jump out ahead of myself and I know sometimes I don't listen. But right now, at this moment, I give this business thing, my relationship with Mia, my relationship with my mother, Karen, all up to You. I'm at a standstill in every aspect. I'm certainly not in control here and I need Your help. What's my next move? Again Lord, I love You and I thank You for what You're going to do in my life. However You direct me, I'll follow. In Jesus' name, Amen."

I lingered on my knees for a few minutes then returned to the sofa. I stretched out and stared at the ceiling. I was at peace; a sense of calmness was in the room, and I allowed it to stay. The anxiousness that I'd felt earlier had dissipated.

I was interrupted by a knock at the door. I looked at my timepiece.

"Yes?" I rose up and planted my feet on the floor.

"Mr. Matthews? I was just letting you know an hour and a half has passed."

"Okay, thanks." I rubbed my hand across my face.

"May I enter?"

I stood up and walked to the door, unlocked it, and pulled it open.

He pushed his way inside and closed the door before I could acknowledge him. I stepped backward with furrowed brows.

"I'm sorry about that, Mr. Matthews. I had to come in here. There's a guy who's been waiting on you since fifteen minutes after you asked me to hold your calls. I told him you were unavailable and he said he'd wait." He rolled his neck, folded his arms, and shifted his weight to one leg.

Is this dude gay? I've suspected it since I first met him but now I'm positive. My thoughts about him being metrosexual just turned to all out assuming he's homosexual. Wow. I wonder if TJ knew this. Or does he even care at this point. I stared at him for a few seconds, distracted.

He interrupted my thoughts. "Mr. Matthews, he won't leave. Well, he left and came back twenty minutes later. I didn't want to call security because he said he was a good friend of yours for several years. But he looks scary."

"What's his name, Alex?"

"Monty. That's all he'd give me."

I tried to suppress my rising irritation that was threatening to take over the peace that was still lingering in my office.

Monty was Dena's fiancé, boyfriend, lover, or whatever they were at the time. He had never been to my office and I don't know what had caused him to show up to talk to me. I had not spoken to him in several months. We weren't the best of friends but we were cordial. He always seemed to have a chip on his shoulder, angry about something. I assumed it was because he and Dena were always at odds about something and although I tried my best to stay out of it, I've stepped in a couple of times over the years when their altercations were headed to physical because of Dena. Dena Thomas, gotta love her. She is a Brooklyn-born-ride-or-die type lady.

Alex had unfolded his arms and was standing with his hands on his hips waiting on me to answer.

"Give me a minute. Tell him to give me five more minutes."

"Okay, sir." He took a deep breath, squared his shoulders, and walked out.

I walked back to my desk and picked up my cell phone. Monty had called me six times, not including two times last night. He had also texted once. He really needed to talk. My mind went back to the conversation I had with Dena the other day.

"Lord, please let Dena be okay." I smiled because it had occurred to me that I probably should've been praying for Monty. I hadn't prayed this much in a long time. I didn't prolong the inevitable. I had to talk to him.

I pulled my office door open and walked into our very small lobby. He leaped from his seat.

"Hey, G man. I'm sorry to come up here and camp out, but I really need to talk to you."

I scanned him for a quick second. "How's it going, Monty? What's up?" I extended my hand to shake his.

He grabbed my hand and pulled me toward him with one arm and slapped my back. "Can we talk in your office? I don't want, uh, I need to talk in private." He tilted his head toward Alex who was pretending to focus on his computer screen.

"Yeah, sure. Come on back."

CHAPTER 28: GARY

DANCING around an issue surely doesn't make it go away. Monty had been in my office twenty minutes talking about weather, sports, jewelry, houses, and anything else he could think of to avoid the real motivation for why he camped out in my office. I tried to listen more than I spoke because I thought he was looking for an entrance to the reason he was sitting in the chair across from me. I had entertained several nonsense small-talks but he still hadn't come out with it. I assumed after some time, he realized it so he just blurted it out.

"Man, G, I don't know how to tell you this but me and Dena got married about three weeks ago."

I shook my head in confusion. "What?"

"Yeah." He studied my expression and waited on a response.

"Oh. Well. Congratulations, man. Was that the plan?" I forced a smile as I opened the left drawer on my desk in search of cigars. I didn't have any. I tried to hide my baffled expression but to no avail. "What happened? Why did y'all choose the route you took? Eloped?"

"Well, it was right after Mia left and went to Arkansas this last time. She came home one day and said let's just do it. We had discussed going to Vegas if we ever got married, so we went away for the weekend and did it."

"Oh, okay." I paused. "So, are you happy?" I was still trying to figure out if that was the reason he camped in my lobby for over an hour.

"Yeah, yeah, man. I couldn't be happier. I love Dena. I'm in love with Dena. But uh, uhh…"

"Is that why you came here?"

"Naw, man, I, uh…" His eyes turned glassy. He wiped his hands across his face. He leaned forward in the chair then sat back. He adjusted his weight by pressing his hands on the arms of the chair. "Before I start, I want to let you know that all of the drama you've seen between us lately has just been the distraction she wanted so you all wouldn't know what was really going on. All of the anger and going off at the drop of a dime was not about me, it was about her."

He paused and leaned forward to place his elbows on my desk. My mind had done at least three world winds of thoughts. I was trying to be patient. I didn't speak because I figured that would only add unneeded fuel to what I conceived was a simmering fire. Monty and I only had one issue that I could remember and that was after Dena caught him in her house with another woman. He later came back to her house for some of his belongings when a fight between the two of them resulted from him calling Dena a bitch and charging toward her. I was only trying to stop them when he landed a punch on my chin, then I hurt my hand when I punched him in the face. We had no issues after that. He stopped his excessive drinking and stopped smoking weed completely. He showed some signs of maturing and we've hung out a few times.

He continued his delivery, "I've tried to get her to call Mia, call you, or any of her other friends she confides in, even her mother, but she wouldn't." He sighed heavily, "Dena found out a month ago she has breast cancer and she needs somebody in addition to me to help her through this." He pressed his fingers into his closed eyes as if to squeeze away the tears running along the rims of his eyelids. "She's so stubborn, man. She wants to beat this and then tell the story. I keep telling her that part of beating it is to have support. Tell somebody." He sounded defeated.

I couldn't speak. Out of all the things that had just run through my mind, that was not one of them. It felt like a golf ball had suddenly lodged into my throat. I looked away from him because I couldn't stand seeing another man cry. I wiped my hands across my face and stilled them in a praying position resting the tips of my fingers under my chin.

"Yeah, man, breast cancer." He began again with more rapid words than the first time. "She's wanted to just up and move but I told her that would not be a good idea. So, we found an apartment near Lake Conroe. We're going to build, build a house somewhere. She put her house on the market and was ready to move. She got an offer on her house she couldn't refuse. I had to talk her out of moving to Austin right now."

He was beginning to talk in circles. "That's what she wants to do but I convinced her to stay here because I think she can get the best treatment here." A tear rolled down his cheek. He wiped his face with both hands. "Man, I just needed somebody to talk to. Somebody I knew who cares about Dena as much as I do. If this mess is tearing me up trying to support her, what do you think it's doing to her going through it? She's angry most days. One day she wants to get treatment and other days she doesn't want it. And with all of that, she doesn't want to tell anybody."

"Breast cancer," I mumbled.

"She really needs Mia, man. I know she hasn't told her anything because I listen to her while they're talking. They still shoot the breeze like everything is normal."

"Okay, man. I will get, uh. I will get uh, I will get Mia." It literally felt like my windpipe was being pinched by an unknown object. I closed my eyes, I couldn't think, I was stuttering. I pushed my chair away from the desk and stood up. I walked around my desk and briefly placed a comforting hand on his shoulder, then I walked over to the small table by the window. "Arrrggghhhh! Damnit!" I let out in a loud voice. I swung the lamp to the floor. "My God, my God," I yelled.

Alex rushed into my office with widened eyes and in a stance ready for a fight. "Is everything all right?"

I was standing facing the window with my face raised toward the ceiling and my fingers pinching the bridge of my nose.

I heard Monty say in a surprisingly encouraging tone, "He's okay, he's okay. Just leave him alone. He needs some time to process."

A few seconds later, I heard the door close.

CHAPTER 29: MIA

had fallen asleep on the sofa. There was so much rolling through my mind about my relationship with Gary. His mother wanting to get acquainted could be a good thing or a bad thing. I had to wait and see which one. I loved him and I had to stop running before he ran off with someone else. My sister and my aunt were scaring me even more with their encouraging words. I needed to stop running away every time there was a problem. If I have to fight, then I have to fight, I'd do my best. I allowed my emotions to take control of me and I "ran" to Arkansas for the third time allowing other woman to tug at the heart strings and the zipper of my man. Just as the thought of him entered my mind, my phone vibrated with a text message from Gary.

Gary: I love you.
Me: Hey babe! I love you too!
Gary: You good?
Me: Yeah I'm good. Just got back from visiting my aunt.
Gary: Oh, yeah. That's cool.
Me: What are you up to?

Gary: I just finished at the driving range with Karen.
Me: Whaaaat? Wow. That is awesome. Did you enjoy?
Gary: I'm getting there. I was at church Sunday and they were
talking about forgiving and how we should forgive as God forgave us.

I scrolled through my favorites contact list and touched the phone and called him. "Hey, baby, that is really awesome." I sat up and placed my feet on the floor.

"Yeah, it is. I'm really trying but she's a piece of work. I just don't want to be praying for things and God is looking at me like, go and reconcile with your mother."

"Wow. Gary that's awesome. I love that. I love you for doing that. It definitely demonstrates forgiveness in action and maturity." I walked through the foyer and up the stairs toward my room.

"Yeah, Vaughn kinda forced it. I stopped by the restaurant one day to see him and she showed up."

"Were you okay with that?"

"Yeah. I was okay. I had a lot going on last week. I missed a couple of Sunday's from going to church. So, I made sure I went Sunday and I decided during service that I would forgive her and at least listen and act more cordial. You know…"

"Gary that is so awesome." I smiled.

"Yeah, I decided to at least listen. She's had an interesting life which makes me understand some of her choices. I'm not saying I totally agree with her choices but I understand."

"You'll have to tell me about it someday."

"Yeah, someday. I really need to figure out her angle though. It'll take some time. I'm not sure I can trust her. So, what have you been up to, babe?" His abrupt change of the subject let me know he didn't want to talk about his mother any longer.

"Nothing, just shopping with Aunt Edna and listening to the same stories she told me the last time we hung out. She's so cute, Gary." I stood in front of the mirror and fluffed my hair.

"I know; sounds like my parents. I swear both of them fight over who's going to tell me the same story again."

"We talked about the time she got upset about my cousins running out of food at the family reunion and she snapped. We laughed so hard every time, as if it just happened." I laughed.

"Sounds like you're having fun."

"Yeah, she's so cute, all four feet eleven of her." I sighed.

"Okay, babe. I just wanted to call you since you said you talked to your mother and I wanted to hear your voice."

"Okay." He paused.

"What? I really did."

"I'm not disputing that."

"What? Is something wrong? Your tone changed on a dime."

"No, nothing's wrong, I just have a lot on my mind, that's all."

"A lot like what?"

"Nothing, we'll talk about it later, but you know I'm ready for you to come home, right?"

"Yes, I know. I'm coming soon."

"Soon, like…"

"Very soon. Okay? I'll talk to you later."

I rushed to the bathroom because I had eaten something that didn't agree with my stomach and it had to come out. I did not want Gary to hear it.

I stood at the mirror looking at myself for a few minutes. My stomach was extremely queasy.

Des came barging into the room and into the bathroom where I stood. "Gosh, I'm glad I wasn't on the toilet, geesh."

"I'm glad you weren't either. I brought some fresh towels."

"Thanks." I leaned forward on the counter to examine my face. "Does my skin look weird to you? Blochy? Spotty?"

"Mia, I think you're pregnant. You may as well go to the doctor. That's why your skin looks like that and your emotions are running so high. Aunt Edna thinks so, too." She opened the linen closet and stacked the towels neatly.

I looked at her trying to figure out why she'd think I was pregnant and I hadn't said anything. I thought I was also but I hadn't said anything to her.

CHAPTER 30: KAREN

S PRING is here, Alex and I am so excited." I twirled toward the sofa where Alex was perched, typing feverishly on his laptop. "Don't you just love this weather?"

"Yes, I do but my allergies do not." He rubbed his eyes for demonstration.

"I got to spend a few minutes with my son today. I think he's coming around." I folded my arms and sat on the edge of the sofa.

"Really? That's wonderful. He seems to be a really cool guy. Very professional, not too much of a talker though." He closed the laptop as I leaned in to see what he was typing.

"What are you working on?"

"A paper for class."

"Hmmm. Okay." I lowered my eyes at him. "I still need you to pay close attention. If he's not talking, then watch him. Does he and TJ have a good relationship?" I stood to walk into the kitchen and went to the sink to wash the vegetables I had placed there for my salad.

"Yes but I haven't heard them talking much."

"Hmmph. I wonder why." I rubbed the back of my neck.

I wondered if TJ had told Gary about the business set up and that I was one of his business partners. I knew he'd be extremely annoyed about it. That's why I need to prove to him that I'm a good person, a good business partner, and not to be messed with.

"I have no idea," Alex said absentmindedly as he flipped through a magazine. "Gary has sort of a quiet intensity about him."

"Hmph. It seems the business has slowed down over there. Do they appear very busy?"

He stood up to stretch and pulled his slim fitting pants toward his ankles. "I guess, fairly busy. Gary does anyway. He literally buries himself in his work. He's in early and leaves late. He spends most of the day reading files, then on the phone negotiating and making deals between people."

"Mediation."

"I see him going through stacks of files on his desk, on the floor, you know." He rocked back and forth on his heels as he stood in the center of the kitchen. "TJ is out a lot."

"Really? So Gary is running the place by himself?"

"Well, kind of. I think TJ is sick." He spun around in an about-face and sat at the table in the nook and opened his laptop.

"What makes you say that?"

"I just believe he is. Lots of doctor's appointments."

I nodded and continued to slice the cucumbers for my salad.

"There was a guy who camped out in the lobby today to speak to Gary. He went into Gary's office to talk and after a few minutes, Gary was really upset. Throwing things."

"What? Throwing things?" My heart sank. What would upset my son so badly? "I should call him."

"No. The guy said he'd be fine, he just needed a moment."

"Who is this guy? Did he say his name?"

"Yes, Monty."

"Hmmm, that's Dena's fiancé. I wonder if there's something

going on with her. Gary loves her like a sister and he wouldn't react like that to anything else coming from Monty. At least I don't think so."

"I'm not sure. They close doors when they don't want me to hear."

"You need to…" I stopped short of telling him to spy and snoop on what's going on. He should understand what I want from him. This job for Alex is getting way bigger than finding out about Gary's personal life with Mia. I figured working in the office; he would eventually end up in Gary's house just as he did mine after I was comfortable enough with him. He can add TJ's health, Monty, and Dena's issues to his list of things to watch for.

Alex printed some documents on his portable printer and slid them into his folder. He folded and placed one document in an envelope and sealed it.

"Do you have my information about Mia? I'm having coffee with her on Monday."

"No, not much more. Most of the information I'm finding is her career and awards and stuff here in Houston. She is a class act." He placed the folder on the counter next to my salad bowl.

"That's nice to know."

"I really hope she is not your cousin and you have somehow gotten mixed up." He shook his head.

"I really hope I'm mixed up, too."

I was pacing back and forth but still watching what he was doing, looking at the phone trying to determine if I should call Gary just to see how he was doing. I wouldn't dare tell him that I was meeting with Mia.

An hour passed, I was still pacing, and Alex had left. I finally worked up enough nerve to call Gary. He didn't answer and I didn't leave a message.

CHAPTER 31: GARY

A drink per day keeps the sorrows at bay. Or does it? Sam had dropped me off at a hotel in the Galleria area. There was usually a nice mellow crowd there. The bartender knew us. I was missing Mia like crazy. I needed to hold her. I wanted to make love to her.

I gulped the last half of my third gin and tonic as I ignored the phone vibrating in my pocket. I wanted to feel numb if only for a moment. Cancer was taking over the world and hitting too close to home. Dena had breast cancer and TJ had prostate cancer. Somehow it just seemed so unfair to both of them.

"Hello, Gary. It's been quite some time since I laid eyes on you and what a beautiful sight I see." She leaned on the bar.

This had become normal. Women approached me all the time if I was out, and especially at a bar. Sometimes I knew them, and sometimes I did not, and this time I was trying to determine which one it would be.

Her voice was familiar. She was tall, medium build, and had long blond hair with loose curls. Before the question, "Do I know you?" spilled from my lips, I remembered her eyes. Her nose was different, a bit smaller, and her lips were filled with too much collagen. I stepped back to give her a full look. The gin and tonic had me buzzed. I pressed my fingers into the corners of my eyes.

She twirled around a couple of times in her fitted black dress. "It's me, silly. You'd better be joking; as if you don't remember me." After her second twirl she place her hands on her hips as if she was at a photo shoot.

I blinked a few times. "Sharon?"

"Yes, it's me." She opened her arms wide and pulled me into her breasts.

"Hey, how have you been? It's been a long time." I immediately felt awkward.

Sharon Stevens was a good friend to me while I was in law school in Seattle though I met her in New York. She was a year ahead of me and the reason I chose Seattle as the place to attend school. She helped me out a lot. She always wanted to be more than friends and definitely made it known. I didn't want to do anything to hurt her but I slept with her the night before I left Seattle.

Her pale skin and brunette bed-hair had been the first thing I saw when I opened my eyes the following morning. I was on my back—spread eagle with no clothes—and she was tucked under my left arm with her arm draped over my body. I remembered leaping from the bed, tripping over the chair next to the bed as I tried to gather my clothes, then ran to the bathroom to get dressed and then out the door.

She had changed. I had changed, and I felt badly about the way I had left her place. We had spoken only a few times since then. I had apologized, she had apologized, but we never discussed what really happened that night. To this day, I assumed we had sex but I don't remember any of it.

"What brings you to Houston?" I managed to say. I wanted to say, *you've changed a lot. What did you do?*

"A really good friend of mine." Her eyes sparkled.

She looked really good.

"Oh, so, you want something to drink?"

"Uh." Her eyebrows rose slightly. "Sure, just a house merlot would be fine."

I leaned over and told the bartender, "One merlot and another gin and tonic."

"Thank you, Gary."

"Not a problem. Sam is coming back to meet me after he drops off a client."

I turned my wrist to look at my timepiece. He must be sitting in traffic.

"Sam? Sampson?" She tilted her head.

"Yes." I fished for my cell phone to see if I had missed a call or text message. Sam walked in just as the bartender set the drinks on the counter.

"What's up, yo?" He pushed his fist toward mine.

I had a lightbulb moment. I looked back and forth between him and Sharon.

"Oh, is this who you picked up at the airport?"

"Yeah." He looked around me to Sharon.

"Sam? Oh, my God, neither of us was paying attention. Oh, my God." She rushed over to hug Sam.

"I saw you and you looked familiar but it didn't register. And I try to stay focused on driving and only talking if the client chooses to do so." He gave her an apologetic expression.

"Oh." She sang and pulled Sam into another embrace. "She didn't tell me who was picking me up and I practically jumped in the car as soon as you drove up."

Sam smiled. "Yeah, I couldn't even get your bags you were moving so fast."

One of the bellman walked over and said, "Ms. Stevens, we will take your bags to your room."

Sam pointed to Sharon and mouthed, "Sharon Stevens?" I nodded.

"Guys, I'll be right back." She tossed her hair over her shoulder. "Will you be here when I get back?"

"Yes, we'll be here," I said.

She turned and sashayed with extra sway in her hips. Both of us watched as she walked away.

Sam tapped my arm. "Look, I did not recognize her, yo."

"Me either."

"When I said to meet me here since I was dropping her off here, I had no idea who I was bringing."

I grunted but didn't say anything. I ordered another gin and tonic.

"How many have you had? Your eyes look glassy as shit."

"I've only had three."

"Well, I need you to slow it down, yo. Remember what happened the last time you were around this chick while drinking." He pulled the stool toward him. "And that will not happen again."

I ignored Sam. He was dating several different women, mine was running scared, and I was horny as hell.

I was on my fifth gin and tonic by the time Sharon made it back.

"Oh great, you two are still here." She leaned in and slid something into my pocket and made sure she reached further than necessary to get it in there.

I frowned and reached into my pocket. It was a card key.

Sam was on the phone so I hope he didn't notice. I wasn't sure what I was going to do at the moment. I knew how I was feeling before I arrived, and if she could help relieve a little bit of the pressure if only for a moment. She was certainly willing. I had to make a decision.

"Look, yo. You ready to go? I think you've had enough for one night." Sam stood up.

"Awww. You all are leaving already?" she whined.

"Yeah, my man has been here for two hours before we got here and we've been here an hour, so it's time to go," Sam explained.

I looked at Sam quizzically as I got up from my seat. It was not like him to pull me away but I allowed it. It was the right thing to do.

"Well here, Gary, take my number." She brushed her hand across my check as she pushed the napkin with her number into the inside pocket of my jacket. "I'll be in town for several days, so maybe we can get lunch or coffee or something." She leaned in and kissed me on the cheek. "It's was good seeing you."

I blinked a few times. I noticed she had reapplied her red lipstick. I imagined her devouring me as soon as I stepped in the door with her lips around my dick then her tongue giving it one long and incredible stroke. "Okay," was all I could say.

Sam and I made it home within twenty minutes. It was only eight o'clock. I went in my room and he went into his. I lay across the bed and tried to fall asleep. Even after drinking as much as I did, I was not sleepy. My dick was hard and I was tired of getting myself off. I tossed and turned until 11:30. I got up and found her number in my pocket. She had written the phone number and the room number.

I dialed the number. She answered, and I said, "Can I come over?"

"Yes, of course."

Thirty minutes later. I walked up to her hotel door and knocked.

CHAPTER 32: MIA

THE time has come; I must pay Nina a visit as well. I mean it only makes sense. I will be in Houston for a few hours. Gary will not know. I will handle what I need to and come back.

Desilyn walked into the family room. "You've got mail," she said in a dramatic tone as she tossed the envelope in my direction. It fell to the floor and slid across the hardwood and underneath the sofa.

"Dang it, Des. I was walking toward you."

"I'm sorry, honey. That must be some juicy stuff in that letter, or some mess."

"You're right since you're making it hard to get to." I got on my knees and stretched to reach the letter and inched it toward me with my fingertips until I was able to grasp it fully in my hand. "Who's sending me something anyway? Very good penmanship."

I sat on the sofa examining the letter.

"Just open it." She leaned on the sofa behind me and then turned and walked away.

"Nosy Rosy." I took my finger and tore the envelope and unfolded a typed letter. I stood up and walked up the stairs. I needed to make flight reservations for Monday.

Hello Mia, you don't know me but I know you and I'm writing you with a bit of caution. Please pay attention to what you're doing and examine your roots. Gary might be your cousin. I'm not for sure but I heard somebody say it.

With eyes wide and trembling hands, I dropped the letter on the floor and stared at it. I placed my right hand on my abdomen and covered my mouth with my left hand as I fought back the tears.

My mind went from normal happy to complete chaos. *Who could send me such a letter? Gary cannot be my cousin. Gary is not my cousin. There has to be a mistake. I met him in Houston and he was born and raised in Brooklyn. This can't be. My parents are from Arkansas and Louisiana not New York. Oh my God, what if I'm pregnant, Oh my God...by my cousin.*

I bent over to pick up the letter. I read it again. I managed to get the laptop from my bag and open it. My bed had become my favorite spot to sit while I surfed the web. Tears were escaping rapidly; my hands were still trembling as I typed in the name of the airline into my internet browser.

Desilyn knocked on the door and pushed it open. "Hey, dinner will be ready in a few minutes."

I nodded but I never looked up to make eye contact. I wiped away a tear. That was the biggest mistake I could've made.

Desilyn rushed into the room. She had on her signature apron and towel in hand. "What's wrong? Why are you crying?" She reached for the laptop and turned it toward her. I grabbed it and turned it back. "I'm just looking at flights to go home."

"Why would that make you cry? That doesn't make sense."

I handed her the letter and folded my arms. I leaned my head on the headboard. She read the three lines then flipped the paper and looked at the back. "Who sent this crap?"

I hunched my shoulders then wiped away a tear.

"Girl, this has to be a joke. We are too far removed from Gary's life to be related to him. You're getting all upset before you learn the facts. Where was the letter postmarked?"

"Houston."

"Ummhmm, that's somebody who wants to throw you off your game. Welp, it's not going to happen here. Pull up ancestry dot come. I'm calling Aunt Edna. We will figure this out."

She left the room.

CHAPTER 33: GARY

MONTY had come into my office a couple of days ago and delivered some news that left me speechless. It was hump day and I was supposed to be working on several cases but I couldn't get past the news that Dena had breast cancer. That thought ran through my mind so many times I couldn't count, and she was trying to go it alone which baffled me even more.

It was six o'clock in the morning and I was still sitting in my office at home. I hadn't started my workout, hadn't made a cup of coffee, and I didn't feel like battling the traffic but I knew I had to. Alex would be in the office alone and I didn't want that to happen. I didn't trust him yet. I had just finalized my plans that I wanted to discuss with him in the afternoon, to test his ability to work solo and execute tasks without my supervision. I really didn't want a male assistant, it just didn't seem right but I didn't have time to find and train a new one. I had to let go of my pride and let it roll. I hoped I wasn't making a mistake. I really wished TJ would've consulted with me prior to hiring him. I still needed to figure out what that move was about. We had released all of our employees a couple of years ago at the same time most businesses went through downsizing, trying to save money. All of them found work at other companies. I guess one employee, especially an assistant, is helpful. Alex appeared okay but I needed time to determine what I'd want him to do, day to day.

I picked up my phone and texted him. *Sorry about the late notice, please come into the office at 12 instead of 8. We'll discuss your goals at that time.* I felt the need to offer an apology although I had mentioned to him that we'd probably start later the day before.

My mind was on its own roller-coaster ride and I couldn't stop it. I didn't know if I should reach out to Dena alone or tell Mia and we do it together. I texted Dena.

Hey, Momma, it's been a few days. You good?

Ten minutes passed. She replied, *All is good on my end, you good?*

Then I thought of something that had raced across my mind earlier. I texted, *I think I'm going to surprise Mia. I want her to come home. I need her.* I wanted so badly to say, *and so do you.*

She responded, *;-) Ha! You're going to Arkansas?*

I didn't understand the Ha! I actually liked Arkansas, the natural state. It was a nice break from the hustle and bustle of the city. I replied, *Yes.*

Dena: Okay, cool. When?

Me: Within the next few days.

Dena: Oh, wow. Okay, bruh. Go get yo' woman man. I like it. :-), y'all call me when y'all get back.

Me: Okay I will.

I leaned back in the chair, bouncing my pen on the leather pad on my desk—thinking. This will be my final offer to Mia. I'll propose again, same ring, different setting, and if she says no, I'll move on.

"What's up, man? What are you doing in here?" Sam leaned on the door frame and looked at his watch.

I wrestled quickly with whether or not I should tell him about Dena. There's no telling how he'd take it. He really liked Dena; he thought of her as a sister, a mini-him. They behaved in the same manner when they became angry.

"What do you have going on today?" I asked him.

"Not much, I have a couple of drops this morning. Why?"

"What time? I want to hit Arkansas for a minute."

"Do you need me to go with you or you need me to drop you off at the airport?"

"Well, it depends. What time is your couple of drops, and what do you have tomorrow?"

"One is at eight at IAH and the other is at nine-thirty at Hobby. Man, what's up? What's going on? Is Mia okay?"

"Yes. Yeah, she's good. Maybe we can go Friday. I need to just get her. I'm tired of wasting time. I'm ready to get married and just move on. I've been thinking a lot about what you said. All of this running bull has got to stop." I bounced the pen more and looked at Sam. Should I tell him about Dena?

"Sam, man, sit down for a second. I need to tell you something."

"What's up?" He sat down in the chair across from my desk. "What's going on?" His eyebrows furrowed.

"Ummmm." I cleared my throat in search for the right words. I had expected him to start small talk as he usually did but this time he didn't. "Monty came to my office and told me that, uhh, that uhh, Dena has breast cancer."

"What? Come on, yo." He grabbed the top of his head. "Aww, come on. No, not Dena."

I nodded slowly as I tried to allow him a moment.

"Where is she? Can I talk to her?"

"We might be able to today but I doubt it. I'll let you know."

He was silent.

CHAPTER 34: GARY

I walked into my office two hours before I had planned. The lights were on and I noticed TJ's door was open. I entered TJ's office but he was not there. No one was there. Our office was extremely small with two offices, a cubicle, and a small area for the printer and the copier, and the tiny break room. It would be hard for someone to hide but I looked around anyway.

I called out, "Alex?"

There was no answer.

I noticed his computer was on and one of those genealogy websites was on the screen. He had papers strewn about the desk and several folders neatly stacked with labels. At the top of the purple folder was *Nina*. On the screen, the cursor was flashing in the last name field behind *Nixon*, the first name was *Mia*.

"What the hell?" I sat down in the chair and read all of the information on the screen. It had Mia's parents' names, grandparents, their occupations, and other detailed information. I pushed back slightly in the chair and loosened my tie and collar.

I minimized the browser and opened the document from the bottom of the screen. It listed three pages of information about Mia S. Nixon.

How does he know Mia? I've never even mentioned her name around him. I wondered if he talked TJ into providing all of the information.

"What in the hell is this guy up to?" I mumbled and loosened my tie some more. "Damn, another assistant with an interest in Mia. This will not be a repeat of Lynn."

I had to think quickly and I did. I printed all of the information from each open application. I deleted the contents of the documents and clicked Save. He'll see a blank document when he opens them again. I pressed and held the power button. After a couple of error messages, the computer went off. I waited a few seconds and powered it back on. I retrieved the documents from the printer and walked into my office and closed the door.

"God, please don't let me have another assistant who's trying to hurt Mia. What is it about her that every assistant I hire is fascinated by her?"

I picked up the phone to call Sam but thought better of it. I know Sam would go ballistic and be in my office waiting to beat the hell out of Alex when he returned. I read through each page which included articles about her speaking engagements, mentoring, the accident, and other public information that anyone can get if they searched the Internet for it.

An hour later, Alex walked in whistling a tune as I struggled to control my cold and flinty eyes. I wanted to fire him as soon as he sashayed into the office but I couldn't and I had no intention of letting him know that I knew he was up to something. My job had just turned into figuring out why he was interested in Mia's background.

Rubbing the back of his neck, he said, "Good morning Mr. Matthews. I really needed to get in here and get some things done so I talked with security and they let me in."

I took a deep breath and clinched my jaw. It took everything in me to not reach across the desk, pin him up on the door, and punch him in his face. Since I did not want an assault charge, I had to remain seated.

He did not enter my office; he leaned on the door and crossed his arms then uncrossed them.

I rested my elbows on the arms of the chair and pressed my fingers together. "Just so that we're clear, the next time you need to get in here early, I need you to call me, not security. They're not paying you, I am." I paused. "So, what are you working on?"

Blinking rapidly, he replied, "Oh uh, I understand, sir. I'm so sorry. I have about five files to review before I give them to you. Well, I have two new ones and then three I think we can close out."

I was careful not to interrogate him and even more careful not to show my anger. I had to remember, I did not hire him, TJ did. "What have you worked on since you've been here? Do you have the Stigler versus Stigler file?"

"Yes, I finished that one." He turned and rushed toward his desk, I'm sure intentionally not answering the first question.

Alex walked back into the office and sat down at his desk. I heard a gasp and I waited a few minutes then slowly walked toward the door. I stood there and watched him stare at the blank screen for a moment, "I can't believe this." He looked all around the desk. "What happened to my documents?" He powered the computer back on.

"Alex, come here for a minute?" I called his name loud enough in hopes to startle him. He jumped around with a panicked expression. I walked back to my chair.

I asked, "What's going on? Are you okay?"

"Yes, yes, I'm fine, I'm fine," he said as he approached my office.

I paused and looked at him with a defiant stare, and then I said one more thing. "For the short amount of time you've worked here, I think you're doing a pretty decent job but never let your behavior cause me to question your integrity. I just wanted to encourage you on that."

"Okay, sir. I won't, sir." He looked as if he had seen a ghost. He rushed back to his desk.

"What's wrong?" I stood up and walked toward the door.

"Oh, nothing." He jumped up from the chair, spilled his coffee, and dropped the folder to the floor. "Damnit, I'm so sorry, Mr. Matthews. I'm so sorry." He quickly grabbed some napkins to wipe the spilled coffee from the desk as I bent down to pick up the folder. He abruptly turned around to snatch the folder from my hand.

I frowned.

"I'm sorry, Mr. Matthews, I'm so sorry. That's the wrong file. Can you give me a few minutes to get myself together? I'm so sorry."

"Stop apologizing." I turned around to walk back into my office. "And stop fucking up." I slammed the door.

I picked up the phone and dialed TJ's number. When he answered, I said, "Who is the assistant you hired?"

CHAPTER 35: KAREN

thought I asked you not to mess this up? Why were you doing research right under his nose? I don't want you to mess this up, and if you upset him, he will fire you, Alex. Who were you telling about his fiancée? Why haven't you finished this?"

"Karen, you're not letting me speak. I'm telling you my computer rebooted. It must have done an automatic reboot after an update or something."

I sighed heavily. I was frustrated beyond belief. I asked him to get me some information on Gary's fiancée. I know this young lady was related to me in some way but I needed sound proof before I told Gary that he's about to marry his cousin.

"I think I'd rather get fired than endure another minute of that look he was giving me. I thought he was going to snap. But thank God he didn't."

"What did you do? Why would he want to do that?"

"First of all, I was there without him after I talked the security guy into letting me in, wasting coffee on the desk, dropping the folder with Mia's information in it, and almost handed it to him for another file that he was looking for." He slapped his forehead. "Oh my God, I was so nervous I just wanted to get out of there."

"Well, I'm glad you got out of there without him getting suspicious," I speculated. "He didn't suspect anything, did he?"

He sighed heavily. "No, I don't think he did. Well, at least he didn't say anything if he did."

"Well, what do you have?"

He pushed a stack of folders toward me. "All of the information is public knowledge. I'll need her social security number to get personal."

"No, I don't need anything personal yet. I might have to have you go to his house to snoop around."

"No, no, I can't and I won't. I'm not doing that."

I began reading the documents. Gary had really chosen well this time. She appeared to be an awesome and admirable young lady. I'm surprised I hadn't seen her on the speaking circuit. She had done well. I'd actually love to have her as my daughter-in-law, the mother of my grandchildren. If I hadn't spent so much time with that other girl with my names mixed up, I would've been further along by now.

"Alex, my dear, you do remember that you work for me and you will do whatever I ask." I never took my eyes off the documents.

He rushed over to me. "No. Please, Ms. Chandler. No. I'm afraid of your son."

"What? Why are you afraid of him?" I frowned. "He's affable, not a mean, malicious, or a violent person. What is there to be afraid of?"

"Have you seen your son? Do you really know him? I've only been around him for a short time and he's cool and mostly calm but I can tell he takes no mess from anybody. I'm afraid to piss him off. He takes no mess from his clients or those attorneys he come up against. And his driver is even worse. He seems like he could really beat the living shit out of me."

I smiled at his rambling and rapidly blinking eyes. "He probably can, but I doubt he will. Gary is not like that," I lied. Sam or Gary would beat the living shit out of him if they caught him snooping and wouldn't think anything of it.

"Hmph. And his driver?" He folded his arms. "His driver looks more like a security guard. I don't mean any disrespect about your son but he looks like he can go from zero to damn fool in a matter of seconds."

"Oh, Alex, you're being dramatic."

I thumbed through the articles and read a few more paragraphs as Alex calmed his breathing.

"Oh my, I wonder why she was hospitalized in Little Rock... and Gary went to get her." This was exciting. I think my daughter-in-law is going to be great. I need to get to know her and she can help me get to know my son. Now, I hope she's not my cousin but I need to figure it out. She and I need to figure it out.

I walked into my office with Alex by my side and we went deeper into the theory, *Is my son engaged to his cousin?*

CHAPTER 36: MIA

"I had spent the last few days researching my family and Gary's. Monday morning was here and it couldn't have come fast enough. Karen sounded genuine enough. I wonder if she had anything to do with the letter. I had seen her only once and that was at our engagement party. I had searched the Internet for her and found several professional headshots from her time in corporate America. She was married to a Caucasian guy but I wasn't sure if she had any children. The article I read stated, *she currently resides in Houston with her family.*

Desilyn fixed a full course breakfast that I devoured.

"Hey, I'm headed to the library to do some research," I said as I hurried to wash the dishes. "I'll go to Little Rock if I have to but expect that I'd be gone all day."

"Research on what? I'm going to talk to Aunt Edna again. If she blows me off, I'll have to figure out if some of our family members here know if Karen Walker is related to us."

"Okay, well I'm just digging deeper into our heritage. That would be awful if I'm about to marry my cousin." I leaned on the counter. I only hope Karen would shed some light that I could share about Gary's ancestors and I wouldn't have to lie even more.

"It'll be fine, Mia. I honestly do not believe you have anything to worry about. I just don't think God would have you going through all you've gone through to lead you to a family member. My goodness, he's not that cruel."

"He's not but Satan sure is."

"Be careful."

I finished the dishes, grabbed my purse, and was out the door. I texted Karen and told her I'd see her at noon. She had changed from having coffee to having lunch and texted an address to a place on LaBranch. My trip to Clinton Airport was uneventful and so was the flight to Houston. I was a bit nervous to meet her. Although Gary didn't respect her like a mother, she would still be my mother-in-law if Gary and I were married. I figured he would eventually come around anyway.

I arrived at the restaurant at 11:35 and found a parking space across the street in the hospital parking lot. I had time to check my hair and makeup. I wore a white button down blouse with black slacks. I got out of my car after I watched several people get out of their cars and walk across the street toward the restaurant. I remembered her being taller than I was so I assumed she was the last one I saw walk in.

"Hi there, welcome. How many?"

"Hi, I'm meeting someone. Karen Chandler."

"Hi, Mia." She appeared from around a corner with open arms. I stepped into her embrace. "It's good to see you again."

The hostess took us to our seats and we wasted no time ordering our drinks and entrées. I ordered shrimp and grits and she ordered soup and a salad. We both had water to drink.

"I really wanted to get to know you so I can get to know my son. I'm just going to be honest. I love my son and I want to get to know him but he's still kind of holding a grudge. I'm sure you've heard the story." She moved her hands a lot as she spoke.

I nodded. "Yes, ma'am, I have."

"I'd really like your help with this, if you can. I'm having dinner with him tonight."

"Well, that's a step in the right direction. What do you need me to do?"

"I don't know, just encourage him that it's the right thing to do."

"Okay, I can continue to do that."

"What's that? Continue?" She beamed.

"Yes, I've always encouraged him to get to know you."

"You know what? You are just the woman my son needs. You're so adorable."

I smiled. "Thank you."

We talked for thirty minutes about her career, my career, our interest, and then the mood changed slightly when the conversation turned to where we grew up.

I folded my napkin in my lap as the waiter refilled my water.

"Karen, I wanted to talk to you about something. You said earlier that you were born in Houston. Where is your family from?"

"My parents moved a few times, I was born in Houston, raised in Brooklyn."

"So, your roots are in Houston not somewhere in Arkansas?"

She stuttered but couldn't formulate an answer.

"Okay, look, let me just cut to the chase." I pulled the letter from my purse and handed it to her. "I was in Arkansas and received this at my sister's house. I'm not sure if this was a coincidence that I was there at the time the letter arrived or something planned but I need to understand it. Both my parents are deceased so I can't ask them. I have my Aunt Edna who you met at Mr. and Mrs. Matthews' anniversary party. She told me that we are not related to James' and Matthews'. So, if this letter is true, then you and I have to be related somehow."

I allowed her a moment to read the letter before I continued. "Mrs. Chandler, you understand we really need to find out. Gary and I have been dating for almost three years and we're planning to get married. We've had one miscarriage and want to try for another one. You understand? We need to make sure."

She rubbed her fingers across her pearls and sadness spread across her face. "My maiden name is Walker and we are related to Nixons in that area, the Pine Bluff, Altheimer area where you're from, even Little Rock."

"Did you send this letter, Mrs. Chandler?"

She shot me a look that said, "How dare you accuse me." She cleared her throat. "I would not do anything like this."

I figured if she didn't send it she knows who did.

"Well, can you tell me about the Nixons you know?"

"Sweetheart, I've done a bit of research on this myself, that's why I haven't brought this to my son." She looked all around the restaurant and fiddled with the salt shaker. "I've thought this since the day I met you all in New York. The more I look into it, the more I think our family trees do not coincide. I can't speak with absolute certainty, but I know some of the Nixons I think I'm related to are Caucasian."

I exhaled mildly. "Okay."

There was something about this conversation that didn't seem true, genuine. I still had a lot of research to do and it started with my Aunt Edna. Somebody was going to tell me the truth.

I drove back to the airport and flew back to Arkansas and decided I'd handle Nina later.

CHAPTER 37: GARY

didn't tell you because I didn't think it mattered. If he did a good job for you as I'd hope he would, his connections are irrelevant. Especially if they're legal," TJ said nonchalantly.

I rubbed my hands over my face. I was angry as hell and I did not want to explode on TJ. His voice was raspy and I'm sure he didn't feel up to getting into an argument with me. "Well, I caught him researching Mia so his connections are relevant. Who the hell sent him here? Where did you get him from?"

He remained silent for a moment then said, "Man, I'm not going to hold anything from you. I don't have the energy or the time. Your mother is our business partner and Alex works for her as a personal assistant. She found him through one of her friends, Leslie, who has a staffing agency. She really likes him and—"

"Hold on, what? Our business partner? Judy?"

"No, your biological mother, Karen. I've known Karen for decades. She has always been there for me. Did you read all of the information on the flash drive? I included all of that in the documents. You have to get to the details. Karen owns the majority of my 50 percent. My name was on it but I never repaid all of the startup money I borrowed. After my first bout with prostate cancer, I decided to let her stay in. Your mother is a smart business woman, G. She's the reason a lot of this has gone as smoothly as it has."

I was so pissed I wanted to strangle the hell out of TJ. If he hadn't been on the phone, I probably would have.

"Let me make sure I understand. Karen, my biological mother is my business partner because of you and you've known this for more than, how long have we been in business? Five years? Six years? And you never thought that was important enough to disclose to me?"

"Yes, she's always been your business partner but as an investor. She has no interest in working the business. She invested when I needed her. I'm indebted to her for the rest of my life. She is really a smart business woman. You could learn a lot from Karen."

I groaned. I didn't doubt she was a smart business woman. Hell, that's why I was raised by adoptive parents because she was chasing a business dream.

"I'm serious, man. Put that pride to the side and get to know her. You could take this firm to the next level with her."

I was so tired of Vaughn and TJ forcing my biological mother on me. Vaughn forced a conversation but TJ has done the unthinkable.

"Your mother has always looked out for your best interest. She wanted to make sure you had a business set up the way you wanted it. She knew all of those instructors in Washington and she knows way more than you think she knows about you."

I suddenly felt violated, like I had been stalked all of my life.

CHAPTER 38: KAREN

I met Mia for lunch two weeks ago and she was in shock about someone sending her a letter stating she was related to Gary. She all but accused me of sending it. She handed me the letter and I remembered Alex folding a letter and sealing it one day at my house. I recognized the paper; it was pre-hole punched so him sending it didn't appear farfetched. When she started asking questions, I had to think of a quick lie. She was so adorable at lunch I couldn't break her heart but the truth was, I didn't know. I want her to be my daughter-in-law and she will make my son very happy.

My son agreed to dinner and I'm going to go and enjoy my time with him at one of my favorite steak restaurants. He opens up more and more every time we talk and I share more and more in every conversation. It was like a light switch that turned on inside him and he just let me in.

I was already seated at my favorite table by the window when I saw the hostess escort him to the table. I quickly slipped the pill into my mouth and chased it with a gulp of water. I stood up and he leaned in to hug me and gave me a kiss on the cheek.

"Hello, son. How are you?"

He assisted me back into my chair. "I'm doing well." He unbuttoned his jacket and pulled out his chair.

"I decided to wait before I ordered anything," I said with the biggest smile I could muster. All of the information I needed to share with him tonight was probably going to send him out of here running.

"Oh, that's fine. I'm sure we can figure this out together."

His comment made my heart palpitate. I truly loved my son. In the beginning, I was only interested in him to get what was due to me. His attitude toward me was horrible and I was not used to begging someone for friendship or a relationship. As time passed and more encounters were in the rear, I genuinely wanted to get to know him. He is definitely a young man I'd love to call my son.

"So, what kind of pill was that you took?"

"Huh?" I shifted slightly in my seat.

He looked at me with a *please don't lie to me* expression.

I raised both my hands as I mocked surrender. "Okay, okay, you win. Pain pills for my shoulder."

"Oh, yeah? What's wrong with your shoulder?"

"Oh, it's nothing. Probably lifting those heavy purses and laptop bags for so many years."

He nodded in a way that demonstrated he did not believe me. "So, tell me about you."

I hesitated because I didn't want to run him away for coming on too strongly. I tried to give up being a bitch about it because that would be no good to either of us. We'd both be miserable. I figured we could just give it a go—he'd be surprised at what we have in common.

"Gary, I want you to understand something, I'm a...well, that's neither here nor there..."

"You're a what? And what's neither here nor there?"

"I should've known the attorney in you would ask questions." I smirked.

He nodded.

"I was only going to say that I'm a powerful woman and that's neither here nor there in this conversation."

He squinted his eyes but didn't speak.

I kept going. "You're my son, I gave birth to you. I decided on my own to allow two beautiful human beings to raise you as their own. You're a grown, mature, and successful young man. They did well with you. But, all of that doesn't negate the fact that I love you as my son and I want to get to know you. And. I want all of this outside noise to stop."

"What outside noise are you speaking of?"

"Vaughn and Emma, his old woman, fiancée, or whatever she is to him," I said flippantly.

"What have they done? Ms. Emma is a very sweet lady."

I brushed my hands through my hair, "Well, I can't really say Emma has done anything. I just feel he's with her so she must be influencing his conversation in same way or another."

He sighed. "What did V do?"

"Vaughn is just—I don't know, he's just constantly trying to dictate what I say to you, when I say it, how I say it."

"Well, we're here now without him, so what is it that you want to say? If you're as powerful as you say you are, V cannot stop you from doing anything you want to do, correct?" He raised his eyebrows slightly.

I hesitated again. I liked his style, his confidence. My son. I couldn't believe how he was saying the simplest things but they stopped me in my tracks and made me stutter. My stuttering was coming from the secrets that were caught in my throat and

I couldn't thrust them forward to come out. "Ummm, I just want you to be happy. I want you to be good with your career, your marriage to a beautiful young woman, your future children, and everything that you set out to do in your life."

"Oh."

"If you don't want to acknowledge me as your mother, that's fine, it could potentially change over time. It the meantime, let's try to develop a relationship, a friendship."

He tilted his head to the side and adjusted the place setting. "So, what about your husband, what is he like?"

I adjusted myself in my chair and cleared my throat. "He's uh, he's a businessman, executive vice president and partner at his firm."

"I figured he was an accomplished career man because you married him, but careers are just the surface. I was speaking of something a little deeper than that. I just want to understand what type of person you married. Is he kind? Does he love you? Is he a provider? A protector? I would like to know."

I was shocked and flattered all at the same time. "He is all of the above, at times," I lied.

"Oh. So what's going on with you and V?"

I smiled at the mention of Vaughn's name. "There is nothing going on with Vaughn and me. We are friends. We have a forever bond in you. We have our differences but truth be told, I never stopped loving him."

The waiter interrupted our conversation to choose a wine and to tell us about the specials. We ordered a bottle of wine and took the waiter's suggestions for the appetizer and entrées. The appetizer, smoked salmon rillettes with goat cheese and toast points arrived promptly.

"So, let's change the subject. Tell me about your fiancée. How did you two meet? Who are her people?"

"She's from Arkansas, her parents are deceased."

"I have family from Arkansas."

"Oh, really. Last name Nixon?"

"Ummm, I think so but I'm not sure."

"I was kidding." He slammed his fork down and stared at me.

"What?" I was surprised by his sudden reaction.

"So, you're related to some Nixon's? How?"

"I have cousins whose last name is Nixon, yes," I stammered.

"So, what are you saying, Karen?"

"Sweetheart, I'm not saying anything. We're just talking about your fiancée." I became too nervous to come out with it. I was surely not going to reveal I had met with her already.

"Okay. So, I ask again, what are you saying?"

"I'm not saying anything. I just know people from Arkansas and I think their last names are Nixon." I patted his hand.

He moved his hand away from me. A suspicious stare rested on his eyes but he didn't pry any more. We finished our meals in silence and fussed over who would take the check. I finally acquiesced and allowed him to pay. I could tell his little wheels were turning as he struggled to maintain control. He shifted in his seat and placed the napkin on the table. "Excuse me. I need to go to the men's room before we go."

Whew, I didn't get to tell him much of anything because I couldn't get one intelligent sentence to formulate in my mind.

CHAPTER 39: GARY

was putting forth the effort but I did not trust my biological mother. I had arrived at the restaurant to meet her a few minutes ahead of plan. I hung out in the bar incognito until I saw her walk in. I did my usual when dining with someone new—scope out the clientele. Before my mother arrived, I decided to go to the men's room. The urinals were occupied so I walked into the stall. While I was relieving myself, I heard the door open and close several times as men left and others walked in. I overheard two men talking.

"I absolutely hate my wife."

"Why do you hate her so much? Is it because of her race?" He snickered.

"That has absolutely nothing to do with it. I hate her because she's a bitch. She's mean, she's condescending, she's not supportive of me or anything I do lately, I think she's cheating, and I'm tired of it."

"Cheating? Yeah, right. You're just being emotional right now."

"Yes, cheating. I had her followed. I think it just started though. I've had her followed before and found out nothing."

There was a pause. His cohort was obviously listening emphatically because he didn't speak.

The hater continued. "We've been married freakin' ten years and she's barely noticed me in the last eight since our daughter was born."

I flushed the toilet just as the cohort said, "What are you going to do about it?"

They both paused and looked at me when I stepped out of the stall. I refused to believe they didn't see me and wanted me to hear their conversation. I walked toward the impeccably dressed brown-haired Caucasian man. He stood less than six feet maybe one hundred-eighty pounds, cleft in his chin. The silver-haired one stood against the wall jingling change in his pocket.

He replied, "I don't know at the moment."

The two men looked at me and I scowled at them, washed my hands, and left the men's room because I didn't want to hear anything else.

After my mother and I finished our dinner and a bottle of wine, I went to the men's room again and saw the same two men there. I frowned and slowed my stride as I passed them to the stall. I heard one of them say, "She's here with a younger guy. I followed her here and she's with a younger guy."

After I finished, I stepped out of the stall and to the sink to wash my hands. The tall guy with the cleft chin appeared as if he wanted to say something to me but he didn't. I looked down at him, dried my hands, and walked out. They were both pathetic for standing in a public men's room whining about his wife cheating and being in the restaurant with a younger man. Even if she was, standing in the men's room crying about it was not going to resolve the problem.

I strolled back to the table. "Are you ready to go?"

"Yes, I am. I enjoyed our evening together." Karen stood up and reached for a hug.

"Yeah, so did I."

She did not admit it, but I believe she and Vaughn were messing around again. She thought I didn't hear the comment when she said her husband was "all of the above, most of the times." I wondered what he was like at "other times." I decided to wait until later to pry more into her personal life. She implied that she was related to Mia. I could not have possibly come from Brooklyn to Houston, met a woman from Arkansas, fell in love, and she's my cousin. No way.

We stood and walked outside. I handed my ticket to the valet and waited. My mother and I shared small talk until the valet pulled my truck around.

I gave her a hug and walked toward my truck. "I'll be right back. I'll wait until your car comes around."

I opened the door on the passenger side to drop my coat in the seat and that's when I heard a scream and turned around to my mother holding her face and crying.

The same guy from the men's room was yelling some obscenities. I rushed back to the valet stand toward the man. "Did you just slap her?"

"Who the hell are you?"

I grabbed him by his tie and slammed him into the valet stand and started punching him wherever my fist landed in his gut. I didn't remember anything for the next few seconds. After two men pulled me away from him. I remembered my mother crying, "Gary, please stop, honey. Please stop."

He started yelling, "I'm going to sue you! You're going to jail."

"Gary, sweetheart just leave, please."

"Who is this man, and why did he slap you?" I barked. I had an idea but I wanted her to say it.

"He's my husband," she mumbled and looked around at all of the onlookers staring at us. "This is so embarrassing."

I threw up my hands in frustration. "How did you get here?" My mother was married to a Caucasian man. Not just a regular, simple, Caucasian man but a rich, well-dressed one who wanted to beat on her.

"I didn't drive. My driver is pulling the car around. I texted him before we walked out."

"Well, where is he? He's the slowest fuckin' driver I've seen in my life."

"He's right over th…" Her hands trembled and her voice trailed off when she noticed there was no car there.

"Did you tell him to leave?" She stormed toward her husband and I grabbed her arm. "Get in the car. You're going with me," I yelled.

"I'll be fine, Gary. I'm not afraid of him."

"That's not the point. Get in the car."

"Sir, I think the cops are coming." The valet guy rushed over to tell me in an accent so thick, I could barely understand him. I had heard the sirens several minutes before he alerted me.

"And?" I yelled at him. "Why the hell you telling me? You need to tell that prick over there. He's lucky his ass is not being life-flighted to Memorial Hermann."

"Sweetheart, just come on, please let's just go." Karen climbed in the passenger side and I closed the door.

I walked around the truck and got in. "I don't understand why you women insist on getting with men who slap you and want to beat on you. Damnit!" I slapped the steering wheel.

She began explaining earnestly. "Gary, my first husband

was an abusive corporate drug addict and Chandler saved me from him. I dated him five years but chose not to marry him because I didn't want to abort my alimony. At the time, I was not working but I left town for a few months to hide from him. I was educated, single. I didn't have children; Chandler helped me through it all. He supported me. I feel like I owe him a semblance of loyalty." Her bottom lip began to quiver.

"Do you realize that fool hates you, and he's telling people he hates you?"

She looked at her trembling hands but did not respond.

CHAPTER 40: KAREN

WE drove around for at least an hour before going to Gary's house. I knew he was trying to ensure no one was following him. He had switched out of his jacket down to his t-shirt and had tossed his tie, dress shirt, and jacket into the back seat as I scrambled to get them hung on the hanger.

"Leave it alone. Put your seatbelt on, that stuff is fine," he yelled at me, and I tossed the jacket back into the seat.

He pulled a New York baseball cap onto his head, and then made a call to Sam, then to Vaughn and informed him to contact his HPD buddy. He turned down several streets and even drove into a cul-de-sac and turned the lights off. For the first time in a long time, I was afraid. He seemed focused and pissed all rolled into one big emotion.

"What are you doing?" I asked timidly. I was beginning to understand how Alex felt. I had heard about Gary's temper when it came to protecting people he cared about but I had never personally witnessed it.

"I know your husband was following me with his goons. Karen, I don't want to have to kill your husband, but I will."

"No, no, no. I wouldn't dare let that happen, Gary. I don't want that. I can handle him myself. I don't want you involved. You won't serve not one day of jail time for that clown."

"Who said I was going to jail? And how are you going to handle him? Your strength is no match for him. I saw how he slapped the shit out of you and you let him."

"Trust me, sweetheart, I can handle him. I was just as shocked as everyone else, actually surprised, he struck me in public; therefore, I wasn't supposed to hit back. Trust me, I can handle him. I'm not talking about murder for hire; I'm talking about self-defense or to keep him from hurting anybody else. I've done it before."

"What do you mean, you've done it before? Where'd you meet this guy? Why does he feel it necessary or okay to hit you?"

I sighed heavily and leaned my head back on the headrest. I had to take several deep breaths before I was able to fill him in on my life. I knew almost everything there was to know about his life and he did not have any insight into the drama that has transpired in mine.

"Gary, this is my second marriage. I've been married to this guy for a long time and he just started this madness when he lost his job over a year ago. He's working at his family's firm now but his position is not as prestigious as he's had in the past. Believe or not, I love him though." I couldn't believe I had said that. I guess I did love Chandler on some level.

"Oh, really? That's funny because I was in the men's room and I heard him say he absolutely hates you, so we need to call the cops."

"No, no we don't. He'll be fine. I'll be fine."

"So, you think I'm gonna take you home? Well, I'm not. I can't believe what I'm hearing. Did you hear me? He told his buddy he hates you," he bellowed.

"I know. I know," I said meekly. My emotions were all over the place and my pill didn't seem to be working. I fumbled in my purse to see if I had taken the right one.

In my haste to slide the pill into my mouth before he arrived at the table, I took a B-12. Damnit. I slide the pill into my hand and then pushed it into my mint tin. I pulled out the tin and slide the pill in my mouth, quickly swallowed then place a mint onto my tongue.

"I bet you money you wouldn't get any sleep tonight because he'll beat the crap out of you." He glared at me.

The illumination from the moon and the streetlight allowed me to see his eyes dancing between my face and my purse then back to the street and all of the mirrors on the car. He was conversing but he never lost focus of why we were sitting in the car.

"No, he won't, Gary. He just didn't know who you were. He thought I was cheating on him with you."

"Oh, really? So, he doesn't know I'm your son?"

"No, he doesn't know you're my son. I don't want him to know who you are or what you do."

"Good, I don't want him to know any of that either, at least until I found out all about him. The guy he was talking to in the men's room looked familiar." He changed the subject. "What kind of pills are you taking? Depression? Anxiety? And don't lie, I saw you popping twice. Putting it in a mint tin doesn't change the substance of it."

It was weird but at that moment, I was proud of him. Nothing could get past him which showed me he was the same in business. I decided not to tell a lie, "Anxiety. They calm my nerves when I'm a little stressed."

"You should probably try smoking weed, fewer side effects, and same end result."

I clutched my necklace, my eyes widened.

He smiled. "I'm kidding. Back to my question, does he know you even have a son?"

"Yes, he knows it. I just hadn't told him who you were and what you looked like." I paused. "Gary, he's the father of my daughter. I had endured so many unsuccessful ways to get pregnant over the years and I was in a funk. I wanted a baby. So in some ways I feel indebted to him." I shifted in my seat to face him. "I really wanted another child because I let you slip away."

"No, you gave me away, remember?" he scolded.

"Okay." I held up my hands. "I deserved that."

He looked toward me for a second and then turned away.

"Well, I'll finish the story. My husband is really good for me and on occasion, he's good to me. He was with me through the entire process until my baby was placed in my arms."

"What?" He frowned. "What process?"

"We used a surrogate." I paused. "You have a sister named..."

"We gotta go. Get down." He put the car in drive and coasted to the end of the street then squealed away.

"Oh my, what's going on?" I said as I got down into the floor as best I could.

"They found us."

CHAPTER 41: GARY

I was one of the main characters in Karen's life story but didn't know I was in it. As she was talking and giving me more details of her life, I had to stay focused on the street and what was going on in the neighborhood around me. I noticed the Ford Expedition pull to the end of the street where we were parked. It stopped for a few minutes then quickly pulled away. I never turned the truck off but I put it in drive and let it coast to the turn then drove quickly in the opposite direction.

We arrived at my house at the same time as Vaughn. Sam was already there.

She beamed. "Oh my, is this your home, sweetheart?"

I frowned. I was not an eight year old. "Sweetheart?"

She ignored my irritations. "This is beautiful. I feel a sense of pride that you have done extremely well with your inheritance and your hard work."

"Your focus is off right now, Karen. We need to figure out what your husband is trying to do. Get out of the car."

"What's going on here, man?" Vaughn met me in the driveway.

"I just witnessed Karen's husband slap the taste out of her mouth."

Vaughn's eyes widened as he rushed to her side looking at her face, examining her. "Where is he?" he barked.

I frowned at that scene. Vaughn was tending to Karen's needs. I was a bit surprised he did it in front of me. I can tell when there's just genuine *you share a son* concern but this was love. They were in love.

We got her in the house and for twenty minutes, she paced the floor while looking at her phone. She walked into the restroom in the foyer and I walked over to the door so that I could hear her clearly. "Alex do not take my baby back home. I need you to meet me somewhere and I will get her from you. Do not take my baby back home. Do you hear me? Do not take Breleigh back home. I need you to call me, Alex."

Breleigh? Who is Breleigh? Is she my sister? Is that what Karen was about to say earlier?

Karen stepped out of the restroom and was startled because I was standing there leaning beside the door.

"What's going on, Karen? I know there's something going on. There's a lot you haven't told me, isn't it?"

Sam walked out of the kitchen and Vaughn stepped around the corner toward us. "Karen, let's just sit down and fill him in."

I looked at Vaughn as I was thinking, *Here we go again. Vaughn is in the middle of a pack of secrets regarding me. Do I really trust this guy?*

We sat down in the formal living room that I never use. She perched on the end of one of my Windsor chairs with confidence and composure. Vaughn opened a bottle of water and handed it to her.

"Thank you, honey." She smiled at him.

I frowned. I walked across the room and sat on the sofa. I needed to look directly into her face as she told the rest of the story. Sam leaned on the wall with his arms folded.

"As I was telling you in the car, you have a sister named Breleigh. I used a surrogate, Sharon Stevens, one of your law school friends, to carry her for me."

My eyes widened and I gasped.

"Sharon approached me with the idea after she found out we were trying to conceive but couldn't. I had really bad fibroids and couldn't conceive."

"Sharon approached you where?" I tried to stay focused after she mentioned fibroids as I understood that all too well with Mia but I didn't want to show any empathy toward Karen.

"I lived in Seattle at the same time you did."

"Where did you live before that?"

"I've lived in several places in New York, Brooklyn, Long Island; I lived in Atlanta for a short time."

"So, everywhere I've lived, you did too?"

"Yes."

"On purpose?" I said as more of a statement than a question.

"Yes."

"Why?"

"Because I was really trying to be close to my son."

I grunted. "I don't know if I should be flattered or furious that you've been stalking me."

"I wouldn't call it stalking. I love you. You're my son and I wanted to make sure you were okay, at all times. The only way I could do that was to see for myself."

I rubbed my hands over my face. "When were you going to tell me you owned half of my business?"

She sighed and looked at Vaughn.

He frowned. "What?"

"V, how much of this do you already know?" Vaughn was a bit of a con artist also. His restaurant burned down and he hasn't said one word about it since that night and I hadn't asked just in case there was some illegal activity going on. I wondered if he was trying to get next to Karen just to get financial assistance. But something told me that Karen was no fool to anybody when it came to money.

Vaughn answered, "All of it before she said she owned your business. Karen, what is that about?"

"TJ and I knew each other for a long time and he wanted to start the firm that you all have together. Gary, I knew that you wanted to start your own business after law school because you had told Sharon, who obviously told me. I knew you had your inheritance so I set it up so that TJ connected genuinely with you until he got the money to partner with you. I'm not into handouts." She shot a glare at Sam. "I never told him about your money, I just told him that I believed you were the best person to partner in a startup business. You were young, hungry for success, ambitious, you had style, you were smart, intelligent." She moved her hands with every word.

"Umph," I grumbled.

"When you all started getting serious about moving forward with the business, he started having health issues and I offered to invest in his portion of the business. I always wanted you to succeed. I did not want you to go into business with someone who, because of health concerns, could not hold up his end of the bargain and have you struggling. To help you fulfill your dreams, I had to step in."

"Why did you just shoot Sam a hateful glare?" I knew I couldn't confuse a pro like her by changing the line of questioning but I wanted to know quickly, so I asked.

Sam didn't let her respond. "She got me out of some tough shit in Brooklyn, and she has never let me forget it. She brings it up every chance she gets. But I'm paying her tonight." Sam walked away.

Her eyes widened. I had no idea how much Sam owed her but her expression showed that she was surprised he would be able to pay up. I pulled out my phone and texted Sam, *DO NOT bring any amount of money out, no cash, no checks, no cashier's checks, nothing!*

"Business must be going well." She smirked.

"Karen!" Vaughn scolded. He stood and walked to the foyer.

"How much money does Sam owe you?" I asked.

"That's between Sam and me."

I pinched the bridge of my nose. I don't know why I asked her that. I'll get my information from Sam.

Sam texted back, *Auight, yo but I'm sick of dis shit.*

I understand we'll figure it out. I texted and dropped the phone on the table.

"You know what, Karen, I don't know if I should hate you or be afraid of you, and since I have no fear… you have manipulated my entire life."

"Gary, it's not in your character to hate. I understand you might be a little furious but I've done everything in your life to protect you."

"Protect me. No, you've done everything to control me." *Oh damn, I sounded like Mia. Now I understand how she felt.* "I didn't need you to protect me."

"That might be true but I did it anyway and the fact still remains you have been protected."

I shot her a defiant stare.

"Gary, sweetheart, I—"

"Please don't call me that."

She pursed her lips and sighed. "I assure you that I have never done anything, anything to harm you. Everything I've

done was for your own good and the good of those around you
if they meant well by you and if they didn't—"

"What does that mean?" I frowned at her.

"Look, I didn't want you to go to jail so I stepped in to help,
that's all."

Vaughn walked back into the room jiggling change in his
pocket but remained quiet. He watched Karen's every move as
if he wanted to catch a secret before it escaped her lips.

"Did you out somebody?"

"No, but I'm not against it, if it helps you," she said matter-
of-factly. "We're not against it." She pointed her finger between
her and Vaughn.

He spoke up. "Karen, you've been holding on to a secret that
you believe to be true. I know you're not convinced but he can
make it without you." He turned to me. "Son, I did know a lot
about Karen's shenanigans to protect you, sometimes after they
had already happened."

"As always V, you're right in the middle of everything con-
cerning me without letting me know any of it."

He rubbed his chin. "Son, we have always tried to help you.
We had, no, we have your best interest at heart."

"According to who?" I barked.

He held up both hands. "Look, you and Sam didn't start
anything with anybody but you left a lot of destruction in your
paths when you got involved and tried to end it. If we couldn't
stop something bad from happening, we cleaned up whatever
and whoever it was afterward to make sure it never happened
again."

I stood up and started yelling in both their directions. "If
you were so big into protecting me and those around me, how
did Mia get put in a coma because of Lynn? How did Roni plow

her car into the nail salon where Mia and Dena were? And how was Nina constantly showing up everywhere Mia went? No, this stuff is not happening to me but it's happening to people I care about. How about you protect them from this bullshit? I don't need your protection."

"We protected you when you were younger. I tried to stay out of everything since you've been older and established," Karen tried to explain.

"Oh, so owning half of Matthews and Jefferson is staying out of my business?"

She looked at Vaughn. "Yes, we did that to protect you, also."

"We?"

"Yes, TJ and I."

"Okay, stop. Don't tell me any more. I can't digest any more of this tonight." I got up and walked down the corridor to my office. I knew exactly what "we" meant.

"We did it to protect you, son. You had your whole life to live," Vaughn yelled in my direction.

CHAPTER 42: MIA

had spent the last couple of weeks rereading this letter sent to me anonymously. I was successful at holding Quan at bay on most days so his drama was not adding stress to the situation.

I wanted to tell Dena about the whole cousin fiasco but she's been out of pocket lately. I'm not sure why. She'd reply to some of my text messages but this was not a text message conversation. I looked at her Facebook and Instagram pages and she hadn't shared anything in awhile.

"Desilyn, I have a confession. Two weeks ago when I told you I was going to the library, I went to see Karen in Houston."

"You did what, Mia? You went to see Karen? Gary's mother?"

"Yes, I went to see Karen. I needed to see if she knew anything about this cousin nonsense. That would be crazy."

"Mia, no. Going to Houston for a day is crazy."

"No, it's not. I needed to see if she knew anything and I didn't want her to know that I was away from Gary."

"Why not? What do you care?" She grunted. "You know what? I'm sorry. It doesn't matter. You're back safely. I'm so sorry. So, what did you find out?"

"Not much more than I already knew." I decided not to tell

her my original plan was to see Nina also. She would've lost her mind. She apologized so I let it go.

"Well, I did some digging in the family tree and found who we're related to and I didn't see any Vaughn James or Matthews."

"Matthews is Gary's adoptive parents' names."

"Ooh my goodness, what a tangled web you're about to get yourself into."

"I know." That saddened me a bit.

"So, who are we looking for? James, Matthews…who?"

I pulled out the letter again. "All of the above."

"What did the letter say, again? You might be cousins or you might be Karen's cousin?"

"It said, Hello Mia, you don't know me but I know you and I'm writing you with a bit of caution. Please pay attention to what you're doing and examine your roots. Gary might be your cousin. I'm not for sure but I heard somebody say it." I stopped reading and looked at her.

"So that means we need to look at both sides."

I nodded. "Eighteen different families."

We both laughed and walked upstairs.

"Come on let's see what we can figure out. We're going to have to talk to Aunt Edna and get her to spill the beans because she's holding tight to her lil' information. Those baby-boomers are relentless, I tell ya. They take all kinds of stuff to the grave."

"I know, right. But she needs to let go. I don't want my baby having any birth defects just because she doesn't want some-body's feelings hurt."

"Girl, I know it."

"Just tell me if I'm about to marry my cousin. It's bad enough we've been sleeping together."

"Umph, I don't even want to think about it. Y'all aren't cousins. You better not be."

We spent the rest of the evening searching through our family tree for the last names of all of Gary's families. We concluded, we still didn't know.

CHAPTER 43: KAREN

VAUGHN shook his head as we watched our son increase the distance between us.

I heard my phone vibrate. Alex sent a text instead of calling me back. I found that odd but I went with it.

Alex: Bringing Breleigh to you.

Me: *Okay, let me get the address.*

Alex: *No worries, I have it.*

Me: *How did you get the address?*

I watched my phone for a few seconds waiting on a reply but he didn't respond. *Why did he text me instead of calling?*

Vaughn and I sat in silence for at least ten minutes as he gave me a neck rub. It was relieving the built up tension from the previous conversation that replayed in my mind.

"I'm sorry, Vaughn. I didn't mean to tell him all of that tonight. He kept asking questions, and I couldn't sit here and blatantly lie to him. He's too dang smart and would've figured that out in a heartbeat."

"Yeah, you laid a lot out there but he needed to hear it. And the sad thing is that's not all of it." He paced back and forth with his arms folded across his chest and occasionally rubbing his chin.

"I know. He also needs to understand my point of view. He has not always had the greatest attitude on the block either." I paused and looked at him. "Thanks to you, Vaughn."

"What the hell is that supposed to mean?"

"You were the one who coached him and trained him with all of those illegal activities and violent altercations, getting into trouble, fighting and all that stuff."

"That's not true, Karen. I was the reason he went to law school. I knew what my son was made of."

"And I did, too."

"You didn't tell him he was related to Mia, did you?" he said abruptly.

I rubbed the back of my head. I wanted to escape. My phone started to vibrate. I picked it up immediately. "Alex, where are you?"

"I'm at the security gate. Hurry and open up! They were following me."

I leaped from my seat and started running to find Gary. I had not been in his house before so I didn't know which direction to run in. "Gary! Gary! Open the gate for Alex. They're after him."

"What?" His phone was ringing. He said, "Hello. Who's after him?" He paused for a second and looked in my direction. "Let him in." He turned to Sam. "Sam, let's load."

"You know I'm strapped," Sam replied.

"Wait, what's going on? Alex is bringing Breleigh over so Chandler won't try to keep her from me. He's done it before when we had an argument." I tried to keep up with him as he walked into this massive media room, pulled open the drawer of the entertainment center, put a clip in a Glock, and headed toward the door.

"Gary, sweetheart, what are you going to do?" I knew what he and Sam were capable of doing.

He glared at me but remained silent.

"Gary, you do not need that gun. Alex probably got in the gate before Chandler caught up to him."

"You better hope he did."

"You're not going to shoot him, are you? I can't let you do that."

"I'm not going to shoot him; you are. He's abusing you, not me." He put the gun in my hand.

My hands were trembling. "Gary, but my baby is coming here. I can't let her see me shoot her father."

"Don't worry, she won't."

I had never seen so much evil resting in the eyes of my son.

Vaughn stepped toward me and eased the gun out of my hand. He looked at Gary. "Now you know we don't handle things in public like this and with Breleigh on her way, too." He removed the clip from the gun.

"Why not? She needs to show him that she will kill him if he continues to beat her and keep her away from her daughter."

"Gary, he doesn't beat me."

"It's amazing you don't call it…"

My phone rang again and stopped his comment. "Alex?"

Gary said calmly, "Go outside to get your daughter and tell Alex to leave. I do not want him in my house. V. you can take Karen and Breleigh to your house. Sam and I have things to do." He took the gun from Vaughn's hand.

He disappeared down the hall toward the media room.

"I need to make a call." Vaughn walked outside and I walked out behind him to get my daughter.

Alex pulled into the circle driveway and hopped out. "Alex, honey, are you okay?" I rushed to get my daughter out of the back seat. Alex was visibly shaken but I had to explain to him that Gary did not want anyone else in the house under the circumstances.

"Yes. Yes, I'm fine." He took a deep breath.

"Did they see where you went?" I examined Breleigh all over.

"No, I came through the gate before they caught up to me."

"Are you okay, sweetheart?" I held her face in my hands.

"Yes, ma'am," she replied. "Whose house is this?"

"I'll tell you when we get inside." We turned to walk inside.

"Here's her bag." Alex stood awkwardly.

"Alex, I'm sorry but Gary is in a mood tonight and I don't want you getting all mixed up. Are you okay to drive home? Or do you have a friend's house to sleep at?"

"I understand. Yes, yes I do. I have somewhere to sleep tonight."

"I have someone to watch him make it home or to a friend's," Vaughn added.

"Thank you, sir. I appreciate it, sir," Alex replied nervously.

The lights on a black dual cab truck came on and started coasting in our direction.

"Vaughn, who is that?' I rushed Breleigh toward the door.

"Calm down, Karen. He came with me. He'll follow you home, Alex. What's your number?"

Alex gave his number to Vaughn and Vaughn gave it to the guy in the truck. I continued toward the door, twisted the handle, and it was locked. I looked through the glass and knocked. "Gary! I know this boy didn't lock us out." He was standing there talking to Sam. "Gary!" I yelled as I pounded my fist on the glass.

I turned to look at Vaughn. Alex got in his car and pulled away. The man in the truck followed him.

"Let's go, Karen." Vaughn gently touched my elbow and guided us toward his car.

CHAPTER 44: GARY

FROM my perspective, I never broke the law. I felt like I had never gotten into anything that I couldn't get out of legally. Sam and I had bad tempers for different reasons growing up and that got us into trouble on occasion but in my opinion it was nothing where Vaughn or Karen needed to get involved. My parents had me under control just as Sam's parents had him.

I decided to allow the two of them to handle Karen and her husband in whatever manner they chose as long as it didn't involve me. If I heard, "We did it to protect you" one more time, I might have lost it. I had more to resolve with Karen but I just had too much going on in one night to address it. I did something I had never done and that's lock them out of my house. I had to do it. I wasn't ready to meet Breleigh. If I hadn't locked the door, Vaughn and Karen would've walked back in with Breleigh in tow and I would've been faking my way through the introduction. Breleigh didn't deserve that treatment. I guess she didn't deserve to get locked out either but I would explain it to her later.

I was sexually frustrated, I wanted to slap Karen, pummel

her husband, and punch Vaughn. I did not need all of those emotional demons roaming through my mind as I met my sister. I had to admit, my heart skipped a beat when I learned that I had a biological little sister.

My phone rang and I saw Desilyn's name flash across the screen. If Mia had not been in Arkansas, voice mail would've caught that call.

"Hey, Des what's up?" I walked into my office and sat down.

"Hey, brother-in-law."

I pretended to laugh. "Hey, how are you doing? What's up?"

"Ummm, we have a little situation that I don't know if my sister has told you about. If she has not, act as if you don't know and please don't tell her I told you."

I leaned back in the chair thinking, *Damn what is it now? It can't get any worse than what I've just heard.* "I'm listening." I put my feet up on the mahogany desk.

"Mia came here to deal with some personal issues between you and her, that part is true but there's another matter that I know she hasn't told you about."

"What is it, Des?" Her saying Mia's name immediately got my attention. I had seen so many conniving issues in my line of work; my mind had already done a three-sixty flip in a matter a seconds. Not to mention my biological parents are manipulative, too.

"There is this guy…"

I felt the fire rise up in my throat. I opened the bottle of water and took the last swallow remaining.

She continued. "This guy who we've known for many, many years. He helped Mia pay for her last year of college and now he constantly threatens her or blackmails her about paying him back."

"What does he have to blackmail her about? Have they ever—"

She interrupted. "I don't know, Gary. I asked Mia if she ever slept with him, she said no." She paused. "And I believe her."

"Do you know if he has anything significant on her?"

"No, she said he threatened to tell lies on her and you know how she is about her reputation and public appearance."

"Hmmm, it's gotta be something if Mia wanted to come there to handle it and not tell me." I could feel anger rising but I had to suppress it. I got up to walk to the kitchen for another bottle of water. I had to remain calm and hear Desilyn out. She was genuine. She loved Mia and me together, and we knew it.

"I don't know. The amount he's requesting from her is three hundred percent higher than what he gave her. He claims it's interest. Every time he talks to her it's a different amount. He gave her this tethered sheet of paper the other day with a bunch of numbers on it. I'm telling you about it because I believe that even if she pays him, he still won't leave her alone."

"What's his name?" I grabbed the bottled water and walked back to my office.

She sighed. "His name is Quan Winters. He's a felon."

"Really?" *Why is Mia dealing with a felon?* "How much time, and for what?"

"Drugs and assault and battery. I can't remember the amount of time but it wasn't his first offense. He's been in at least twice."

"Okay, I'll check him out." *Quan Winters.* I wrote the name on a piece of paper.

"Thanks, Gary. You know I'd die if something happened to my baby." She sounded worried.

"Thanks, Des. I got it. I'll be there tomorrow."

"Oh." She sounded shocked but pleasantly surprised. "Okay, I'll see you tomorrow."

"Please don't tell Mia."

After hanging up with Desilyn, I pulled up an Internet browser and logged into a site I used for background checks and keyed *Quan Winters* into the search box. Everything I needed to know about the guy flooded my screen. I made a few phone calls and within minutes I had even more information that I could use against him to stop any kind of blackmail he thought he'd use against Mia. He's had a tough life and even more so behind bars.

Sam walked into my office and sat down. He had been in a somber mood all day since I had told him about Dena. I'm sure that blast of information from Karen didn't help the situation either. He didn't look in my direction; he stared at the TV and didn't speak immediately.

I had never seen him get so close to tears although he didn't let go. He took the news about Dena worse than I'd expected. His grandmother had passed away from breast cancer about a year ago. She meant the world to him. He used to go by her house every morning to take her a cup of Starbucks coffee and a newspaper and she'd cook breakfast. If he didn't have clients that day, he'd take her for a ride around town. After she passed away, he said Brooklyn was not the same anymore.

I know that was not the only reason he wanted to move away but certainly one of the main reasons. And I should not have encouraged his move. The two of us together plus my brother, Vance, could get us into a lot of trouble. Sam knew me better than I knew myself sometimes. We created a lot of chaos when we were growing up. Some that we have not and will not ever speak of again. Sam started it and we'd finished it or vice versa. I started it and he assisted from smoking weed, selling weed, fighting, you name it we did it from the age of eleven to fourteen. My parents moved from Brooklyn to Long Island

and when we left the environment, we made different choices until I found out I was adopted. I created more chaos out of anger but it didn't last long. I have matured, I live a different life now and so did he. We had changed. At least I thought we had. I know that if he had not been in the chair in front of me, I would've thought of a better solution to one of my current problems—Alex.

"Sam. Two things. We need to talk about how much money you owe Karen, and then I need you to get some information for me."

"We can talk about Karen later. I can't deal with any more of her right now. What kind of information you need me to get?"

"Okay, fair enough." I let out a long breath. "Alex is researching Mia for some unknown reason and I need to know why. I stumbled upon the lil' conniving prick when I went into the office early one day. He had sweet-talked the security guy into letting him in early. He wasn't actually in the office when I got there but he had Mia's information on the screen. I'm not sure what he was doing."

"What? What kind of information? Like a background check or something?"

"Exactly that plus some. He had her genealogy information and everything. I deleted the information on the document and saved it then rebooted the computer so he'd lose whatever he was working on."

Sam knew how we did things in the past and he didn't hesitate. "Oh, so I need to get an understanding of why he's looking at Mia's information? Okay," he said casually. "Where is he?"

"He'll be in the office by eight-thirty in the morning."

"Do you have a panic button in your office?"

"No."

"Does he carry any weapons?"

"Not that I know of."

"Hmmm. I'll find out if he does."

"Thanks, man."

CHAPTER 45: GARY

THERE is definitely no sleep for the weary. I had packed an overnight bag for my trip to Arkansas thinking the time of night and my exhaustion from the entire week would render me unconscious in a matter of minutes but that was not my story. Reading books, listening to white noise, praying, none of it seemed to have worked. I tossed all night and ended up in my office after a workout, reading the paper and having coffee at six o'clock in the morning. I was productive for two hours before Sam interrupted me.

Sam texted me, *I'm outside.*

I replied, *okay.*

I got up and walked into TJ's office and closed the door. I noticed Alex had arrived but he wasn't at his desk. I was glad and I needed to find something to distract me until Sam finished whatever he had planned to do.

My phone buzzed again and I looked at the screen. I had made the last minute reservations to Arkansas so it cost me quite a bit, but I didn't care. I got a text message alerting me that the flight was delayed. I didn't want any delays today. I was trying to get to Mia. She'd been gone two months too long and

I needed her. I missed her. I sat back and reminisced about the night before she left and how I had loved her hard. That night I had made love to her incorporating every single act I had ever performed on her, plus some. The way we made love, I'd thought we'd never part again. If there was an open spot, we licked it. If it was suckable, we sucked it. We made love in the missionary position, from the back, in the chair, against the wall, and every other direction she could handle. I wanted to kiss her passionately and I couldn't do that from behind her. I curled her. I did it on the side of her, in the down stroke, butterfly, bridge, wheelbarrow, and every other exotic position and she hung in there. I understood that relationships were not all about sex but it was a very important part to me and to her. She screamed, she moaned, and enjoyed everything until she couldn't take it anymore and she yelled out in passion, "Gary!" I loved when she called my name. That night Mia got pregnant again. I just needed to confirm it. Yes, I needed to go get Mia sooner than later. My flight time couldn't come quick enough.

I turned on TJ's computer and began to look around the office as it booted then I logged in. I found the office lease and read through the early termination clause we had negotiated. "Yes! This lease expires in four months. Just enough time for me to determine my next move."

A few minutes later, I heard Sam talking to Alex.

"Is Gary here?" Sam asked.

"Yes, but he's not available at the moment. How can I help you?" Alex said in the most authoritative voice he could muster.

"Uh, I need to get something from his office." Sam started walking towards my office.

"No, you can't go in there," Alex screamed.

I heard a scuffle.

"You can't go in there," Alex continued.

"Shut up! Now sit down. Why were you researching personal information about Mia? What do you want with her?"

I searched the internet for other office space. I thought a virtual office space would be perfect. I had decided in an instance to move out of the office to save on rent expense by working from my house. My phone vibrated and I swiped my finger across the screen to answer.

"Hey, dude. What's up?" I began speaking first. It was my car dealer, Jorge.

"Hey, dude. I know you thought I forgot about you. Just wanted to let you know I hadn't. I found the car you've been waiting months for me to find. Exactly what you wanted, well, I found one of the two. The black S5 Coupe, with red interior, staggered black rims, wait a minute, let me look at something here; it might have the red rims. No, I think they're all black, I'll have to go look when it arrives later today." Jorge gushed with excitement.

"Man, that is good news. It doesn't matter, if she wants the trim, we'll figure that out later. When can I get the keys?" I had been on the hunt for this car for Mia for months and my car dealer couldn't find it, until now. Mia is going to flip out when I hand her the keys.

"We can get you the keys tomorrow. You know I have to check it all when it arrives and make sure everything is okay, then we'll go from there."

"Okay, that's cool. She's out of town anyway. I've had this fake key fob for some time just waiting to hand it to her."

"Well, it's all yours, man. I'll call you tomorrow when I check it out."

"Thanks. This is awesome."

I hung up the phone and the smile turned into a frown. The call came in as soon as I touched *End* on the other call. I sighed trying to decide if I wanted to deal with her this morning. I had promised I'd try to respond better to her request, especially after locking her out.

"Hey, Karen."

"Hey, son. What are you doing?"

My eyebrows furrowed. Her voice irritated me. "Nothing, I'm headed to the airport."

"Well, actually you are doing something then." She let out a nervous chuckle.

I didn't respond.

"Oh, so what time are you leaving?" she continued as I struggled to suppress my irritation. I felt like I was giving it a try at developing a relationship with her but she was too sneaky by giving me bits and pieces of information instead of telling me and showing me all I needed to know at once.

"Now."

"Oh, I wanted to go to lunch with you today. Can we go before you leave?"

"That's a no go. My flight leaves in less than two hours."

"Oh, I wanted to tell you some things. I've been hesitating to tell you but I think it's time."

I sighed. "What do you have to tell me? You seem to be always full of unwanted information all the time."

"Well, not this time."

"Okay, speak."

"I'm so sorry that Vaughn and I have disappointed you but I honestly wouldn't have it any other way. You're my son and I love you. Hindsight is definitely twenty-twenty and if I had to do it all over again, I would have raised you myself, by myself if

I had to. I didn't enjoy doing everything in the shadows when I was the one who gave birth to you." She sniffed.

"Is that what you had to tell me? If not, tell me what you have to tell me. I have a flight to catch," I said calmly. I was trying my best not to let her crying get to me.

"Well, I prefer to tell you in person."

"Well, that's not going to happen. You need to tell me now or never."

"What does that mean?"

"Exactly what I said, Karen. I have a flight to catch so I can't meet you. If you choose to tell me something, you need to do so now or never."

"I just wanted to say I'm sorry for delivering so much bad news to you."

"Okay. Apology accepted. Life must go on. And if you are sincere about getting to know me, you're gonna have to stop all of this hiding and sneaking around, doing things behind my back. I can't deal with sneaky, manipulative people."

"I understand. Please understand that nothing I've ever done for you was to harm you. I've always had your best interest in mind."

I really didn't want to hear anything else she had to say but I keep hearing my mother Judy's voice: *Gary, she is your mother and she loves you. I'm still your mother, too. Listen to what she has to say.* Karen had done just enough damage in my life to last me for the rest of my life. I know she did it all to "help me" but the way she went about it was all wrong. I was disappointed that they kept so many secrets and didn't allow me to be the mature person raised by Clive and Judy Matthews to handle anything life threw at me.

"Sweetheart, please, I just need a few minutes of your time. We don't have to meet."

I sighed. "Okay, what?"

She stopped pleading and just blurted it out. "Gary, you have some more inheritance coming to you from my parents."

I remained silent because I couldn't believe what I was hearing and I didn't believe it. I knew there had to be a catch in her comment. There had to be a loophole in it for her to benefit from all of this.

She continued. "You got your first installment after college, now you're due one just because you are successful and contributing to society six months after your 35th birthday."

"What?"

"Yes. My parents were working parents who were very savvy in their finances, including the windfall from the patent my father had on an airplane part. You were their only grandchild and you will get an additional five hundred-thousand dollars at every milestone, complete college, marriage, and children, and then continued after that until the funds are depleted."

"Really?" I was obviously intrigued; any normal human being would be at the crossroads of their business.

"Yes, they really loved you, Gary, as you can tell by the amount of time they spent with you. I'm sorry the truth didn't come out about your adoption until you were a teenager. Me and Judy didn't think the time was right. God, my mother was so angry with me." I shook my head. "That's the reason she told you at a very young age to call her Grandma. Kept me in suspense if she'd spill the beans."

"Yeah, I know."

She repeated, "They really loved you, and so do I." She paused. "Look, as you can see, I want to develop a relationship with you. Surely you can tell how I've been clinging to everything about you all of your life hoping that you would change your mind about getting to know me." She paused again. "I know you're not too fond of me these days but if I reconciled my relationship with you, I'd receive a onetime amount of seven hundred thousand dollars."

I lowered my head. I knew there was a catch. But I had no more fight to give her. I guess I really didn't need any. I'm not sure when Karen figured out her portion of the money but she thought she was doing the right thing by protecting me all of these years. None of her actions harmed me physically but the emotional turmoil of constantly discovering a new scheme she created was my heartache. She went about it all wrong but she did it out of love, wicked love, but love nonetheless. I came to grips with everything last night after the altercation with her husband. She just might go to any lengths to assist me but I wondered what would happen if her husband and I were on opposite ends of her crossroad.

"Okay. We can meet when I get back to discuss it."

"Okay. One more thing. I know this question might seem random but do you have a prenuptial agreement? If not, you should consider one."

I sighed. "We've already discussed it." Mia and I didn't have a prenuptial agreement and didn't want one.

"Yes, well, that's good because she might be good now but you never…"

Sam had Alex by the neck and stormed into TJ's office. I didn't hear Karen complete her sentence.

"Tell him what you told me." Sam growled at Alex.

Alex was sweating profusely and wincing from the obvious pain Sam had inflicted upon him.

"I gotta go." I pressed *End* and set the cell phone on the desk and stood up. "What's up, man?"

"Tell him what you told me." Sam growled in his ear again.

Within five minutes, Alex gave me information that made me distrust my biological mother even more.

CHAPTER 46: MIA

SOMETIMES you just have to let go of foolish fear and go for it. I've been running for the past two years from the man I love and the man who loves me more than any man has ever loved me. I am going to ignore the speculation that he might be related to me. I just can't deal with that or believe that right now. He has never been abusive, always supportive, willing to provide for me and protect me, if I would only allow him to. I was targeted twice and severely hurt once by women he had no control over. I had prayed about it, studied scriptures to support my prayers, and realized that this could happen with any man. There is something that I'm supposed to learn from this. Only God knows what it is and I plan to get quiet and listen.

I slipped into black velour running pants, a red sorority t-shirt, and sneakers.

"Hey, Des." I walked into the kitchen.

"Hey, Miss Mia," she replied with such a motherly smile as she pressed End on her phone and slid it into her apron pocket. Des reminded me of my mother. She calls me "Miss Mia" and she looks so much like her. Sometimes I look at her and just want to burst into tears because I miss my mother so much. The entire house still reminded me of my parents although they had remodeled and replaced the furniture with the exception of my room. She kept the same furniture from my teenage years. "You okay?"

"Yes, I'm good." I smiled. "May I borrow your car again?"

"Sure." She placed a skillet on the stove. "How long will you be? I'm getting ready to cook lunch. Then I'm cooking all of your favorites for dinner."

I twisted my face as if I was contemplating if I wanted to borrow the car after all. "All of my soul food favorites?"

"Yep."

I needed clarity. "Greens, yams, black-eyed peas?"

She nodded teasingly.

"Mac and Cheese, fried fish, and fried chicken?"

She continued smiling and nodding and leaned over to pull more pots and pans from the cabinet.

"Peach cobbler and pound-cake?"

"Now don't run out, Missy." She rose up and pushed both fists into her hips.

I started dancing a jig in the middle of the floor and singing "Ola ola eyyyyy, rollin', rollin', rollin'…"

She fanned a towel at me. "You're so silly, girl. Where are you going?"

My sister always interrogated me like my mother used to, but for some reason, I didn't care. I had nothing to hide.

"I'm going to the cemetery."

"Hmmm. Okay. Are you sure you're okay?"

"Yes, of course but I think this will be my last time."

She turned to look at me with lowered eyes. "Are you sure you're okay?" she emphasized.

"Yes. I told you, I'm okay. I'm standing in my truth. I need to grow up and bring some closure. I think I keep it lingering and use it as a crutch in a way, to come home and stay for a time, to run away to keep from confronting my issues. I've never had to handle anything; my relationships always ended before they got to this point of major issues and I darn sure have never been close to marrying my cousin."

"Girl, stop it."

"I pray I'm not, but I'm serious about the other stuff. I need to grow up, again. I finished college, I started my career, I saved money to start my own business, and I was doing fine. Then I met Gary, drama from these crazy women ensued and every time there's an issue, I run home. I've never met a guy with so many women issues. It's crazy, Des. I feel like I want to hurt somebody. That's not me. When I was working full time, I didn't run away at all. Well, my issues weren't petty like this either but I handled stuff like a strong woman should or buried myself in my work. Perhaps I should do that now before Chris tells me to stop coming here," I rambled.

"Girl, please. Chris is fine and you know you're always welcome here. That's why I kept your room as it is. Maybe I need to change the furniture out, and maybe you won't feel so much like a little girl when you get here."

"No, you don't have to do that. I'll get it together. I'll at least reduce it to normal visits, events, just for the weekend, some holidays. I understand Mom and Dad are not in the grave and I can feel just as close to them everywhere I go. I think it makes me sadder by doing this, so I'm going to make it my last time. You know?"

"I understand, my dear. I do understand." She walked over and rubbed her hand through my hair. She patted my shoulder.

"I go twice per year, on their birthdays. That is my way of grieving and coping. So whatever it takes for you, honey, as long as it's healthy. Okay?"

I nodded. "Maybe I'll start going to the library or something." I smiled.

I lounged around for another two hours then gathered my items, including Chris' gun, and headed to the cemetery. The cemetery was in the country, far off the main highway and the gun was for my protection. Desilyn insisted on giving me a lunch that I devoured before I arrived at my destination which was less than thirty minutes away.

I stepped out of the car into a cool breeze brushing against my face and the smell of fertilizer from the nearby fields lingered in the air. I scanned my eyes into the beautiful blue sky with fluffy clouds and watched as the clouds rolled pass the others. My parents' graves were near the front and about three rows in from the half gravel, half dirt road. I spread the quilt I borrowed from Desilyn's closet. I sat down facing the tombstones. I recalled doing the same thing when I was younger. I always sat between them on the couch and drew pictures, wrote notes, or read books. I felt a sense of peace sitting with them and I had created that same peace many years later sitting between their tombstones.

After writing ten pages of my feelings, I placed the journal on the quilt and began to pray with my eyes open staring across the field as far as my eyes could see. My prayer and tranquil thoughts were halted by the noise of a car speeding down the dirt road with dust billowing at least ten feet above and behind it. The green sedan slowed then came to an abrupt stop at the front of the pavement where the church used to sit. The dust was settling and lucky for me the wind carried it in the opposite direction. The door flung open and out stepped Quan.

Great, him again. He walked toward me with a purposeful stride. He walked so close, he stepped on my quilt. I shot him a hateful glare and jerked the quilt and sent him stumbling backward.

"Dang, girl. You could've asked me to move."

"How about I ask you to get the hell away from me? I don't need you or the drama you bring," I retorted.

"Mia, baby, we're better than that."

"Please do not call me baby. You're gonna make me throw up."

"You didn't used to throw up."

"I wanted to." I paused to think because I didn't want to go back and forth with him. I needed to nip it. "Listen to me, Quan. I paid you what I owed you, now you need to leave me the hell alone."

"No, you didn't pay me all of it."

I looked at him angrily.

"But I might be willing to let it slide if you act right."

"Look, I do not want you. I am so happy in the relationship that I'm in. With Gary. You need to go home and pacify your little fat wife, because if she shows up here, I'm going to do something bad to her. And you."

"Man, forget her. She ain't coming nowhere." He fanned his hand.

"The only reason I agreed to talk to you is because we had been friends for a long time and I figured that would mean something for you to act like you have a little bit of sense. I am not, I repeat, I am not trying to have anything other than a friendship with you. You went and married a crazy woman who thinks I'm trying to take you from her because you failed to tell her the truth. You want her to think you're stepping out on her. I don't want any parts of your freakin' mess."

"Man, forget her." He sat down in the grass.

"Is that all you can say, forget her? Quan, that's your wife."

"Look, she's always tripping and I'm tired of her."

"So, work it out. That's not my problem. I'm sure you knew you had drama when you went down on one knee and asked her to marry you."

"No, I didn't, and for your information, she asked me."

I simply looked at him with a *you're pathetic* expression.

"And why can't we have something more?"

"'Cause I don't want anything more. I don't want you. And you constantly hounding me and threatening me about money you said was a gift, boy please." I barked with hand gestures to match. "And you're married. Dang it, leave me alone."

"Slut, you don't have to be hateful."

I glared at him. I thought about pointing the gun and shooting him just because of his last statement but then I thought more about the rest of my life and he wasn't worth the jail time especially since I didn't appear to be in any immediate danger. I sighed and calmly stated, "You used to be such a nice gentleman, a real man, a caring man." I shrugged. "Now you're just a sorry-ass man who wants to run around pretending to be powerful and all you are is a wounded little boy who needs to grow up." I ended with a growl.

"Why you gotta get all mad, Mia? You weren't mad when we were—when you were taking my money when you were in college. I practically paid for everything for you. For what? Nothing. How would you feel if I told you I wanted my money back?"

"You have fool! And trust me, I do appreciate everything you've ever done for me but when you gave me the money, you said it was a gift, which means I shouldn't have to pay you back. Now you're constantly bringing it up, which is way I paid you," I yelled.

I thought for a moment regretting every penny I had accepted from him because back then, something told me that he'd want payback in the future. He always said he'd do anything for me because we were friends since the first day we met as kids in vacation bible school. His dad was very abusive to him and his mother and eventually left them. Quan was immediately thrust into manhood at age twelve and was used to working hard and making it happen for himself and his family. I never wanted to date him because I saw a mean streak and an abusive side that I didn't want to deal with from a girlfriend perspective but he always had my back in any situation. I once saw him punch his girlfriend in the face and then picked her up and threw her in the dumpster on campus. That was the day I called the cops on him and we were never close afterward. But at that point, I had already accepted gifts from him so I was already in his debt.

"Man, whatever," he mumbled.

"How much?"

"Huh?"

"How much do I owe you, now? I'd really hate to be indebted to someone who will always throw that back in my face. I don't want nor do I need that feeling over me."

"Well, feel it. Because you owe that much. You can't even come close to paying me back. Ever."

"Try me. How much?"

"I told you, eighteen thousand." He raised his head higher as he seemingly grabbed that number out the sky.

"Is that all? Is that what it will take for you to leave me alone, forever?"

"Yeah," he said with confidence as if he didn't think I had that much money.

"Okay, I'll get it to you. What's your email address?"

"Man, whatever." He stood up. "You trippin'."

"No, Quan, I'm not trippin' but you definitely are. What's your email address?" I asked again.

He walked away as I was talking. He had no clue of new technology. He probably didn't have an email account and surely didn't know you can transfer a certain amount of funds between accounts using email.

I stood up and positioned myself to move swiftly just in case he decided to drive forward instead of backward. "Yeah, you should go hop right back in that car and speed along the dirt road in the same direction you came and go home to your wife."

He got in the car and sped away with dust billowing behind his car just as he came. I had a feeling that was not going to be the last I saw of him. I had to figure out a way to make him go away. The amount I owed was marching uphill every time we spoke.

CHAPTER 47: GARY

Y OUR mother is conniving and a master manipulator," Alex hissed through gritted teeth.

I didn't trust Karen either but hearing another person hurl insults at her, although it may have been true, pissed me off. I wanted to punch him. I stepped closer to him, "What did you say?"

He recoiled his attitude and started speaking humbly. "I work for Karen. I've been her personal assistant for two years. She knows TJ and that's why he hired me. She wanted me to work for you so I could get to know you and tell her what you had going on. Sort of like a spy. It was twofold; she wanted to see how you were doing and to check into your fiancée to make sure she was legit and not trying to take your money."

My head started pounding. I wondered if he was making this stuff up because he read an article about my last assistant, Lynn, and her granddaughter. They had an article in the newspaper after Mia's accident so this could very well be a made up story. Why does it seem that everybody is trying to protect my money from Mia as if she's a gold-digger? Mia works hard for her own money just like me. The current story was way too close to the last one with different characters. Karen had gotten me again and I couldn't decide at the moment if I wanted Alex to pay for Karen's mistakes or she paid for her own.

Sam squeezed the back of Alex's neck and said, "That's not all. Tell him everything."

"Okay, Sam, let him sit down before I knock his ass down."

Alex eased into the chair and looked timidly in Sam's direction. I sat behind TJ's desk and placed my hands in the steeple position. "What else do you have to tell me, Alex?"

He rubbed his wrist. "Karen basically hired me to work for you. She asked me to just do my job and not get in your way or piss you off."

"Well, you failed the first assignment."

He blinked rapidly. "I understand." He looked down at his hands. "At first she just wanted me to work then she asked me to find out any information I could on your fiancée. I didn't want to do it, I promise I didn't. But I've enjoyed working for her for two years until this stuff came up."

I pulled my lips in and sighed heavily. "Keep going. I saw the information on your screen. I just want to know why."

He struggled to get his words out. "Your mother—"

I interrupted, "Karen."

He rubbed his wrist again. "Karen had been talking to a lady she thought was your fiancée, a lady named Nina."

I felt like my head would spin off my body. "What?"

"Yes, she even took her to lunch. She thought your fiancée's name was Nina. I reminded her that she told me her name was Mia. She figured it out when she went to lunch a few weeks ago and Nina left the table when she realized that Karen had figured out that she wasn't Mia. Apparently Nina was milking it, too, because she knew Karen had it mixed up."

He sounded like an idiot trying to explain it all but I clearly knew that he wasn't.

"Gary, your mothe—, I mean, Karen can be really persuasive, even intimidating."

"How long was Karen communicating with Nina?"

"For a few months. She reached out to Nina and it all started from there. I think she really thought Nina was your fiancée."

That's why Nina came back with a vengeance. My mother, Karen, had been filling her head with hope and lies. Lies I don't think she realized she was telling.

"Why were you trying to research information on Mia? How did you know where to start?" I was so glad I knew how to stay calm in stressful situations because had I not known how, I would've turned the desk over on him and kicked his ass.

"Karen had a folder with your name and her name on it and she frequently went over the story with me, all the details of your life. That's how I remembered that you were marrying Mia and not Nina."

"So, Karen had you researching what?"

"She had me searching for her lineage so that she could..." He adjusted in the chair twice before answering. "So she could see if, uhh, if uhh, you were, uhh, you were..." He pressed his lips together. "To see if Mia was related to her."

Sam grunted.

"What did you find?" I didn't react although I wanted to but continued my line of questioning. Karen had already hinted at this but I blew it off because I think she's very calculated and untrustworthy, so I wasn't surprised by his comment. But this is the second time this has come up so I needed to consider looking into it. Mia and I couldn't be related.

"I didn't finish because," he blinked rapidly, "my computer rebooted," he mumbled.

I walked around to the front of the desk and stood directly in front of him. He started to tremble. I heard the main door to our office creak.

"Hello." I heard a female voice sing. I recognized the voice right away. Karen walked into the office still singing. "Hello."

Neither one of us said a word. We waited until she figured out where we were.

"Oh, here you are," she continued in her high-pitched voice. She stepped into TJ's office with a crisp white button down blouse, black patent leather heels, carrying a bag that I'm positive she paid a lot of money for.

She appeared surprised to see Alex sitting in the chair wounded. "Oh, my, Alex! What happened to you? Gary what happened? Alex, are you okay?" She rummaged in her purse for a handkerchief. She pulled it out and dabbed Alex's forehead.

"Yes, ma'am. I'm okay."

"Gary?" She hissed. "Oh my God, what have you done?"

"I haven't done a thing. I only asked him a few questions."

Karen looked over and saw Sam standing in the corner and gasped. "You hurt him, didn't you?" She didn't wait on Sam to respond although I didn't think he would answer. "Alex, let's get out of here."

"You're not going anywhere. Not yet anyway," Sam grunted.

"I came in to protect Alex because I knew something was not right when I heard a man growl, 'Tell him what you told me.'" She changed her voice to mock a man's voice. "I knew that pain was imminent for someone in this room, so I made a b-line over here to see what was going on. I was already in the area because I thought I could convince you to go to lunch. I wanted to take you to Breleigh's school for lunch," she rambled.

All of us stared in her direction but did not say a word.

She looked at Sam then to me then back to Alex. "Yes, we need to get out of here, Alex."

Sam repeated, "No, you're not going anywhere." He folded his arms.

Her voice trembling started to resemble Alex's. I tried to avoid eye contact with her.

"Sam, please don't hurt him anymore."

All of us remained silent and continued to stare in her direction. She apparently hated silence because she kept talking, "Please Sam, listen, you won't have to pay me. I promise, you won't have to pay me one red cent; just please don't hurt him."

"Exactly what I wanted to hear." Sam pushed Alex's head.

Alex chimed in, "You have a thug lawyer and a goon and you're begging—"

She turned and slapped Alex. "Shut up! I'm trying to save your life here, boy."

He looked shocked.

I laughed heartily. "Now that's funny. Dude, she slapped the shit out of you. I didn't even expect that. But who are you calling a thug?" I grabbed him by his neck and bent him backward in the chair.

"Gary, let him go." Karen started pulling on my arm.

I let him go.

"Nobody." He jumped up and fell into Karen's arms as he struggled to respond. "Nobody."

"Look, Alex, I didn't want to hurt you but you lied to me. You snaked your way into my office and you snooped around. I don't like that, dude."

"She told me to." He pointed at Karen and she narrowed her eyes at him.

"Oh really, she told you to? How do I know that? For all I know you acted on your own. You could've been devising a plan to steal from me and stalk Mia, kill Mia, kill Karen. How do I know?" I hunched my shoulders. "Man, I have your finger prints, every document you've created, every website you've searched, basically every move you've made since you've been here." I stepped closer to him with every sentence. "You thought I was a dumb lawyer who was not technologically savvy, didn't you?"

He shook his head.

I continued, "Young man, this thug lawyer not only knows the law, the theory of it, the process, but I'm damn good at practicing it, which means I'm damn good at confusing the hell out of you and with my line of questioning you'd think everything you did had criminal intent."

He held his head higher and pushed his chest out. I guess he was trying to demonstrate he wasn't afraid of me. "I told you, she had me doing all of it."

"Alex, sweetheart, let's go. Please don't dig a hole you can't get out of. I have asked you to be quiet. You don't really know the depth of my full power, do you?" Karen threatened.

"Yes, ma'am, I do."

"Okay, then." She pointed her finger. "Call my son a thug again and you'll regret it." She turned to Sam. "Sam, you don't owe me. I'm sorry I used you as a pawn. I sincerely apologize for my misdeed." Then she turned to me. "Gary, I cannot help myself, I will always snoop into what you have going on. I owe you that much. No one will ever harm you in any way. If something ever happens to me, there are others who will take my place. Understand?"

I stood there with a frown plastered on my face.

"Right now, I have Nina and Roni on the list, I haven't forgotten," she continued.

I had already taken care of Nina with a threat and I had not heard from Roni but if she felt she needed to add some extra pressure, I didn't stop her.

"Get your things, Alex. I'm sure you're no longer welcome here."

I looked at Sam as Karen exited the office. "Let's go, man. We have a flight to catch."

CHAPTER 48: MIA

OKAY, Mom and Dad, I think it's time for me to go, here comes another car slowly coming down the road," I mumbled as I squinted my eyes in the direction of the car. I eased my hand toward the nine-millimeter. "I'm getting pretty sick of this today. I really don't want any issues but I must admit, this is beginning to get a bit scary." My heart started palpitating rapidly. My hand was shaky as I cocked the hammer back preparing to bust a cap in someone. I should've done this earlier; maybe Quan wouldn't have been so cocky. "I hope this thing is like riding a bike; I haven't fired it since my last visit down here." I took a deep breath.

Who have I become? This behavior was not indicative of who I was. I was ready to shoot to kill someone from my perspective, in self-defense. Could I live with this for the rest of my life? I was not ready to be handcuffed, lying prone on the ground, placed in the back of a police cruiser, and possibly jailed for life. As I'm sure my family is not ready to identify a body, pick out a casket, and watch them lower me into the ground. There was no more time to think about it. I stood up as the black Lincoln Continental slowly came to a stop and the passenger door opened.

"Mia, put that gun down," Chris yelled in my direction. "Throw me the keys to the car." He moved swiftly, closing the distance between us.

"How was I supposed to know it was you? Who is that in the car? What do you want with the keys? You better not leave me. Quan already came down here acting crazy." I still had my finger on the trigger.

"What? Did he hurt you?"

"No, just talking crazy, that's all."

He paused and stared at me inquisitively. "Okay, I'll find him. Was that him leaving just now?"

"Yes."

"Whose car was that?"

I hunched my shoulders. "I have no idea, probably his wife. Whose car are you in?" I kneeled down to put the gun underneath the towel on the blanket then stood back up.

"Where are the keys?" he asked again.

I pointed to the keys with my foot. He didn't answer me but walked over, threw the towel to the side, and picked up the gun and the keys. "You don't need this anymore. You're riding back to the house with them." He pointed toward the black car.

Within a matter of seconds, Chris was in the car and slowly going in reverse. The back door on the driver side of the black Lincoln opened and I gazed in the direction. I was expecting my Aunt Edna and my Uncle Herman to step out of the car to give me a lecture for any random reason. I could not believe my eyes when Gary stepped out of the car wearing a brown t-shirt and relaxed fit jeans with a rib knit cap. When I spoke with him, he did not tell me he was coming.

Gary pushed the door closed and walked toward me. My heart started to palpitate. I hesitated. *Is he my cousin?*

The smile spread across his face and I swore I could see all thirty-two teeth. I could not resist and at that moment I didn't care, he was my man.

"Gary!" I screamed as I ran toward him, leaped into his arms, and wrapped my legs around his waist.

He chuckled. "Hey, girl."

"Oh my gosh, I can't believe you came here!" I kissed him all over his face and hugged him. "Oh my gosh, Gary, I'm so happy you're here. I miss you so much. I thought you were my aunt and uncle."

"No, sweetheart, it's ya boy, in the flesh," he said as he caressed my butt and I kept kissing his face.

I could not believe my behavior. I was in such a funk when I left him to come to Arkansas and was nervous and panicked just a moment ago. It seemed that my time away from him had created a lot more emotions that were good toward him. I loved him so much and when I saw him, after a short hesitation, I leaped into his arms. I had to hug him, kiss him, and tell him how much I loved and missed him. I eventually placed my feet back on the ground.

"Gary, I'm so glad you're here. I missed you so much."

He wrapped his arms around me and squeezed me. He cupped my face into his hands and planted several kisses from my forehead to the tip of my nose, then my lips. He rubbed his hands down my shoulder and my arms to my hands, then interlocked his fingers into mine. "How have you been? I missed you, too."

I motioned for him to walk toward the blanket with me and we sat down. "I missed you." I smiled up at him. "Who's that in the car?"

"Samson." He smiled.

"Oh, so you talked Sam into coming to Arkansas with you?" I sang.

"Not exactly; he wanted to come. I didn't have to talk him into it. I only asked him to take me to the airport and he decided he wanted to come." He hunched his shoulders then smiled again. "I'm lying, I asked him to come." He looked around the horizon for several moments. "It's extremely quiet and peaceful out here."

"I know. This has been my ritual every time I come here. I come several times during my stay and sit on my blanket with my food. I write in my journal and I talk to my parents."

He nodded but didn't speak. He had a way of looking at me while I'm talking that made me feel warm and fuzzy, hot and horny, and shut up and kiss me all at the same time. He adjusted his position on the blanket and scooted closer to me but still didn't speak.

I kept talking, "I think this is going to be my last time coming here. I wanted to bring closure to this, this time, because I feel like I've been running."

He nodded his head in agreement and never removed his eyes from studying my face.

"Just stupidity," I mumbled.

He reached for my hands and rubbed the back of both of my hands with his thumbs then he brought them to his lips and kissed them. He scooted closer to me as I sat in a rested yoga lotus position. He placed his right hand gently around my neck and placed the other on my forehead. "Heavenly Father, thank You for this day, thank You for safe travels, thank You that Mia is safe. Please, God, forgive us for our sins and remove any unrighteousness from us. Father You said in Ephesians chapter five that a man will leave his father and mother and be united to his wife and the two will become one flesh and that husbands should love their wives as their own bodies and he must love his wife as he loves himself, and that the wife must respect her husband. That's exactly what I want for me and Mia. I know there had been a lot going on since we met and we want it to stop. We want to be together as one without the type of drama and issues we've been dealing with since day one. Help both of us to stop intentionally and unintentionally causing the drama. Everybody knows I'm with Mia and I want her only and I want her to know that. I want her to know that I will protect, provide for her, and I'm praying for her. Give us the words to say, guide our hearts to make the right choices and actions. I asked that You help me lead her, help me to take care of her, and love her as You loved the church. Give her peace of mind and heart. In short time, God I will make this right according to Your will. Thank You in advance, Heavenly Father. In Jesus' name, Amen."

"Amen. Gary I'm about to cry; that was beautiful."

"Please, don't cry."

"Thank you for praying for me."

"Mia—I feel like I say this so much, that you don't believe me, but I do love you and I don't want to be without you. I just showed up here because I want you to understand how much I love you and how much I want you in my life." He paused. "I certainly hope you feel the same about me. I want to ask you something again." He wiped both of his hands over his face. "Will you marry me?"

"Gary, I—" I opened my mouth to answer and he placed his finger on my lips.

"Shhh. Hold on a sec," he said, gently. "I want you to really think about it. I asked you to marry me after several months

of dating and although I didn't like the two years of engagement and breaking up, I did enjoy the getting back together
and just basically really getting to know you. I have definitely
changed because of you. My pace is a lot slower and I'm pretty
happy about it." He leaned in and kissed me on the corner of
my mouth. "I. Love. You. I'm glad we got to know each other
better. You're a bit crazy, but…"

I scrunched my face and he laughed. "But that's part of the
reason I love you." He leaned back and rested his hands on the
blanket. "If you say no this time, I will leave you alone for good.
I promise. I don't want to go through what we've been going
through for the past two years. It's ridiculous. I want you. I want
you to be my wife. I want to live with you forever but if you
don't want the same thing," he pointed his finger to emphasize
his point, "I think I've put up a pretty good fight but I would
need to stop bugging you. I need to step out of your way."

We allowed a long pause to linger as our eyes danced a Samba.

"So, again, Mia Nixon, will you marry me?" he asked.

"Gary, you know I love you, too. And you know I want to
marry you."

"I feel a 'but' coming. Mia that was a yes or no question." He
appeared slightly irritated and struggled not the show it. I felt
like he came to give me his final offer, an ultimatum. Gary had a
few control issues. He wanted things to go his way—no drama,
no issues, and sometimes, no question, just go.

"Gary, there's no 'but' coming. I was going to say, I love you
and yes, I will marry you, you grouchy man."

He smiled and reached for my hand then reached into his
pocket and pulled out my ring and placed it on my finger. He
said, "Will you marry me, soon?"

"Yes, Gary. I love you and I will marry you. Soon."

He leaned in and kissed me, tenderly. He held my face in his hands and kissed me.

I moaned.

"Hold on. I have something else for you." He reached into his pocket again as I waited in anticipation. He knew that I loved gifts and surprises. He held whatever it was closed in his massive hand. "Hold your hand out."

I opened my palm and he placed a key chain with four circles into my hand. "Oh, my God! Baby, you got my car? Oh my God!" I lunged forward and pushed him back on the blanket. "Thank you. Thank you. Thank you. This is awesome. You are awesome. How did you find it? Gary, thank you. You know this is what I wanted." I squealed. "It's been so long since I had a car."

"I know."

I ogled the key chain again and kept kissing him. "You're the best fiancé ever. No, you're the best husband ever."

"Oh, be quiet. Let's get out of here." He got up from the blanket and started gathering my things.

He helped me up and I stood there stumbling around as if I didn't know how to gather a blanket and basket to leave.

CHAPTER 49: MIA

WE made it back to Desilyn's house and I was still beaming about my new car. I quickly showered and changed into jeans and a t-shirt. We enjoyed the food Desilyn had prepared. Gary and Sam showered her with accolades.

After dinner, Sam and Chris went outside; joining forcing over something since we arrived but I didn't know what. I assisted Desilyn with cleaning the kitchen until Gary pulled me into the hallway with an intense look in his eyes. He ran his hand softly along the length of my arm, then up around my waist, up my abdomen, across my breast until it rested gently around my neck. I tilted my head back and he kissed me. *Oh my gosh, what if we're cousins?* Those crazy thoughts had returned.

"You just don't know how badly I want to take you upstairs and work on getting you pregnant, if you're not already." He leaned in and sucked my bottom lip.

What if I really am? I think I am. And what if we are cousins? I swallowed hard but didn't speak.

"Look, I need to hear something from you?"

"What?" I whispered, sincerely hoping he was about to devour me in the hallway since Desilyn had made her way outside.

"I need to know how much money you owe Quan?"

"What?" The needle scratched that record from one side to the other. "Where'd that come from? How do you even know about what I owe Quan?"

"How much do you owe him, Mia?" he said firmly.

"Babe, he paid for my college tui—"

"Shhh." He grabbed my arm and turned my body toward him. "I didn't ask you why, I asked you how much."

"Almost six thousand. I have the receipt, I'll show you. But I paid him that already. But he'll say fifteen thousand one minute and now he's up to eighteen. Interest." I twisted my mouth.

"Will he walk away for good if you gave him eighteen grand, or will I have to kill him?"

"I'm not giving him eighteen grand."

"You don't have to, I'm going to."

"No, Gary, you're not."

"Yes, I am. I owe him that much. If he hadn't paid, perhaps you wouldn't have your degree which means you wouldn't have your masters nor your doctorate not to mention your experiences. You've accomplished a lot from that push and I'm benefiting from it. So, I owe him. I'm thankful." He strained a smile.

"A lot of good my degrees are doing me now, huh?"

"Stop it, Mia. It's only temporary, remember? You were going strong until you had surgery. All it takes for you is a few phone calls."

I sighed. He was right. I had accomplished a lot in my career. I had made a name for myself. I was on the move traveling all over the country until my world was turned upside down when my fibroids unleashed their fury on me just before I left the hotel room while I was at a conference in Little Rock, Arkansas.

I had completed my panel discussion on executive presence that morning and was headed to moderate a discussion on personal branding for a different group in the afternoon. I started to cramp during lunch as I sat outside networking with a group of women. I excused myself from the table to retreat to my room for a quick break before the afternoon session. I made it to the room just in time. I started bleeding so heavily I had to be carted off to the emergency room. I was in the emergency room for six hours, long enough for Gary to fly from Houston to get me. I would not allow them to perform surgery there but we went to the doctor the next day and schedule to have a myomectomy. I had not scheduled any events since then and that was over six months ago.

"Come, let me show you." We walked upstairs and into my room. As soon as he closed the door, he stood behind me and wrapped his arms around my waist. He rested his chin in the top of my head and held me for several minutes.

"I missed you so much. I just need to hold you for a moment."

I turned to face him and my eyes met his with a yearning expression. He pushed his hands into my back pockets then wrapped them around my body. I leaned against him and buried my head in his chest. His embrace caused every ounce of stress to leave my body. He reached down, lifted my chin, and kissed me. I felt a fluttering in my stomach and a racing in my heart. At that moment I felt safe and whole with him.

This can't be my cousin.

We were locked in a passionate embrace when we heard a gentle knock on the door. We paused for a moment but he kept trying to kiss me.

"Wait, Gary." I flirted. "You know she'll just bust up in here if I don't answer her."

I walked to the door and Gary sat in the chair at my vanity.

"Oh, hey, Sam. Come on in."

"Nah, I'm good. I just wanted to let you know I'm headed to the store with Chris for a minute. We'll be right back. What time did you want to head to the hotel?"

"We'll be ready when you get back," Gary said.

I spun around on my heels to look at Gary.

"Auight. I'll see y'all later," Sam said.

"Uh, what hotel?" I walked over to him and pushed him back in the chair. I straddled him and started kissing him again. "What hotel? Why do we need a hotel? We can get it in right here?"

He shook his head. "No."

"Why not?"

"Because…"

I stood up and pulled him toward me, toward the bed. We kissed and fell onto the bed as two melded into one. My insides were tingling and clit was throbbing for his attention.

"Okay, okay, we need to stop, Mia."

"Why?" I whined.

"Mia, I'm not about to make love to you in this house. That's why I got a hotel room."

"Why not? We've done it before."

"That was a quick hit in the shower and we had not been away from each other for several weeks, several months." He leaned in, kissed me softly, and stood up.

"But why, Gary?"

"Babe, cut it out."

I pouted.

"Do you realize what I'm going to do to you when we get to the hotel? Trust me, you'll get too loud in here."

I smiled and eased off the bed. "Okay, I can wait." I pushed him back into the chair and straddled him again. "Another quickie?"

"Stop. Stop. Stop, Mia. You play too much. I'm not doing a quickie."

"Please," I moaned softly in his ear.

He held the small of my back and lifted me up. I held on to his neck and wrapped my legs around his waist. He walked toward the bed and laid me down without separating us. Our tongues danced passionately, slowly. He tasted so good. He whispered in my ear, "Girl, you know I missed you, right?"

"Ummhmm."

He kissed my neck as he tugged to raise my blouse. My breast escaped the underwire. "I have dreamed about this moment for so long." He kissed softly from my neck to my chest and landed on my breast. "I really want to make love to you slowly, tenderly." He opened his mouth and took my nipple softly into his lips. "But you keep begging for a quickie. Should I give you a quickie, sweetheart?"

"Yes. You. Should." The gentleness of his touch and the smoothness of his lips had me gasping for breath.

He lingered for a moment then switched slowly to the other breast. I let out a long sigh softly and then louder. I had an orgasm from him suckling my breast.

He slid his hand into my panties. "Oh, you were waiting for me, huh?"

I pulled him toward me and tugged at his zipper.

We made love quietly and quickly. It had been too long. I made a promise to myself at that moment. I will never leave him again.

We lay on the bed until we heard noises in the hall and he went into the bathroom to freshen up.

"Mia, guess what?" He paused.

I assumed he was waiting on me to respond in some type of way. I didn't say a word. I was basking in the glow of being held so tenderly, I almost missed the tone of his voice, which concerned me and ripped all of the words that came to mind from my mouth. I remained quiet. He kept talking.

"I need you."

"What's new?" I offered sarcastically.

"Smart ass. I need you. Seriously. I need you to help me with my business and I'll pay you a salary."

"What?" My brows were furrowed as I rose up to rest on my elbows.

"Yes, I'm moving out of the building and working from home after our lease expires. TJ can't work anymore."

"What? Why? What happened?" I stood up to smooth out the wrinkles on the comforter.

"I told you I hung out a few times with my mother since you left. She could be okay, eventually. She's sharp, intelligent, and knowledgeable business partner; at least I thought she was until she shared some interesting information with me."

I thought, *Shit! Did she tell him that we met?* Silence lingered in the air as I walked into the bathroom to wash up.

He placed his hands on my shoulders and spun me around. My voice trembled when our eyes met.

"What is it? I know it's something bad. I can tell by your expression."

"Babe, sit down. Please? And calm down. Geesh, you get worked up so easily."

I plopped down in the chair and folded my arms. "What is it?"

"Look, I know I'm full of bad news at times but not always." He sat on the edge of the bed.

I didn't move but my eyebrow rose slightly.

He continued, "Listen, I will not promise you that our lives will be drama free. I cannot, because you know it won't be. Matter of fact, there could be more, who knows? But I can promise you that I won't cause you any heartaches and I will give my life trying to protect you. I promise you that I will provide for you. I will.

My palms started itching, my heart started to flutter, and my head spinning. Where was this going? "What is it?"

"When was the last time you talked to Dena?"

"Yesterday, why?" My heart started to race just because he asked the question. "We've talked a lot mainly via text though unless one of us gets excited about something and need to talk. I texted her this morning but she didn't respond. Should I be worried?"

He reached for my hands. "Sweetheart, Dena and Monty got married last month and—"

"They did what?" I was astounded.

"Yes, they got married, but hold on a minute. It was for good reason, they—"

"There is no good reason for her to just jump up and marry that clown without saying a word." I leaped from my seat and yelled as I started fishing for my phone.

"Mia! Hold on. You need to calm down and listen." He grabbed both of my hands.

"Listen to me. Dena married Monty because...you know what, never mind. They're just married. They need each other. She needs him. And honestly, that's why I came here to get you. I need you. There's a lot going on and we need to handle this together."

"What is it, though? What else is going on?" I sighed.

"Mia, sweetheart, sit down. I have more to tell you. I wanted to wait until we were back in Houston but I feel like I need to tell you now."

"I don't want to sit down. Your tone is making me nervous so just tell me. Lordy, my best friend got married and didn't tell me. What else could there be?"

He lowered his eyes. "Come here, please. Sit down. Sit here on my lap."

I slouched over to sit on his lap. I wrapped my arms around his neck and squeezed him.

"Whoa, hold on. What are you doing?"

I stood up. "Nothing. I just know it's going to be bad. You always tell me to have a seat when it's something bad."

"Yes, babe it's pretty bad."

I got up and sat on the edge of the bed. I rested my arms on my knees.

He pulled the chair closer and reached for my hands. He kissed them and looked up at me. "Ummm, I wanted to tell you, ummm," He cleared his throat. "She doesn't know that I know this…and you cannot reach out to her, but ummm, Dena has breast cancer."

I couldn't breathe.

CHAPTER 50: MIA

I could not believe what I had just heard. Gary had taken me on multiple highs and now I was at a low. He told me that my best friend had breast cancer and I couldn't reach out to her.

I reached for my phone. "What do you mean I can't reach out to her?"

He covered my phone with his hand. "Mia, you can't. Monty asked me not to say anything. I need to contact him again before we do anything. Apparently she wants her privacy since she hasn't told us."

Tears and sobs immediately gushed from my face as if someone had flipped a switch. "What do you mean privacy? We don't have privacy at times like these. She needs us, Gary," I screamed. I tried to find her number in my phone again.

He removed the phone from my hand and pulled me into his arms. "Listen, listen. Stop crying. I understand how you feel, baby, but we have to respect her wishes, pray for her, and be there when she's ready."

"What if he's lying and she thinks we've abandoned her?"

"She doesn't think that. We've talked to her and she hasn't said a thing. I went to lunch with her and she didn't say a word. She was cussin' Monty out about making her late for her mammogram."

"Well, why do you think she hasn't told us?"

"I'm not sure, Mia. I'm just not sure. All I know is Monty camped out in my office until I was able to speak to him and he said she really needed someone in addition to him to support her through this and I totally agree. She does."

"Well, why can't I call her then?" I whined.

"I want you to call but you're going to have to calm down." He paused. "And don't chastise her about being married nor about her not telling you. You have to be supportive."

"What?" I shouted. "Yes, I am. She's going to hear from me on both of those. Give me that phone. She'd be doing the same thing. Makes me think I'm not her friend. Who else would support her more than me?"

"Mia, you can't do that." He held her phone out of reach. "We'll call when you calm down."

"Can I text her then?" I huffed. I was just mad. I wanted to scream.

He handed me the phone. I wiped my tears and texted Dena. *Hey Sissy, whatchu doin'?*

"I'll text Monty also," Gary said.

"Okay."

"Wow, that was fast. He said he's still working on her to tell us herself."

I wiped my tears. "Can we pray for her?"

"Sure, baby." He reached for my hands and we both prayed. Fifteen minutes passed and she texted back. *Chillin...whatchu doin?*

Same. I'll be home tomorrow. My knight came to get me. ☺

I knew he would.

☺ *I'll see you tomorrow, okay.*

K

After I finished crying my eyes out and giving Dena a death sentence without knowing the details, we decided to visit my aunt to ask her questions about her experience with breast cancer, her remission, and for advice on how I could support Dena.

"Hi, Auntie. Thank you for allowing us to come over so late," I added as soon as she pushed herself back from a powerful embrace pressing a book into my back.

"Chile, you're fine. Y'all just come on in." She stopped in the center of the floor and turned to look at Gary. "Boy, you are one handsome young man. Who is this twin you got with you?"

"Thank you." He glanced at me. "This is my cousin, Sam. You met him in New York."

She squinted her eyes and raised her glasses as she examined him.

"How are you, Auntie?" Sam chimed in.

"Yeah, that shol' is him. I remember you," she sang. "How you been doing, baby with that deep voice of yours?" She shuffled over to her chair and placed the book on the table.

"I've been good." He grinned.

"So baby, I'm so glad you came to see me again, with your cute self."

"Yes, ma'am." I smiled at her.

"That Sam is handsome, too."

"Thank you, Aunt Edna," Sam added.

"Mia, you look like something is bothering you. What's going on?" Aunt Edna asked.

"Oh, uh. We just found out that my best friend has breast cancer and—"

"Oh baby, I'm so sorry to hear that," she said as she patted my knee.

"I wanted to talk to you about your experience so I'll know how to support her." My eyes became glassy as I tried to fight back tears.

"Baby, there's no need to cry. She will be all right. Do you know if they caught it early?"

"From my understanding, they did," Gary added.

Aunt Edna talked for the next hour sharing her experiences from finding a lump to chemo treatments and radiation to hair loss and pain to remission. I must admit I felt much better about how to support Dena if she wanted it. I couldn't believe she hadn't told us though.

She pointed toward Sam. "Baby, turn that big light on over there. Be careful though, it might shock you. Henry needs to fix that thing but he can't see well enough."

Sam frowned. "Huh, Auntie, are you trying to kill me?"

She fell back laughing. "Chile, no, if I was going to kill you, I'd go straight for it. I wouldn't try to kill you on the sly. I'd just do it."

We laughed and Sam pulled out his cell phone to shine light on the trick light switch. "Let me use my light so I don't commit suicide over here."

"What's going on with the light, Auntie?" Gary asked.

"I don't know. It's a short or something. It won't come on sometimes and sometimes it does."

Sam flicked the light on then off, on then off.

"Well, look at that, it's working now because you're standing over there by it. If I did it, it wouldn't come on at all."

Sam smiled at her. "I know what to do to fix it. Do you have a screwdriver and a knife?"

"Mia, get him a knife out the drawer in there," Aunt Edna said.

"Yes, ma'am." I got up from my seat and Gary replaced me. I could tell he wanted to ask Aunt Edna something. I came back into the room and handed Sam the screwdriver and knife then took my seat next to Gary.

"Gary, how is your mother?" Aunt Edna asked.

"Oh, she's doing well. She asks about you all the time," Gary replied.

"Really? That's good. That's my girl, yes she is. You know I talk to her from time to time. It was so good to connect with her again. I hadn't seen her in years. Well, how's your biological mother?" She rocked back and forth rubbing her knee.

"Oh, she's doing okay, too. We're working on our relationship. We've been hanging out."

"You know God is good. I've been praying for y'all because it's important to know your folks and where you come from. I know your mother's folks. They're from down there where Henry's family is from."

"Which mother, Judy?"

"No, Karen."

"Really?" Gary's voice raised an octave. "What were their names?"

"Same as ours, Chapman, Chapman is the name."

"Really, so Mr. Henry's family are Chapmans not Nixons?" He appeared excited again.

She nodded.

"I'm sorry I'm asking so many questions."

"Oh, you're fine." She rubbed her knee. "You can ask all you like." She smiled at him and then looked at me and winked.

Now I was intrigued. *Did he know what I knew? Why was he asking so many questions about our family? Had he gotten a letter, too? I needed to reveal what I had.*

I took a deep breath. "Wait a minute. I got this in the mail the other day." I handed the paper to Gary.

He scanned the letter and looked at me with a stunned expression. "What is this? Who sent this?" He rubbed his hand over his face.

"What is it?" Aunt Edna fanned her hand in a beckoning gesture.

Gary handed her the paper. He fell back in the chair then leaned forward and stood up.

"Who sent this nonsense, chile?" She frowned and looked up at me. "Desilyn mentioned this nonsense to me, too. I didn't believe her. Who would do such a thing?" She pushed the paper back toward me.

"Auntie, I don't know. Des got it out of their mailbox."

"Lord, have mercy." She shook her head.

Gary was pacing back and forth looking at me then Aunt Edna.

I prayed that it was a practical joke by someone in Houston who didn't care for Gary or me. I did not want to be his cousin and I can promise it would not stop me from loving him.

"Come here, Gary. Sit back down. Sit down, Mia. Let me tell y'all something," Aunt Edna ordered.

Gary trudged every step as if weights were in his shoes. He sat down and rubbed his hand over his face again. I wanted to hug him but I didn't. I wanted to hold him but I couldn't. *What if we were cousins?*

Aunt Edna was shaking her head. "Chile no, you two are not cousins. You two are not related."

I wanted to shout and do a couple of cartwheels but I waited. I wanted to hear more.

Sam turned toward us and frowned. "What the…" He walked over to the couch and sat down next to Gary.

"What is that then?" Gary pointed to the paper dangling from her fingertips.

"Nixon is my side; Mia's dad is my brother. Your mother is down the line related to Chapmans. I ain't related to Henry, just through marriage."

"So?" He looked into the ceiling and then back to her. "My grandma Mabel and grandpa Harold were related to Chapmans down the line."

"No," she replied.

"Because their last name was Walker, well at least my grandfather's name was Walker," Gary said.

She frowned. "No."

His eyebrows furrowed.

She continued, "No, uh, umm, umm."

He raised his right eyebrow.

She continued, "Baby, you are a blessed young man is all I'm going to say. It's so complicated." She shook her head as if she was fighting off something evil.

"Aunt Edna, please, I just want to know my family," Gary pleaded.

"And I need to know if I'm in love with my cousin." That sounded selfish and insensitive but I needed to know why she started stuttering. *What was she not telling?*

Gary continued, "I spent a long time not knowing my family because my adoptive parents and my biological parents decided not to tell me for seventeen years. Please." His eyes were pleading. "Matthews is the name that I use but I know I'm really a James. Vaughn's last name is James and then we get this asinine letter, so I really need to know what you know, Auntie."

My aunt has never been one to mince words. She has always told everybody, everything, just like it was but she did it out of love. Everyone in town knew that truth came from her if she wanted to tell it. People confided in her but she held on to a lot more than she told. She was very influential and on several occasions talked people into telling their truths regardless of how much it hurt. She facilitated the reconciliation of many relationships in our little town.

She stared at Gary for a moment then said, "I'm sorry, Gary." She patted his knees and sighed. "I just don't want you hurt no more than what you've already been."

"I'll be fine, I'm sure."

"I talked to Judy when I was in New York and we've been keeping up ever since. I haven't talked to her in a long time though, maybe a week."

"A week Aunt Edna, really? That's not a long time."

"It is for elderly people. What if you didn't check on me for a whole week and I done died."

"Aunt Edna!" I exclaimed.

"I'm serious." She leaned over and rubbed her knee.

"She has a good point, Mia," Gary added.

"You're right." I smiled as I tried to lighten the mood.

"Well, I'll tell her to call you, Aunt Edna," Gary continued.

She leaned over and patted his knee.

"Aunt Edna, will you tell me, please?" Gary pleaded.

"Okay, here goes. I guess you need to know your folks, baby."

He tilted his head slightly.

"Your mother is not a Walker."

"Huh?"

"Your mother is not a Walker as she thinks. She's a Yancy."

CHAPTER 51: GARY

DID I hear her correctly? My mother is not a Walker as my grandparents were. Oh, my God. I cannot believe this. My biological mother was raised by Harold and Mabel Walker in Brooklyn, New York. She grew up thinking they were her parents but they weren't. I grew up thinking they were my grandparents but they weren't. I wondered if she knew that.

"Baby, I hate to tell you but…" She paused and looked around the room at each of us. "Sometimes family secrets are best kept untold. Your blood family got some crazy shit going on there, baby. I tell you. It sounds like make up. Not real." She rocked back in her chair. "Your mother, Karen, has a brother named Lardell. He's also her uncle because her aunt and brother had the same father, no wait he's her first cousin, too. Oh shit, I don't know. Her daddy was a hoe and slept with several women in the same family. Chile, cheating didn't just start with y'alls generation."

My mouth was agape. "What? Does Karen know this?"

"No, she doesn't know. She doesn't even know who her parents are. After all that mess, Harold and Mabel scooped Karen up and took her to New York with them. I think they lived in

Houston too or maybe it was Dallas. They couldn't have children and they loved Karen like she was their own." She fanned her hand out. "They never told her."

I paused for a minute to gather my thoughts and try to determine my next question.

Mia walked over to me and stood directly in front of me. I adjusted in my chair so she could sit on my lap.

I rubbed my head and she stood up in front of me. *Why did I start asking so many questions? I have some messed up roots.* I buried my head in Mia's abdomen.

"So, I'm not related to Karen in any way?" Mia asked.

"No, you're not, sweetheart. That crazy family." She covered her mouth and looked at me. "I'm sorry, baby. But the Yancys are related to the Chapmans, Henry's family."

Mia whispered in my ear, "This is great news. I love you, baby."

I hugged her and Sam squeezed my shoulder and got up to finish working on the light switch.

"Baby, there's so much about these families down there in Alabama. But your mother made a good life for herself. She's all right and so are you. Forgive her for the wrong she's done. She acted out of love for you. Me and Judy been praying for y'all."

"I understand. So, let me make sure I'm clear. There is no way that I'm related to some Nixons?" Gary asked.

"No. Well not that I know of, not those Nixons anyway." She pointed at Mia.

"Babe, Karen had hinted that you and I were cousins and she even had my new assistant checking into your background."

"What?" She frowned.

"It's cool now; Aunt Edna just cleared it up. God, I'm glad she cleared that up."

"Why didn't you tell me?" Mia said.

"Mia, this man is not going to tell you everything that goes on, you can get used to that," Aunt Edna chimed in.

I wanted to say *just like you didn't tell me about that letter* but thought better of it.

Aunt Edna continued, "If it's going to hurt you, you can forget it, he's going to handle it and tell you 'bout it later if necessary. Do you realize how much that man in there has kept from me so I wouldn't lose my mind or my cool? Count your blessings. He's a protector."

I felt good after my conversation with Mia's Aunt Edna. Here we are thinking that we were two different worlds and our worlds had collided in the south a long time ago. Thank God they hadn't collided in the way we thought they had. She's not my cousin and we don't have to bring that up again. I just hope Mia's Aunt Edna doesn't have her families mixed up or just made the story up to protect our feelings.

Sam remained quiet. He came back and sat down in the chair that was butted up against the sofa.

"Thank you, Aunt Edna," I said.

We heard a knock on the door. Mia sat down close to me.

Mr. Henry walked from the back and answered. A man walked in.

"How you doing, Mr. Henry." He brushed past quickly.

"Whatchu doin' here, boy?" Mr. Henry looked concerned.

Sam stood up. I stood up.

"What's up, young blood," he said to Sam. He turned to me. "What's up, man?"

Mia shifted in her seat then she stood up. "Quan, what are you doing here? What do you want?" She folded her arms.

"I want my money; you know why I'm here."

I stepped in front of Mia because he was walking with purpose in her direction. Sam grabbed him from behind and put him in the Full-Nelson as I immediately searched him for a weapon. He had a gun and a knife. I handed them to Uncle Henry.

"Lord have mercy, Quan. Why would you come up in my house with all of that? Lord have mercy, Jesus," Aunt Edna sang.

Sam slammed him onto the stool and he leaped up and swung at me. I blocked his punch and landed a punch in his gut. Sam put him in the Full-Nelson again.

"That was a sissy punch you got there, Quan." I shook my hand. "So, you're the guy who's trying to blackmail my fiancée? Nice to meet you, Quan. Why do you feel Mia owes you fifteen thousand dollars?"

"Is this who I was out looking for earlier?" Sam asked as he tightened his stance.

"Wait a minute, y'all? She owes you what, Quan?" Aunt Edna looked at Mia. "And don't lie, Quan. How does Mia owe you fifteen thousand dollars? What cost that much?" She shuffled over and stood directly in front of Quan.

"He helped to pay for my last semester of college and…" Mia added as she stepped closer to Aunt Edna. Her hands were visibly shaking. I put my arm around her shoulder.

"It cost fifteen thousand dollars? Back then? I don't believe that." Aunt Edna shook her head and started back to her chair. "Let him go, Sam. She owes you what, Quan?" She walked back toward Quan. She leaned in closely to his face. "I want you to tell that lie up close. She owes you what?"

"She owes me."

"She owes you what? And you better not say fifteen thousand dollars because we gon' have to take it out your ass because she ain't payin' it. And why you come up in here with all those ol' guns and thangs. Probably ain't got no bullets in it." She laughed at herself.

Sam and I were accustomed to scaring people into the truth and hurting them if we had to. We were ready to use the scare tactic but the respect tactic worked much better. We were in Arkansas and Aunt Edna and Uncle Henry had it under control.

I had passed the gun to Uncle Henry. "No, he got some bullets in it. I guess we were gon' play Wild-Wild West, and trust me son, I don't miss."

"Me either and he ain't gon' use 'em anyhow," Aunt Edna scolded.

"Ms. Edna, I wasn't gon' try to use 'em," Quan responded. "It wasn't even in reach."

"I know damn well you wasn't. What would your grandmother say about you down here acting a fool with a gun, lying about somebody owe you some money? You know you didn't like the amount of time you spent in jail the first time. I heard about you. And yo' ass will go right back fooling with my baby or to yo' grave."

Quan lowered his head.

Aunt Edna kept talking, "This girl went on and made a good life for herself in her career, she's doing well. You should be thankful that you were able to bless her. You married Constance, though I can't believe she married you while you were locked up. You should want that for somebody else." She turned to Mia and whispered, "Do you have the money to pay this fool?"

"I paid him already," Mia added.

"No, you didn't. I didn't cash that check. I tore it up," Quan barked as Sam eased his grip. "Nah, you don't have to pay me nothing." He glared at Mia.

"Well, why in the hell are you here then? Are you crazy?" Aunt Edna scolded. "Oh yeah, she gon' pay you. 'Cause we don't

want you comin' around here talking this nonsense ever again."
She shuffled her way to the phone. "I'm calling your grandma."

"Yeah, you're right. We don't have to pay you because one
phone call will have you back in the cell with Bunky. You
enjoyed being cot mates with him, didn't you?" I leaned in then
stood back and folded my arms.

He started trembling and breathing heavily.

Mia's eyes widened and her mouth opened. Aunt Edna
couldn't hold her shocked expression. "Sayyyy whaaaattt?"

I almost laughed.

I kept talking, I needed him to know about all of the information I had found on him. "And one more thing." I leaned in
to speak in his ear. "I could send you right back to prison with
this gun charge, and guess what? Levell will be right back in the
bed with yo' wife. But you don't care, do you? Because Bunky
is still down there and you like the way he made you feel, huh?"

He still had no words. His eyes had turned red and his heavy
breathing continued.

"So, tell me, how much does Mia owe you?"

"Nothing," he mumbled.

"Oh, really. Nothing? Now, how is that? Mia, was it a gift he
gave you?"

She didn't speak so I turned toward her. "Mia, did he give
you the money as a gift?" I walked around and pretended I was
in a court room and Mia was on the witness stand.

"Yes, that's what I thought it was."

"But do you remember? Is that what he said? It was a gift?"

"Yes."

"Oh. Can you recall that day for us, Mia?"

She huffed slightly. "I told him that I wasn't going to be able
to finish school because me nor my parents had the money.

When he first offered, I said no, I'd figure it out. He said no, I'm giving it to you as a gift because we're friends and he wanted me to do well with my life."

"Do you recall that same scenario, Quan?" He had long stopped fighting with Sam to get out of the Full-Nelson.

"Yeah."

"But you entered the home of an elderly couple, headed straight for my fiancée with a gun and a knife on your person? Is that correct, Quan?"

"Yeah."

"So, technically, they can call the cops right now and have you arrested and that'll be it for your freedom, right, Quan?"

"Yeah."

"Then why on earth would you do that, Quan?"

"Because, I wanted Mia."

"How is that, Quan when you know you're married? And, you know Mia is engaged to someone else? What did you want with Mia?" I questioned.

"I'm calling his wife, is what I'm gon' do," Aunt Edna piped in.

"I'm sayin', I wanted her back then, I'm not talkin' 'bout now," Quan explained.

"Oh, should I be excited because you don't want her now?"

"I ain' sayin' that, bro."

"Mia belongs to me. Anything you want from her, anything she owes you, you come to me. No more threatening, no more blackmail. Understand?"

"Yeah."

"Uncle Henry, Aunt Edna, what do you think we should do? Should we call the cops to have him go back to prison? Or do you trust him enough that he wouldn't come back around here trying to harm you all again?"

Aunt Edna chimed in, "No, I don't trust him."

Uncle Henry added, "Send him to jail. I don't trust any of them."

Aunt Edna called 9-1-1 and the cops came to get Quan. His grandmother showed up and his wife. I slipped his wife a cashier's check and told her what it was for and prayed we didn't hear from them ever again.

CHAPTER 52: MIA

WE arrived back in Houston on Saturday afternoon to rainy and sunny skies; away from my issues in Arkansas and back into Gary's issues.

I had begged Gary to go straight to the dealership to get my new car. Sam dropped us off and we drove away in my new wheels. I loved it.

We stopped in the bookstore, one of my favorite past times. I was addicted to books, addicted to reading, addicted to shoes, and handbags. I stopped at the book store at least once per week, if only for ten minutes.

This time I wanted to do some research on breast cancer. I had searched the internet thoroughly enough but I ran across a couple of book titles that would provide more details in the area of supporting an individual. I attempted to connect with Dena several times but she was not responding and I was worried. Monty wasn't answering either. I thought maybe he'd answer Gary's call but he hadn't yet.

Gary and I walked in and went our separate ways. Gary looked at magazines and the biography aisle. I found my way to the nutrition and health area, located several books I had found in my research and plopped down in the chair at the end of the aisle. I placed my purse and all of the books on the table, then pulled out my phone and called Dena's number and took a deep breath. Monty answered.

"Hey, Monty. It's Mia."

"Hey, Mia. How are you doing?"

"I'm okay." I didn't know whether I should say I'm fine, I'm doing well, I'm great, or what. I was confused under the circumstances I was calling. I had texted with my best friend but I had not spoken to her since I found out she had breast cancer. "How are you? Where's Dena?"

"She's resting. She had her first chemo treatment yesterday and she's not up to talking or anything. She said she was nauseous. She asked me not to mess with her for any reason."

Tears filled my eyes and I could barely speak. "But I told her I was coming home today and I was coming to see her."

"Mia, don't cry. She's going to beat this thing. You know she's a fighter in a lot of ways. She'll get past this."

"Okay."

"How much has Gary told you?"

"Everything I guess. He told me she has breast cancer and they caught it early. He also told me you all are married."

"Yeah, we got married at the justice of the peace."

I sniffed.

"But, we're really happy, Mia. We were doing fine until this came up and she shut down. She gets a little feisty at times but I'm trying my best to support her. We'll beat this, Mia. You have to be strong when you and Gary come over."

"Okay. I will." I sniffed again and wiped tears with the back of my hand.

"I'll check with her and text you, okay?"

"Okay. Thanks, Monty. I appreciate it."

"No problem."

We hung up and I sat in the chair at the end of the aisle and cried. I eventually pulled myself together and forty-five minutes later, Gary and I ended up on the same aisle. I heard him bark, "Look, you need to stay your lying ass away from me."

I rounded the corner and he almost mowed me over exiting the aisle.

I saw a tall, blond, and voluptuous Caucasian woman leaned on the shelf. I could tell they knew each other by her body language.

"So, I guess you're ready to go? I have a couple of additional books I don't need. Dena would be proud of what I have become in a matter of minutes—an expert." I strained a smile.

"You ready to go?" I said.

"Yeah, let's get out of here," Gary replied.

"Oh, what do you have?" The lady Gary was arguing with said as she made her way toward us and reached for the books.

I took a step back. "Ummm, who are you?" I asked puzzled.

"Mia, this is Sharon, someone I knew from college in Seattle. She knows Karen also."

"Hi, pleasure to meet you." She extended her hand and I looked at it then back at her.

"Sharon, this is Mia, the love of my life, my fiancée."

"It's very nice to finally meet you, Mia." She bit the corner of her lip.

Finally meet me? Did they just meet up here or is this happenstance they are here at the same time? Had I become so predictable that he knew he'd have a minimum of thirty minutes uninterrupted so he asked her to meet him? Did I just catch my fiancé in the act? Or is this an innocent encounter? There is never an innocent encounter.

I was still looking at Gary waiting on him to explain some more about this aggressive woman he knows from college. *Who is Sharon Stevens? Could she be another Roni?* I didn't want to sound as insecure as I felt at the moment. I know I ran away from Gary a few times. I know he has needs. I know he's attractive. I know he's approachable. But this is different. This is history. All I know is I'm not running away again. This time, there will be some fight in me.

"It's a pleasure to meet you, Mia." She stepped closer to Gary as if she was with him. He stepped away from her giving a frustrated expression.

"Likewise, Sharon," I said straight-faced with no emotion.

She stood there. Silent. Staring.

CHAPTER 53: GARY

MIA and Sharon had gone into a standoff. Mia certainly didn't deserve this. I went to Sharon's hotel room a few weeks ago. I did not sleep with her although I wanted to just to feel the walls of a vagina wrapped around my penis. I came to my senses and stopped myself so that I wouldn't end up in a situation like this. I had gone back home and jacked off again. I thought she had left town and she showed up here today telling me that I disrespected her again and leaving without calling. She wanted revenge.

"Listen, Mia, I love Gary just as much as you do." Sharon exited the aisle we were standing in.

Mia folded her arms and said, "I tell you what. I will not deal with another bitch about you."

"No, no, no, there's nothing to deal with. Let's go." I gently touched Mia's arm to guide her out of the store.

She snatched her arm away from me and stormed away, yelling, "I will not go through this again!"

"Come on, Mia."

I grabbed my head. This was so crazy. I was simply looking at some biography books and Sharon walked into the aisle where I was standing. I tried my best not to acknowledge her and she kept talking until Mia walked around the corner. That last statement she yelled, I was shocked and embarrassed. She did not love me. She could not love me.

Luckily no one was at check-out. Mia paid for her books and stormed out the store. I caught up to her and we made it to the car without saying a single word. She appeared mad enough to fight. I knew she was pissed because she walked to the passenger side of her new car and got in. I walked toward her door to make sure it was closed, then walked around the car and got in.

I noticed her hand move toward her face several times. *Shit, she's crying.*

I reached over and squeezed her thigh. "Mia, baby, things are not what they appeared in that store. I don't want Sharon. She showed up in town to see Karen." I was not going to tell her the complete story until I had to. There was no need.

I slowed toward a yellow light and stopped instead of speeding up as I had in the past.

I continued talking. "I want you and you only. I don't know what it's going to take for you to believe that. I sincerely do not want to be with anyone else. I want you. I love you." The light changed and I pressed the gas pedal lightly. "Sharon was a friend to me in law school, a good friend. We used to study together."

She looked at me and blinked and a tear rolled down her cheek. I turned away.

"Mia, what man would profess his love for a woman and do all the things I'm trying to do for you and still have women on the side? That's crazy."

Her eyes shot daggers in my direction.

"Okay, Mia that may have been a bone-headed comment but I'm not that guy. I'm not the cheater, the womanizer. You know that already. I want to be with one woman." I pointed one finger upward on the steering wheel. "And I need you to understand that."

We arrived home within thirty minutes of leaving the store. The trip was usually ten to fifteen minutes but I drove slowly so I could talk to her.

She got out before the car came to a complete stop and I had to hurriedly put the car in park, hop out, and make it to the door before she did. I moved swiftly and I made it.

"Mia." I wrapped my arms around her.

She burst into tears. "Gary, move. Let me go. Just let me go." She tried to push me away.

I released one hand to push the button so the garage would go down.

"Mia, hold on. I'm not letting you go." I pulled her closer and she cried harder trying to push me away. "Baby, calm down. Please. I honestly do not know where the hell that came from. I had no idea she felt any kind of way about me," I lied.

Sharon had expressed interest since the moment she arrived in town. I needed to make sure Mia knew that I loved her and only her. I was not about to let her run away again. The moment at the cemetery was the final offer for us. I would not continue to go down the path we had gone for almost two years.

She stopped crying, wiped her face with both hands, and said, "I'm fine. I'm fine."

I let her go slowly. I studied her face as I opened the door to let her into the house. She walked to our bedroom. I knew exactly what she was getting ready to do.

CHAPTER 54: MIA

I did not understand what I was feeling at the moment. I was pregnant and Gary didn't know it. I had to think about that when I was in the store because I refused to physically harm myself or my baby. I was emotional because my best friend had breast cancer and I was waiting on a text message for permission to go see her.

Gary walked into the room and I turned to him. "Gary, I'm not running anymore. My first thought was to switch out the clothes in my luggage and give up. But I'm never giving up. I'm not running anymore."

He looked toward the ceiling. "Oh, thank God."

"I'm not going to fight either but I'll kill her."

"Mia, don't say that. You don't have to fight or kill."

"I'm just telling you. That's how I feel right now."

"Mia, I'm so sorry." He reached for my hand. "I promise you there's nothing there. I'm sure my word means nothing to you right now, especially after this happened, but I promise I have nothing for Sharon."

I took a deep breath. "I'm not losing another baby, Gary."

"Wait, what? Another baby? Are you pregnant?" His eyes beamed.

I nodded my head as I smiled through my swollen eyes.

He scooped me up and lifted me off the floor. "Oh my God, Mia, that's great news. How do you know?" He started examining me.

"My sister and Aunt Edna had been saying it from the moment I arrived in Arkansas and I've had a little bit of morning sickness and of course my period is late."

"Let's go get a test." He rejoiced. "Let's go."

His phone buzzed. "Let's go," he said again as he looked at the phone. "Oh, it's Monty. Hold on a sec."

He read the text message. *Hey, G man tell Mia Dena is not feelin' well after her treatment yesterday and don't want visitors. I'll let her know 2morrw if she feels better.*

I turned the phone so Mia could read the text. She started sobbing uncontrollably. "Gary, what should I do? My best friend doesn't want us to support her."

"Baby, that's not it."

We heard a knock and both of us looked toward the door.

"May I come in?" Sam leaned his head into the room.

"Yeah, what's up?" Gary turned to him.

"I couldn't help but overhear." He walked over to me and placed his hand on my shoulder. "Mia, it's not you. It's her. My grandmother passed away from breast cancer." His voiced cracked.

"Sam, I'm so sorry to hear that," I whined.

"Thanks. I remember watching the side-effects of that chemo and it's tough. Some days it'll have her messed up. Sometimes nauseous, sometimes her skin hurts to touch, sometimes diarrhea, sometimes constipation, you name it. It was always something but it had her feeling bad right after the chemo."

"Thank you, Sam. I understand," I lied. While I was thankful he was shedding some light on the situation. I didn't understand why my best friend who's been with me through everything doesn't want me around. I wanted her to know I would be there with her.

"It's not you. She wants the support; it's just how she feels physically. But then again you know Dena. She's not one for pity parties."

"And probably the best way to avoid that is to not have visitors," Gary added.

"I get it." I sniffed and wiped my face with both hands.

"Come here. Maybe you should lie down for a few minutes. Come on. We can go to the store later."

"What do you need at the store? I can go get it. By the way, I left your luggage in the laundry room."

"Okay, thanks, man. I'll get it," Gary replied.

"What do you need at the store?"

We both looked at Sam. Gary paused as he looked at Sam then at me. "Can I tell him?"

I nodded.

"We need a pregnancy test."

Sam grinned widely, laughed heartily, and rushed toward Gary and pulled him into an embrace and slapped him on the back.

He pointed at me. "I'll be right back." He rushed toward the door. "Can I get you anything else? Food, drinks, cigars?"

"Yes, all of that."

We took a bath and sat in the tub until our skin was wrinkled, both of us falling asleep. We got out of the tub when we heard the garage door. Gary dressed quickly and went to meet Sam. I chugged a bottle of water and stretched out on the bed and watched TV. He walked back into the room twenty minutes later with four pregnancy tests.

"Oh my goodness, Sam couldn't decide." I laughed.

"He said he wanted to be sure. Are you ready?"

"Yes. We can do two today and two tomorrow."

"Okay, go for it." He sat on the edge of the bed as I walked toward the bathroom, then he followed me and leaned against the sink.

I emerged a few minutes later and ran into him standing at the door. "Oh my goodness, you may as well have been in there with me."

"I was close." He reached for the test.

I handed it to him. "A big ole plus sign."

He pulled me and kissed me so tenderly it made my knees buckle.

CHAPTER 55: GARY

HOW many times should I forgive someone who sins against me? I thought about that scripture many times as I struggled to obey it. I needed to do it because it was not only the right thing to do but also because I knew Karen could get away with a lot more than I could. And I needed her to take care of a couple of people for me whom she already had on her list. Mia was pregnant and I didn't need one ounce of stress headed in her direction by Nina or Sharon. I think my threat to Nina took care of her but I couldn't be too sure.

Karen wasn't going to leave her husband for slapping her in public and I couldn't make her. She said he had never hit her so I let it go. Wanting a divorce and actually filing were two different things. Apparently emotional abandonment could affect alimony. Chandler knew she had a son but didn't have a clue what I looked like, which is why she claimed he acted out. She never addressed the issue of him hating her.

We played golf and discussed her marriage and a boatload of other things including her biological parents.

I drove the ball over three hundred yards. "Damnit, I put too much power on that one," I mumbled as I watched the ball land underneath a tree.

"Good shot." She smiled. "You are really good."

"I'm working on it. Trying to be like you."

"Oh stop it." She blushed.

We walked back to the cart.

She said, "As I was saying, everybody thought I didn't know who my parents were. I always knew something was not right with that entire family. That's why I stayed as far away from them as I possibly could. Nothing escapes my inquisitive spirit, sweetheart. My parents told me a long time ago and I considered them my parents and didn't acknowledge my biological parents. So I guess all I've experienced with you, I had it coming. Karma."

I remained quiet and listened.

"Gary, I never meant you any harm, although sometimes, I made Vaughn think I would because he always acted as if his love for you was so much greater than mine." She got off the cart to set up her drive.

"Hmph." I got off the cart and walked over to the box with her. "Why did he think that?"

"I don't know, Gary. Pompous I guess. Both of us were wrong. He was married and didn't tell me and I was messing with an older gentleman against my mother's wishes."

"What made you start messing around with him again? You're married now and he's well, engaged," We walked back to the cart.

"Love. I never stopped loving Vaughn. Never. I don't know why."

"Was he your first?" I couldn't believe I asked my mother that question but it was out now.

She made a playful gasped and clutched the collar of her shirt. "I'm not telling."

I smiled and pressed the pedal on the golf cart.

"Do you have dinner plans tonight?" she asked.

"No. Mia and I just plan to watch movies."

"Why didn't you bring her today?"

"Karen, can I tell you something? You have to promise me you won't say anything until I let you know that you can." This was me and Mia's first test to see if we could trust her. We discussed it before I left.

She sat up straight and turned toward me. "Yes, of course you can."

"Mia is pregnant."

"Oh, my. Oh, my God. Oh my, Gary, that is wonderful. Oh, my God. I'm so thrilled to hear that." Her excitement appeared genuine. Her eyes turned glassy.

After she stopped beaming, we walked to find our balls and took a swing to get it on the greens. After she hit her ball, she trotted toward the greens and I drove the cart. She squatted down to get her angle and with one stroke her ball went into the hole.

"Good shot." I pushed my fist toward hers.

"You know Alex was the one who sent that letter to Mia. I was being sneaky but he was worse than me. I had to let him go. He was too much. I fired him and I needed him more than ever this past week but I realized I'd have to hire someone else. I attend at least one women's business retreat every year and I can't wait to get there and connect with my friends and foes but I had to prepare for it alone. It's inspirational, renewing, refreshing, and so much fun and there's always a new corporate buzz phrase or something everyone is harping on, but I love that, too."

I ignored all of her comments prior to the retreat comment. I didn't want my mood to change. "Where is it?" I inquired.

"It's in Naples, Florida. You and Mia should join me at the end of the week. I can get my travel agent to set it up for you. It's at the Ritz. I'm sure you can get a direct flight into Fort Myers."

"What is there to do on the weekend?"

"Honey, relax, sit on the beach in a bikini or sit by the pool, take in some sun rays, just unwind."

"Sounds nice."

"Yes, I assure you it is. And you know the Ritz's staff is phenomenal. They get what you need before you ask."

"Yes, I know."

"Why don't you and Mia come for dinner tonight at my house?"

"Ummm."

"Oh come on, Gary. You haven't met Breleigh formally and you need to really get to know Chandler. You might like him."

"I don't want to like him, though."

"Gary, oh, stop it."

"Can V come too?"

"Oh, you are a mess. Let's go in. It's starting to rain."

CHAPTER 56: GARY

MIA and I got dressed and went to Karen's for dinner. I had briefed her on every encounter I had while she was away. My goal was to minimize any potential stress she could experience that evening including the part where I met Sharon at the bar and then later on went to her hotel room. I was torn about telling her about the hotel room. Although nothing happened, Mia probably wouldn't believe me.

Chandler and Karen greeted us at the door.

Karen hugged Mia and pushed back and hugged her again. Mia handed Karen some fresh flowers. I leaned in and kissed Karen on the cheek then shook Chandler's hand. I handed him a box of cigars. I purposely left the alcohol off the list.

"Mia, thank you so much. These are beautiful. You two come on in."

Chandler added, "Thanks for the cigars. These are my favorites."

"Chandler, you finally get to meet my son. This is Gary."

"Please to meet you, Gary." He appeared nervous. "Welcome to our home. Both of you." He nodded toward Mia and smiled.

Was this the same guy I punched in the face? I agreed to dinner with them but I still didn't trust them one hundred percent. I was strapped.

We walked into a formal living area. Their home was immaculate.

"Your home is beautiful." Mia beamed.

"Oh, thank you, Mia," Karen chimed.

We kept the conversation light. We talked for a few minutes about sports. I guess Karen was trying to get Chandler to settle in.

I noticed a little girl running down the stairs so fast she almost tumbled.

"Be careful, sweetheart. Come on over, we have someone we want you to meet." Chandler reached for her hand.

"Come here, sweetheart." Karen hugged her.

Breleigh bounced out of the room. "She has a lot of energy," I said.

"Yes, she does," Chandler exclaimed.

Karen leaned over and said something to Chandler and he said, "Breleigh come here, sweetheart. We have something we want to share with you."

She did cartwheels from the foyer all the way to the sofa. Mia laughed. "I love her energy."

"It can wear on you. Maybe Chandler and I waited too long. Breleigh, honey, please walk."

"Yes, ma'am," she whined.

"There's a story about someone in this room that I think you'd be delighted to know," Karen said.

"What's that?" She twisted her body from side to side looking at Mia then me.

Karen's eyes sparkled, "Sweetheart, this is Gary, your brother."

She covered her mouth with both hands to contain her excitement and her eyes looked like two large marbles. "Mommy, are you for real?"

"Yes, I'm for real." Karen laughed.

She looked at Chandler and he said, "I agree, Breleigh. Gary is your brother."

She was frozen in place for a second then she stumbled toward me and fell into my arms. "You're my big brother. I've always wanted a brother."

"Well, now you have one." I hugged her. I could not believe the instant love I felt for her as I hugged her. I now had someone else to love and protect.

Karen held up her phone to take pictures.

"Is this your wife?" Breleigh asked Gary.

"Soon to be wife," Gary replied.

"She's pretty." She reached over to Mia for a hug.

"Thank you, Breleigh. Breleigh is a beautiful name for a beautiful little girl," Mia said.

Breleigh grinned widely "Mommy, I'm so happy I have a brother. Does that make her my sister?" She rested her arm around Gary's shoulder.

"Yes, her name is Mia," Karen said.

"Yes! I have a brother and a sister. Can I come to your house?"

"Yes, we can make that happen in the future," I added.

We enjoyed dinner and fellowship until Chandler brought up purchasing Matthews & Jefferson and that was my queue to exit. I didn't realize his partner was the guy who accosted me in the parking lot at Pappadeaux's until he revealed it during dinner. Karen scolded him for that and I'm not sure how their night ended.

CHAPTER 57: GARY

A month had passed since dinner with Karen and Chandler, and Mia and I were getting dropped off at Intercontinental Airport on our way to Naples, Florida to enjoy a weekend with them if Chandler decided to show up.

It's true, men can be so stupid and succumb to the powers of a woman no matter the relationship. I was once determined to ignore my biological mother, determined to ignore the pressure and encouragement to get to know her from my mom, Judy, the woman who raised me, and I wanted to ignore the marriage counselor who was also pushing the same agenda—build a better relationship with my biological mother. An all expense paid trip to Florida to relax and golf probably clouded my judgment a bit but my determination fizzled and I acquiesced. It was the right thing to do.

The flight was uneventful. Karen arranged for a car to pick us up at the airport. The car pulled into the drop-off area of the Ritz Carlton Beach Resort. The bellman pulled my door open before the car came to a complete stop.

"Hello, sir. Checking in?" he asked.

"Yes, we are."

"How are you doing today?" He held the door until I stepped out of the car.

I nodded. "Doing great, sir. How are you?"

"Couldn't be better." He stood to the side as I tipped the driver. I walked around the car to assist Mia. The other bellman already had the door open but she waited until I walked around to take her hand.

I leaned into the car for a final check for items as I asked her, "You good? You get everything?"

"Yes, I think I did."

"If you step over here, we'll take care of your luggage for you," the bellman said.

I put my hand in the small of her back and guided her inside.

The place was buzzing inside and out with a lot of African-American business woman with designer clothes, shoes, and bags. A lot of them had on the same bedazzled t-shirts and hats as they bid each other adieu. I didn't expect anything less especially since my mother was always raving about her conference and her friends.

I was pleasantly surprised I hadn't seen her saunter through the crowd to find us.

We walked across a massive and elegant entrance to registration and stood in line for several minutes. After what seemed like fifteen minutes, I stepped up to the counter and handed the lady my license and credit card. "Matthews."

"Mr. Matthews, welcome to the Ritz-Carlton. I show two adults will be staying with us for two nights."

"Yes."

"Oh, Mr. Matthews, this card you gave me is…" Her eyes widened and darted back and forth between the monitor and me.

"Is what?"

"It's not working." She swiped it again.

"Babe, did you bring your other card?" Mia asked as I was embarrassed and becoming more aggravated at every breath I took. I didn't know if this lady was playing a trick or if Karen had played one. "No, just my debit card."

"Here, I'll put it on mine. We don't want them to put a hold on your debit card." Mia handed the lady her card and driver's license as I stepped away to contact my credit card company. If there was really such a thing as blood boiling, I believe mine was.

It took a few phone prompts and entries to get to a representative but I finally spoke to someone and she said my card had been cancelled. I almost dropped my phone. "Who cancelled my damn card?" I was trying to keep my voice low and my temper under control. I walked toward a bar area that was closed near the exit.

"Sir, it shows here that you did. There's a note that shows cancelled by the card holder. It was a few days ago."

"No, I did not cancel my card. Why would I do that?" I asked

"Sir, people cancel cards all the time."

I sighed heavily. "What do I need to do to reactivate my card?"

I felt so stupid. I know Karen had something to do with this. I'm sure she had my social security number and everything. My monitoring service I have on my credit card always alerted me when someone was trying to obtain credit or check my credit but I don't recall getting a cancelled card notification. I talked the representative and her supervisor into issuing a new card but that was doing me no good now. The card would arrive at my home in a few days. They acknowledged how long I had been a customer, how much I paid them on a monthly basis, and apologized profusely for the mix-up. I ended the call and walked back to Mia standing and chatting with some of the women as they tasted all the beverages displayed on the credenza. She handed me a cup of water.

"You okay? Taste this, it's really good."

I took the cup from her hand, took one gulp, swallowed, and tossed the cup in the trash. "Yes, I'm good. They're sending me another card."

"Okay, well, I used my card for incidentals and we'll use our debit cards and cash for anything else we need. Your mom paid for the room already so we're all set."

"Karen paid for the room and I bet she cancelled my card, too." I shook my head. "Let's go, I need a damn drink." I guided her and headed toward the elevator.

"They moved us to a bigger room with an ocean view."

"That's cool," I mumbled.

Before we reached the elevator corridor, I heard Karen's voice. "Oh, here you two are."

We stopped to turn toward her.

"I have looked everywhere. I wanted to greet you when you arrived. Welcome." She spread her arms with an inviting motion. She reached out to hug Mia then hugged me. "I'm so happy you all could make it."

I was glaring at her trying to determine if she was behind the credit card saga or someone else. "What did you do?" I asked calmly.

What? Is there a problem with your room? They can connect your incidentals with mine. Let's go over here," Karen said.

"How did you know there would be a problem, Karen. Did you cancel my card?" I barked.

"Oh heavens no, I did no such thing." Karen placed her hand over her chest. "Why would I do that, Gary? I brought you here to relax, not stress you out. I want to spend some time with you and Mia, and I want you to meet my friends."

"I don't wanna meet your friends," I barked again.

Karen threw up her hands and stormed away.

"I told you that wouldn't work." I heard a lady who she did not introduce tell her.

I was close to grabbing one of the apples on the desk and hurling it at her head.

"Gary, honey, come on. Let's just go to the room." Mia tried to pull me away.

I started walking toward the elevator. The bellman had told us he'd bring our bags up shortly and I wanted to be there when he did.

"She had my credit card cancelled so we'd have to depend on her for everything during this damn trip," I said after the elevator door closed. "Baby, I'm so glad you're with me because I promise, I was about to throw one of those apples at her."

Mia guffawed. "Baby, no you would not. I would not let you do that."

Her laughter almost made me smile but I was too upset to do so.

"Baby don't worry about it, I had my card with me."

"It's not about that, Mia. She cancelled my credit card. What if I would've been at dinner with one of my clients?"

"But you weren't. It didn't play out that way. Did you get it straightened out?"

"Yes," I said in a tone that was not meant for Mia.

She frowned.

"I'm sorry. I'm so sorry. You know I do not talk to you in that tone. I'm sorry."

We arrived at the fourteenth floor and I grabbed her hand. "Where's the key?" We walked down the long corridor to our room with the ocean view.

CHAPTER 58: MIA

GARY was on the phone with his mother for a few minutes after we got in the room. She still denied cancelling his credit card. I believe she got caught up or she's just plain evil. She went too far in trying to get to know him. I couldn't believe she went that far though.

I heard him ask her, "Karen, do you pray? Do you even go to church?" He didn't give her a chance to answer. "See that's part of your problem. You think your money is your power and that you got it on your own volition and I'm sure some scheming, too. Just like you got all this money, you can lose it. You can't control everybody with your money, Karen. My God."

I closed the door to the bathroom and turned the water on to drown out the conversation. I felt bad for Karen. I really thought something was mentally wrong with her; some days she appeared normal and some days it seemed she had overmedicated or under medicated. I had spoken to her over the phone after we came from Arkansas. I mentioned my Aunt Edna had verified we were not cousins and she appeared deflated. She mumbled, "Your aunt was lying." Her comment really hurt my feelings but I never mentioned it to Gary. He was already on a slippery slope trying to get to know her and I didn't want to be the reason he changed his mind.

I took a quick shower, pulled on the robe, and slid my feet into the slippers provided by the hotel. I loved staying at the Ritz-Carlton. I'm sure Gary allowed Karen to speak some but he was still going when I walked out of the bathroom.

"Why would you imply that I was about to marry my cousin? You couldn't just come out and say it; you had to keep hinting at it and had your little flaming assistant snooping around my office." He growled. "Why can't you be like a normal mother and be genuine and not devious? My God, I feel sorry for Breleigh."

I didn't want to hear any more of that conversation so I walked across the room as Gary watched me. I struggled to open the door leading to the balcony. He rushed over to open the door for me.

"I have to go, Karen. I'll talk to you later," he said abruptly and tossed the phone on the bed.

"Come here." He pulled me close and buried his head in my neck. I giggled. "I promise you, this will be a relaxing trip for both of us. Even if we have to change hotels."

My eyes widened. "Ummm, there's a golf resort down the street." I pointed in the direction. "You would love that, wouldn't you?"

He winked and buried his head into my neck again. I allowed it for a few minutes then wiggled from his grasp and we walked over to look out the patio door. He opened the door and I stepped out.

"Are you okay?" I asked.

"Yeah, I'm good. I'm sorry for all of that. I'm trying, I'm really trying." He moaned. "But she is making it so difficult."

I kept all of my comments to myself because they were not nice. I prayed she'd seek help for her issues. I hoped he'd one day be able to develop a good relationship with her. That was my prayer anyway.

"Babe, would you still want to marry me if we were cousins?"

"Ehhhh, Gary, I'm pregnant. I think it would've been too late for that question."

"Not necessarily." He raised his eyebrow.

"What about you?" I returned the question.

"I don't know but I'm in love now. It would've been too late to stop it. I think." He looked out across the property.

I paused, thinking about the comment his mother had mumbled about my Aunt Edna. "I know Aunt Edna loves me like her daughter and I sometimes wonder if she made the whole story up about Karen's family to keep me away from heartache."

"Mia, no she did not. She would not do that."

"I pray not."

He pulled me close to him. "Like I said, I'm in love now. It would've been too late to stop it." He planted a kiss on my forehead.

"It's easy to say it now, though, because that's not the case but if we were indeed cousins, I think both of us would've been gagging, honey."

He grunted, kissed me again, and squeezed both of my butt cheeks. "Yep, I think you're right." He walked back into the room to put on his robe also. "I need to take a shower, too."

"Baby, let's just get married and not wait or plan or gather all of these people," I blurted out as I stood up and ran my fingers across the terracotta painted rail.

He turned to me and frowned. "Are you sure?" He paused then shook his head. "No. We can't do that."

I held up my ring finger. "Why not?" I turned the chair and plopped down and put my feet on the table.

He stepped onto the balcony and sat down in the chair bedside me. He wiggled it to test the sturdiness of it. "Where'd that come from?"

"I just think it's going to be too much drama with planning, organizing, and everything."

He started laughing and grabbed my hand. "I thought Dena was planning our wedding? You think Karen is going to take over, don't you?"

I smiled. "Yes."

"Well, we won't let her."

"I can see her and Dena now." I shook my head then pumped my fists together and fanned my hands in the air. "Explosion."

He lowered his eyes and smiled. "We can't let that happen. How have you imagined your wedding day? Describe it for me."

"Well, I've imagined it for years. It used to be a dress with the train from the altar to the door and my groom is brought to tears when he sees me walking down the aisle as fourteen bridesmaids, fourteen groomsmen, and our three hundred guests look on."

He raised his right eyebrow. I swatted his hand. "I wanted lots of bridesmaids and groomsmen, flower girls, ring bearer, fresh flowers in every nook and cranny, friends and family who are so happy for us."

"And apparently lots of guests, but if that's what you've always dreamed of, then you should have that. Why settle?" he insisted.

"Well, the older I've gotten, the more weddings I've been in, the less hassle I desire on my wedding day. I realized that back then, I wanted all of that as a show for other people. I'm not sure what I wanted to prove but after all I've experienced, I just want me and my groom saying I do."

He nodded as his eyes scanned out over the ocean. "That's understandable. Five years from now, do you think you'll regret it?"

"No, I really don't."

"You're not planning to spend money renewing our vows every year, are you?"

"No." I smiled.

He stood up when he heard a knock on the door. "But, you shouldn't destroy your dream because of other people. Make it what you want. Please don't change your desires because of Karen." He stepped back into the room and headed toward the door. "Call Dena."

"Well, I think it'll be less stress for both of us if we kept it small." I called out to him as I scooted down in my chair, leaned my head back, and closed my eyes for a moment.

I heard the door open and Karen sang, "Heyyyyyy, we're headed to the pool. You two want to come?"

"Nah, Mia is not dressed and we were in the middle of a discussion."

"Oh, what are you talking about?" she asked.

I was quite surprised that she had asked that question. I heard a pause. I just knew "none of your business" was coming next until I heard, "Our wedding."

She must have made an attempt to enter the room because I heard, "Mia is not dressed. We'll see you when you come from the pool."

"Oh. Okay." Her voice spoke surprise.

"Okay, we'll see you later."

Gary stepped back onto the balcony. "Did you call Dena?"

"Oh, no, I didn't." I sat up and placed my feet on the floor. "Gary, I was so happy when we got the opportunity to visit her."

"Yeah, me too."

"I tried to control my tears but I couldn't," I reminisced.

He snorted. "I know. You couldn't? You sure didn't."

"She was stronger than I was. After she told you, Sam, and Monty to leave the room, she said, 'Look little girl, you're gonna have to get it together. The only reason I'm allowing you in here crying and carrying on is because you haven't had the same amount of time as I've had to come to grips and deal with it. I'm fine. I will be back to my healthy self soon. My mind is still healthy. God has not failed me. Everything happens for a reason.'"

"Yeah, she's giving Monty hell though."

"Really?" I lowered my eyes.

"I know deep down she feels like she's going to beat this, but when she's in pain, he's hearing and feeling a different side than what we experienced when we were there. That's why he came to my office to tell me. He needed relief that particular day. I was glad to hear him say that there's nothing she can do that will make him not love her and support her."

"Good. Because I don't want to have to hurt him."

He twisted his mouth. "You ain't gon' hurt nobody," he said playfully. "And I didn't wanna have to kill him."

"Yes, I will. And you ain't gon' kill nobody," I mocked him.

"Okay, Mia."

"She was like, 'get it together Mia' and I was like 'okay, okay' through my tears." I paused. "Although she had lost all of her hair, she was still beautiful and her spirits were up. She said she was not about self-torture so she shaved her head. Well, Monty shaved it. She wasn't gonna sit there day after day just watching it fall out."

"She told me Monty has been great though. She wanted us to think he wasn't. All those times when she pretended to be mad at him, she was really mad at breast cancer. She has known this for a minute and she hadn't said a thing."

"I know." I groaned.

"Okay, change the subject, I see the tears coming. She was happy to hear about the baby, though."

"Yes, she was. I can't believe she sold her house and moved."

"I think we should do the same thing, a whole different city," he responded. He grabbed my chair with both hands and pulled it toward him. "What do you think?"

"I'd moved anywhere with you, Gary." I smirked then pulled my phone out and dialed Dena's number. Both of us leaned forward on the table as I activated the speaker phone.

"Hey, Miss Missy. What's up?" she answered her voice was strong.

"Heyyyy Sissy, how you doing?"

"I'm good," she said flatly. She had warned me not to get mushy every time I talked to her.

"What are you doing this weekend, like tomorrow?"

"Nothing, y'all aren't here. We're chillin', can't talk Gary into grilling for me." She had drastically changed her diet after her diagnosis. She said Monty was okay on the grill, he was still learning. Gary was better.

He smiled and playfully rolled his eyes. "You didn't try, but I got you as soon as I get back."

"Cool. Imma hold you to it. What's up?" she asked.

"We called because we want to get married down here." I paused. "This weekend."

"Ummm. Now, what now?" She squealed.

"Yeah, just something small on the beach." I bit the corner of my lip.

"Sounds cute, but is this what y'all want?"

"Yes, and the honeymoon will still be in St. Thomas." I bit the corner of my lip again in anticipation of Dena snapping off with our new idea.

"Dena, I don't think she'll be happy with it in the long run but she seems to think it'll be okay. She's afraid of too much wedding day drama in Houston," Gary chimed in.

"Hmph, well she does have a point though. I like the idea. I'll make some calls and get back to you in an hour or so. In the meantime, go to the concierge and ask for a nearby boutique to try on a simple dress."

My lips made an "O" shape and my eyes widened. Silly me, I hadn't thought about a dress. Not a wedding dress.

It was as if she saw me, she said, "Mia that's why you called me to think of things like this. You and Gary do, I plan."

We both laughed and said, "Thanks, Dena."

"Yeah. I'll call you back."

Dena was true to her word. She had masterminded our wedding plans within a three hour timeframe, complete with Gary's suit, my dress, rose-bouquet, hair, facial, and makeup, after the wedding massages, pampering, and treats. She called back and told us where to be and at what time.

I never thought things would come to this…me and my heart, my love, my fiancé, Gary Lamont Matthews standing on the beach, the cool breeze kissing our skin, our feet pressed into the sand, holding hands as our eyes danced a tune that we created for ourselves. The night before, we had walked hand in hand along the beach toward the spot where Dena told us to meet the chaplain at eleven thirty Sunday morning. Dena was awesome and it helped that she had planned several weddings at the same hotel. She had called the concierge to give me directions to the boutique. She called the boutique and asked for three dresses by name in a size ten. It was a tough decision but I decided on the strapless, slim line dress that had corset closure and beaded detail on one side of the hip. It was chiffon with a notched neckline overlapping and an asymmetrical bodice.

I left the room early before the sun was up. Gary and I didn't want to see each other before the wedding. Our wedding was planned quickly and on the beach but we stuck to tradition in some ways. I had to do a facial, hair, makeup, and get dressed before eleven o'clock. I knew I would need at least thirty minutes to make it to the destination.

His mother had called several times and knocked on the door. Her friend Leslie had texted Gary and said she would assist us by keeping Karen away from us until we finished the ceremony. Dena knew Leslie very well and had gotten her involved. They had told Karen that we had a tee time at eleven o'clock because they knew she'd catch the shuttle or get a car to take her to the golf resort. I felt bad but we needed to avoid Karen. I wanted Gary to have a relationship with her but she needed to stop all of her shenanigans. I still couldn't get over the canceled credit card.

I had completed my facial and makeup and the stylist was putting the finishing touches on my hair when a lady walked into the salon with intention.

"You must be Mia, the bride?" She grinned.

"Yes, I am. You must be Leslie." I tried to remain as still as possible as the stylist placed the flat iron close to my hairline at my forehead.

"Yes, I am." She smiled.

"It's so nice to meet you." I extended my hand toward her.

"Nice to meet you, as well." She peered around the stylist to look at me. "You are simply gorgeous."

"Thank you." I blushed. "We really appreciate your help, Leslie."

"Sweetheart, it is my pleasure." She stood silent for a moment as the stylist appeared to pick at every single strand of hair on my head and another one dabbed on the clear lip gloss on top of the nude colored lipstick. "I just saw Karen get in the car, headed to the golf resort. We have to hurry. It won't take her long to figure out that I lied to her. I'll tell her everything eventually but right now, we need to get you down to the beach before she sees you."

"Okay, I'm ready. Thank you ladies." I nodded to the stylist who was still picking at my hair as I stood up.

"You are so beautiful." The stylist beamed.

"Thank you. You really did an amazing job and I appreciate it." She reached for a hug. "Good luck out there."

"Thank you." I pulled my robe tighter and headed toward the dressing room. Leslie helped me get into my dress. I stepped closer to the mirror as I fought back tears. "My mother would be so tickled. I'm sad that my dad can't give me away but I promise to hold it together."

She turned to me. "Your parents would be proud and happy for you." She placed her hand on my cheek. "You look very beautiful and radiant, Mia. I wish you and Gary nothing but happiness and so much joy. You both deserve it."

"Thank you so much, Leslie." I felt more tears brewing and quickly looked toward the ceiling to keep them away.

"Are you ready?" She placed the veil on my head.

I nodded. "Yes, ma'am. I'm ready." I held up the dress and we rushed through the lobby, in the salon, and then outside.

We walked along the cobble stone pathway then down the steps to the sidewalk by the pool, and down the steps to the beach. There was a nice, cool breeze that danced across my skin. The sun was shining brightly in my face. I heard 'oohs and ahhs' as we walked past. When I reached the sand, Leslie said, "Enjoy yourself, I'll be watching from up there." She gave me a hug and turned to walk away as I removed my shoes and walked toward Gary.

My heart was racing because I couldn't believe it was happening. I was still afraid something would happen to stop us although I felt beautiful, pure, in love, and loved.

There were very few people on the beach at the time and I still couldn't see Gary at the place where we were instructed to meet. As I sauntered closer to the gazebo, my heart was pounding and my steps were getting slower as I thought of every possible worst case scenario including being jilted at the altar or ambushed before I got there. It was too early to feel my baby's kick but my stomach played a part in the orchestra going on in my body. I started fanning myself. I needed a drink of water. I stopped to look behind me, I wanted to bend over and rest my hands on my knees. *Did I walk in the wrong direction?* I thought.

I turned back around to see Gary walking down the steps toward me. He was beautiful. I exhaled loudly. I almost started crying but I held it again. He stopped, pressed his hands together in a praying position, and then started walking toward me again.

"You okay?" he asked.

I nodded. I decided not to tell him what I was thinking and feeling before I saw him. I would've turned into a big ol' teary ball of mess.

"Calm down, babe. I'm here. I gotchu." He pulled me close.

I closed my eyes and exhaled.

He leaned in to kiss me on my nose, and then whispered, "You are so beautiful. I love you so much." He held my hands and kissed them. "So you're absolutely sure you want to do it this way?"

I smiled up at him. "Look at me. Yes, baby, I'm sure." He pulled a handkerchief from his pocket and dabbed my nose and my face. He pulled me close and gave me a gentle squeeze that let me know I was definitely making the right decision. "I love you so much." My breathing had returned to normal.

"Gosh, you're so beautiful. I just want to hold you." He held me for a long time and when he let go, I was looking into the faces of my other loves standing in their appropriate places for a wedding on the beach—Judy and Clive, Dena and Monty, Desilyn and Chris, Aunt Edna and Uncle Henry, and Sam.

"Oh, my God." Tears of joy started flowing. I waved excitedly at them. I wanted to run to hug each of them. "Gary, how did you get all of them here?" Under the clear blue sky, I whispered. "Thank you, Jesus. This day is perfect."

"Our God is an awesome God, isn't he?" He smiled at me then turned to the chaplain and extended his hand. "Thank you for coming, sir. We're ready."

Discussion Questions

1. You can vow to give someone the best you have to offer, which is you striving for continuous improvement of yourself, but outside influences can still cause you grief in your relationships. Discuss the issues Gary and Mia experienced and discuss how similar occurrences could happen in any relationship? What are some ways to prevent it?

2. Mia was back in Arkansas for the third time; did you think her behavior was ridiculous or definitely warranted with all that was going on in their lives? At what point in a relationship is enough, enough?

3. If you were married to or dating a man like Gary, how much would you be willing to endure? Discuss relationship issues you've endured.

4. On page 47, Gary told us his feelings about his biological mother, Karen. "Who cares that Karen was at a football game…She only showed up when it was glamorous or newspaper worthy and something that would impress her colleagues." What did you think of Karen? Did your opinion of her change over the course of the novel? Discuss some of the decisions she made.

5. What are your thoughts on adoption? Some adoptions are closed. Do you think a child should always know their biological parents? Discuss the pros and cons.

6. Do you think attending family reunions are important? Discuss the issues of families and family reunions and the importance of knowing who's who.

7. Sitting at the feet of the more seasoned family members asking questions and learning of our family's history can be rewarding. Beginning on page 288, Gary and Mia went to visit Aunt Edna to find out more about his family. Do you think Aunt Edna told the truth or is it possible she fabricated the entire story? Why?

8. Beginning on page 286, Mia found out about two secrets that her best friend, Dena had kept from her. Revisit the moment when Mia found out. Do you think that it was selfish of Mia to respond the way she did or was Dena selfish by not sharing? How would you help a friend in a similar situation?

9. Discuss the hardship and challenges some college students face and the methods they pursue to complete their degrees? What are some other options Mia could have taken? What do you think of Gary's response to her past? See page 279.

10. Can you relate to any of the characters in any way? Do you know anyone who would relate to any of the characters?